D1035803

THE TALE OF
HALCYON CRANE

**Center Point
Large Print**

**This Large Print Book carries the
Seal of Approval of N.A.V.H.**

THE TALE OF HALCYON CRANE

Wendy Webb

CENTER POINT PUBLISHING
THORNDIKE, MAINE

This Center Point Large Print edition
is published in the year 2010 by arrangement with
Henry Holt & Company LLC.

The text of this Large Print edition is unabridged.
In other aspects, this book may vary
from the original edition.
Printed in the United States of America
on permanent paper.
Set in 16-point Times New Roman type.

ISBN: 978-1-60285-763-6

Library of Congress Cataloging-in-Publication Data

Webb, Wendy.
  The tale of Halcyon Crane / Wendy Webb. — Center Point large print ed.
    p. cm.
  ISBN 978-1-60285-763-6 (library binding : alk. paper)
  1. Family secrets—Fiction. 2. Large type books. I. Title.
  PS3623.E3926T35 2010b
  813′.6—dc22

                                                    2009053558

To those who have gone before, especially my brother, Randall Edward Webb, and my grandmother, Elma Katherine Herrala Maki, both of whom I miss every day. Although they're not here to read this dedication, I know they're delighted to see it, all the same.

PART ONE

I was the only passenger on the ferry crossing to Grand Manitou Island. As I stood on deck holding tight to the railing while we dipped and tumbled on the green, roiling waves, I understood why tourist season grinds to a halt when the November winds blow.

I was called to the tiny island in the middle of the Great Lakes by a dead woman. I traveled there at an unwelcoming time of year to learn the story of her life, hoping to discover my own story as well. A few whitecaps and swells wouldn't keep me away.

A summons from the dead is a strange way to begin a tale, but, as I have since learned, it's really no stranger than any other story in my family. As it turns out, I come from a long line of people who hover on the edge of reality. My family history isn't merely a chronicle of births and deaths and weddings and accomplishments, though it includes those things. No, the stories of my relatives sound more like fairy tales— Grimm's, unfortunately—with witches, hauntings, and malevolence all wrapped up in regrettable and sometimes bloody mishaps.

Until recently, I knew nothing of this. Growing up, I had an altogether different notion of who I was and where I came from. Then the truth began to reveal itself, as it always does. Truth seeks the light of day, needs it just like we need air, and so it finds ways to seep out of the sturdiest, most skillfully hidden boxes—even those buried deeply in the hearts of the dead.

My truth took its first breath one foggy autumn morning, nearly a thousand miles away from where I stood on the tossing ferry. That particular day didn't begin with anything out of the ordinary. Isn't that always the way? Life is thrown into chaos while you're making your way through mundane everyday tasks—an accident on the way to the grocery store takes your beloved, a heart attack interrupts a lazy Sunday morning, or, in my case, life-altering news arrives with the morning mail.

I awoke in my little bungalow overlooking Puget Sound and lay in bed awhile, listening to the barking of the seals. Then I pulled on a sweat-suit and sneakers and headed outside for my usual morning walk. I had already crossed the street and started up the hill before I noticed the fog settling in, dulling the edges of the world around me.

Some people find the sound of a foghorn romantic, evoking images of travel to faraway places with strange-sounding names. But I've never liked the fog. It obscures reality with what seems to be sinister intent, erasing all that is not within arm's reach. Anything could be out there, beyond.

I knew it was silly, being unnerved by fog in a seaside town, so I continued to walk my usual route, listening to the tinkling of the wind chimes—*tubular bells*—that were hanging from the eaves of various houses along the way.

I can't explain why—did I sense what was coming?—but the back of my neck began to tingle with a thousand tiny pinpricks. I paused, holding my breath, dread seeping off the cold pavement into the bottoms of my feet and working its way up my legs. Then something convinced me to hurry home, and I arrived at my door just in time to see the mailman materialize out of the fog.

"Pea soup," he said, shaking his head as he handed me a stack of mail.

"You be careful out there, Scooter." I smiled at him. "I couldn't see you until you were on my front step."

"Don't you worry about me, Ms. James. I'm old friends with this fog."

I watched him disappear into the whiteness and took the mail inside, where hot coffee was waiting, and poured myself a cup as I sorted through the stack. Along with the usual assortment of letters, bills, and catalogs was a large manila envelope labeled ARCHER & SON, ATTORNEYS-AT-LAW. I noticed the postmark: Grand Manitou Island, a popular tourist destination in one of the Great Lakes, halfway across the country from my home.

I sat at my kitchen table sipping coffee, turning the envelope over and over in my hands. What was this about? What did this lawyer want with me? Finally, I took a deep breath and tore it open to face whatever it contained.

I found two letters inside. One bore my name and address handwritten on the front of a thick creamy envelope, the back flap sealed with crimson wax. It was old-fashioned and lovely, reminding me of an invitation from another time and place. (As it turned out, that's exactly what it was.) The other was a white business-sized no-nonsense envelope. I opened that one first.

Dear Ms. James,

It is with deep regret that I inform you of Madlyn Crane's death. I am Ms. Crane's attorney and the executor of her will.

Please contact me at your earliest convenience.

Respectfully yours,
William Archer
Attorney-at-law

Madlyn Crane. The name sounded familiar, but I couldn't quite place it. Why did this lawyer regret to inform me of her death? A feeling of undefined, unexplainable apprehension began to cling to me as I picked up the second letter. Why was my heart pounding so? Why were my hands shaking? I broke the seal on the back of the envelope, unfolded the letter, and began reading. It was dated almost one month ago.

Dear Hallie,

Thirty years ago, my daughter and my husband were killed in a boating accident near our island home. Imagine my surprise to find that they—you and your father—are very much alive.

I don't quite know how to continue this letter. What do I say to my only child, for whom I have grieved all these years?

I'll start here. When I learned that you were alive, I was as stunned as you must be now. I had the impulse to pick up the phone and call you immediately, but then it hit me: I could not do that. I had no idea what you had been told.

Did you believe I was dead? Did you believe I had abandoned you? Your father could have told you anything. But now you're a grown woman. If you had any inkling I was alive, you would have found a way to contact me. I came to the conclusion that you and I must have been told the same lie, each believing the other was dead. We were both deceived.

How does a mother rise from the dead and enter her child's life? I thought of coming to see you, but simply showing up on your doorstep did not seem wise. A letter seemed like the gentlest way to turn your world upside down.

I know you must have many questions, as do I. I'll tell you a little about myself now, but really, can one sum up a lifetime in a few words? My name is Madlyn Crane. I still live in the house where you were born on Grand Manitou Island. You may recognize my name. I am a photographer. You may have seen my work in various magazines.

I imagine you grew up grieving for me, wishing to have a mother to shepherd you through the heaven that is childhood and the purgatory that is adolescence. I'm so sorry that I was not there for you. But Hallie, every time you wished for a mother's love, you had it. I loved you before you were born, I loved you during the empty years when I thought you were dead, and I love you now. That will never change. Although you did not know it, you have always had a mother who loved you more than anything.

I know you must be wondering what to think about this—a letter from a stranger who is alleging to be your mother. Is it true? I'm sure it flies in the face of everything you have believed about your life for the past thirty years. I'm sorry to create such a tempest for you; believe me, I considered staying "dead" to spare you this confusion, but I concluded that the truth, no matter how painful, must be told.

By way of authentication, please look at the photograph I am enclosing. It is you and your father, a few days before you "died." I took it myself. I also offer this—an invitation. Come back to Grand Manitou Island. So much time has been wasted already.

Love from your mother,
Madlyn Crane

The photograph fluttered out as I let the letter drop to the ground. It was a small, square, black-and-white print with a white border. I saw a little girl with a strange sheen in her eyes. Was it me? It certainly looked like me, but I couldn't really be sure. It might have been any dark-haired girl. But there was no mistaking my father—younger, thinner, with more hair, but unquestionably him. This was the man who put me to bed and dried my tears and took me ice-skating. I had no doubt.

I picked up Madlyn Crane's letter and read the words over and over again, until they blurred into meaningless symbols. I don't know how long I sat there, staring at it: a letter from a ghost.

2

The drive from my house usually took twelve minutes. On this day I did it in six, a lifetime of questions and more than a few accusations flying through my mind.

My mother's name was Annie James, and she died in a fire when I was five, or so my father had told me. He said he carried me out of our burning house and tried to go back to save her, but the flames were too intense. The house was engulfed before the firefighters arrived. That's why there were no pictures of her, no records, no mementos of our life together as a family. He was hailed as a hero at the time, but he certainly didn't feel like one. Annie James had no other family, he told me. No grandparents, aunts, uncles, or cousins from her side. I had no surviving grandparents on his side, either, so we were alone in the world, just he and I.

Even as a child, I realized that the story of my mother's death was a tidy little tale, with no loose ends for a girl's questions to unravel. When I asked my dad about her—*What was she like? Did she have hair like mine?*—I could see his grief, as tangible and blinding as a snowstorm. *Please don't ask, Hallie. Put it out of your mind. She's gone.*

As I sped through yellow lights, my questions

morphed into a mix of anger and defensiveness. Over the years I had created a tangible mother in my mind—brown hair, brown eyes, medium build. She had a sort of Jackie Kennedy quality. She liked those colorful pantsuits that were so popular in the 1970s, but we wore mother-daughter dresses to important events. She was kind but firm, loving but playful. Graceful. Elegant. If this letter was true—which it couldn't be—it would negate the only mother I had ever known. I wasn't about to let a stranger kill off my mother in a few short paragraphs.

Not to mention the fact that, if this letter was true, Madlyn Crane was accusing my father of something horrible. I loved my dad with the fierce feelings of protection common to children of single parents. How dare this woman, this stranger, flutter into my life and call my father—*my dad*—a liar? She accused him of faking our deaths and whisking me off across the country. She was basically saying I was an abducted child, someone whose photo might have appeared on a milk carton.

Where did she get off? Men like my dad don't abduct children from their mothers and assume new identities. Men like my mathematician father find rational solutions to problems. It was absurd and insulting, the whole thing. I couldn't imagine what would motivate this woman to make up such a cruel pack of lies.

But wasn't it a little odd that there were no photographs of my mother? No relatives? No friends who could talk about our life together? What if it wasn't grief but fear that I had seen in my dad's eyes when I mentioned my mother? What if he had lived for thirty years afraid that every day would be the day his abandoned wife, my abandoned mother, would show up on our doorstep? That would certainly explain his reluctance to talk about her.

Funny thing is, I remember the fire. I can see the flames and the smoke, hear the screaming and the roar of the fire trucks, feel the spray from the hoses. Was this nothing but a shadow of what never was, a memory deliberately implanted by years of storytelling? That's how powerful stories are. They can actually create the past if told often enough.

Janine, the day nurse, looked up as I walked in. Her smile faded when she saw my expression. "What's the matter?" she asked, but I put a hand up, as if to stop her words in midair. I walked by the nurses' station toward the recreation room, where I knew my father would be sitting.

I found him in front of the window, where he spent most of his days. He loved to watch the birds at the feeder. Their movements entranced him, or perhaps he was simply fascinated by those strange, flitting bits of color hovering in the air outside. It was impossible to know. I pulled up a chair and took his hands in mine.

"Dad?" I said gently. "Dad, it's Hallie."

He turned his head carefully. His deliberate slow-motion movements reminded me of a fetus in the womb, floating in another dimension, one with a thicker, viscous atmosphere, suspended there awaiting the time when he would enter a new world. He looked at me, a mix of innocence and confusion in his eyes.

"Did you bring my lunch?"

My conflicted emotions melted into the sorrow and grief that always overcame me when I visited my father these days. The great man, the profound thinker, reduced to this. I smiled sadly at him. "Janine will bring your lunch in a little while, Dad."

What was I doing here? I wanted answers, but he was clearly unable to provide them. I sighed and squeezed his hands, the love and loss filling my throat.

"Hallie?" My father's voice brought me back into the moment. A smile crept onto his face.

It was to be one of *those* days, then. I had been hoping for it. Most of the time, my father didn't recognize me, his eyes expressionless, his spark extinguished. It was as though his spirit was submerged deep inside his body, exploring some hidden world within. I often wondered where his spirit had gone and what it was doing while the husk that looked like my father sat motionless in his chair, staring at birds.

Every so often, though, he would have moments of lucidity. His eyes would become clear and bright as he rose to the surface, animating the lifeless features with his familiar spark. He would know me again. He would smile and say, "Come to see your old dad, eh?" And we'd be able to have a conversation, albeit a brief one. Soon enough, I'd lose him as he descended back into the depths of his being. The doctors told me that was typical of Alzheimer's patients.

"I've come to ask about Mom."

"Your mother?" He frowned at me, confused.

I knew I didn't have much time, so I dove right in. "Did you take me away from her on purpose, Dad?" I couldn't believe I had even said the words. They sounded so idiotic, so untrue.

He leaned in and put a finger to his lips. "I saw your mother yesterday," he admitted, his eyes darting back and forth, making sure nobody was listening. "I looked out of my bedroom window and there she was, walking in the courtyard."

I was silent for a moment. "You saw Mom?"

He slowly nodded his head. "She was wearing that long purple dress she used to like so much." A smile, then. "I think she's come for me this time, Hallie."

His earnestness gave me a chill. "Dad." I held his hand. "I got a letter today from somebody claiming to be Mom."

"Madlyn wrote to you?"

I took a sharp breath. *He said Madlyn, not Annie.* "Did you do it?" I managed to ask. "Why, Dad? Why did you take me away from her?"

He smiled, his eyes brimming with tears as he stroked my cheek. "I had to save my little girl."

"Save me from what?"

The tears spilled onto his face. "From that place, Hallie. It would have destroyed you."

And that was it. My window of time was gone, at least for that day. He turned back to the birds. I held my hand to his cheek, as if I were trying to transfuse all the love I felt for him into his veins.

"And I thought he was having such a good morning." It was his nurse, there with his lunch tray.

"He was, Janine. It's just. . . ." My words trailed off into a long sigh. I looked up at her in silence.

"I know, honey, I know. It never gets any easier. For us or for them."

I hugged my father tight as I got up to leave. "I love you, Dad," I said, hoping, wherever he was within that shell of a body, he heard me.

The next morning I got the call.

"Did he say anything?" I choked, the emotion shredding my voice to a rasp. "Did he ask for me?"

"I've seen a lot of death in my years here, honey," Janine told me softly. "They almost never have any last words. Dying is too hard."

3

Before I lost my father, I never understood all the rituals surrounding funerals: the wake, the service itself, the reception afterward, the dinners prepared by well-meaning friends and delivered in plastic containers, even the popular habit of making poster boards filled with photos of the dear departed. But now I know why we do those things. It's busywork, all of it. I had so much to take care of, so many arrangements to make, so many people to inform, I didn't have a moment to be engulfed by the ocean of grief that was lapping at my heels. Instead, I waded through the shallows, performing task after task, grateful to have duties to propel me forward.

Three hundred people, maybe more, crammed into our small church for my dad's funeral. His colleagues and former students came, as did my friends and their spouses and parents. Old pals I hadn't seen since high school—the entire flute section of the band I marched with in tenth grade—my colleagues at the newspaper, town restaurant owners, and shopkeepers and fishermen. Most of the stores on the main street closed for the afternoon with signs on their doors: GONE TO THE JAMES FUNERAL. No matter what else he had done, my dad was beloved in this town; all these people standing with me in my grief were proof of that. Simply by being there, they were telling me what a good man my father had been, and I desperately needed to hear it, in light of what I now knew.

Midway through the service, the minister nodded in my direction. It was time. I stood up and made my way to the front of the church to deliver my father's eulogy, my steps achingly slow, as if I were treading through quicksand. It took an eternity for me to reach the lectern, but, finally there, I took a deep breath and looked out onto the sea of stricken faces, friends, neighbors, and colleagues, many dabbing at their eyes or blowing their noses.

I could see their emotion hanging in the air. Grief covered the room like a black shroud, but I also saw relief, wispy and white, swirling around friends whose parents were still vibrant and living; it was not yet their turn to bury the most important person in their lives. Fear radiated from some of the mourners, a hazy almost colorless thread that wrapped around their throats, pulled their gazes to the ground, and twined around their hands. But it was the intense sadness that moved me the most, a blue mist that fell throughout this congregation like gentle Seattle rain, pooling on heads and laps and pews and trickling through the aisles. Somehow, I saw all this as I stood before them—I had a long history of seeing peculiar sights that nobody else seemed to notice—and I felt comforted.

I cleared my throat as I fumbled with the sheets of paper in front of me, but when I looked down to begin reading the eulogy I had written, I saw that my sadness had slipped onto the words, transforming them into vibrating, watery symbols with no real meaning. I had no choice but to speak from the heart.

"My father was a wonderful man," I began, my voice sounding strange and foreign to my own ears. Was it really me speaking? Was my father *really* the one being eulogized? *How can this be happening?*

"I never knew my mother, so my dad was all I had. While most of us would probably agree that it's difficult enough to bring up children with two parents in the household, my dad did a spectacular job of being both mother and father to me. It was his life's mission. He made sure I never missed out on anything because I didn't have a mom—he even took me to the mother-daughter picnics at school, which amused my teachers no end."

A slight chuckle rumbled through the congregation.

"He took me whale watching even though he hated the water; he went shopping with me for my prom dress. And he made hot chocolate on damp winter nights, when we'd sit up talking about everything from the beauty of the universe to small-town politics to the latest dramas in my

24

life, whatever they happened to be. He was always there with his mathematician's mind, making sense of the nonsensical, calmly explaining that there had to be a reason for even the most absurd event. In these ways and countless others, my dad protected me from the harshness of the world, as he also tried to do with many of the students he mentored. I felt safe when I was with him; I knew he could ward off any impending storm."

More nods and smiles from the crowd.

"And now he's gone ahead to prepare the way, for me and for everyone in this room. When it's our time to go, he'll be there to greet us with hot chocolate, helping us make sense out of the unfathomable reality of death and what comes next."

I looked out across the room, and although it was probably the tears welling up in my eyes and clouding my vision, I could've sworn I saw my dad standing in the back of the church, smiling. *Good job, Peanut,* I heard him say softly, in my ear. *Thanks for the kind words. I love you, too.*

After the service and the reception were over, after my friends had put the last plate in the dishwasher and turned it on, packed the remainder of the food into the freezer, and left, I heard a knock at the door. I didn't have to open it to know who was standing on the other side.

He was just as I had last seen him, black over-coat, slightly rumpled hair, electric blue eyes. He smelled of salt air and memories, pain and for-giveness. We didn't say anything for a moment, and then I flew into his arms.

"God, I'm so sorry, Hallie," my ex-husband whispered into my hair. "I know how much you loved him. I loved him, too."

Finally the tears came. I burst into sobs, there in Richard Blake's arms, crying for my father and for a little girl who had lost the only parent she had ever known—and the one she hadn't known—in the space of a few days. The crushing sadness I felt at the passing of my dad mixed with confusion and rage. I had been grieving for my mother my whole life, and she apparently was *there all the time,* while she spent a lifetime mourning the loss of a child who was very much alive. All because of the man whose death now left a gaping hole inside me.

Richard led me to the living-room sofa, my body shaking with the force of the grief running through it. I don't know how long I lay there, my head in his lap, as he stroked my hair. When I finally dried my eyes, he got up and opened a bottle of wine for both of us. "I think you could use this." He smiled sadly, handing me a glass, the rhythm of his accent reminding me of our years together in London. It seemed like a life-time ago.

A mouthful of cold, oaky chardonnay slipped down my throat. "You came all this way. I can't believe it."

"Of course I came," he said softly. "Where else would I be?"

I could think of a thousand places, none of which was at my side. "You might have just sent a card." I took his hand.

He squeezed back. "What other chance would I have to travel halfway around the world from one depressingly rainy city to another?"

I suddenly ached for the lack of his wicked sense of humor in my life. I was grieving every loss now, it seemed. "Did Ethan come with you?" I asked, referring to Richard's new husband. The man who was once the love of my life had sealed a union with the love of his as soon as they were able to do so in London. I hadn't gone to the ceremony—I *was* invited—but I did send a place setting of their china. What else was I to do? The battle had been lost long ago, when I realized it was never really mine to win.

He nodded. "He's got friends in Seattle and is staying with them. I rented an utterly dreadful car and drove up here alone. I thought you'd rather . . ." He didn't finish this thought. He was right; I was grateful he hadn't brought Ethan, but I didn't want to get into that conversation just now.

I grinned at him instead. "You *drove?* In America?"

"Apart from everyone else driving on the wrong side of the road, it went fine," he replied, sighing and slumping into a chair. Both of us were trying to lighten the mood, but it wasn't catching fire. "Seriously, I missed the funeral, didn't I? I didn't get here in time."

I shook my head. "Don't worry about it. I was in a daze anyway. The last few days have been a blur. But I'm so glad you're here now. I didn't know what I was going to do with myself, after it was all over and everyone had gone home and I was alone."

"You're not alone," he said gently. " 'Ain't no river wide enough.' Isn't that what they say?"

I held his gaze for a long time, both of us, I think, remembering how much we loved each other, until I broke our silence. "And what do *you* say, Rich? Dinner? More wine?"

"Both would be lovely. And then let's sit and reminisce about your dad for a while."

Later, after we had laughed and cried, remembering my father, I handed Richard the envelope that had flung my entire existence into the abyss a few days earlier. "I haven't told anybody else about this." I fidgeted in my chair, eyeing him as he began reading the letter from Madlyn Crane.

He looked up at me with wide eyes. "Good Lord. Is this true?"

I nodded, shrugging. "I asked my dad about it

the day before he died. I told him I got a letter from someone claiming to be my mother, and he said her name. *Madlyn wrote to you?* he asked. That was all the confirmation I needed."

Richard took my hands and held them tightly. "But why?" His eyes were searching mine for answers I didn't have. "Why the devil would he do something like that? I know your dad. He wouldn't—"

"I have no idea. He said something about saving me. That's all I know."

Richard let out a sigh and leaned against the back of his chair, staring at Madlyn's letter as if trying to will the words to reveal their secrets. "I can't believe Madlyn Crane is your mother," he murmured. "I mean, of all people."

"You say that as if you know her."

"Well, I don't *know* her, but I know *of* her. So do you. I've got one of her books on my coffee table. You've seen it a million times."

An image shot into my mind: Richard and me, sitting with cups of tea in our flat, looking through a book of photographs of London.

"Where's your laptop?" he asked, and I pointed up the stairs. In moments he was back with it, sitting next to me at the table and typing her name into the search engine.

I watched as page after page of hits came up on my screen. *Time, Travel & Leisure, National Geographic, Vanity Fair, Vogue,* and many more,

29

all having published her work. Madlyn Crane was famous.

"Let's go to her website," I suggested, and I held my breath as it loaded.

A list of headings ran down the left side of the screen: WATER, ANIMALS, PORTRAITS. Richard clicked on them, one by one. We found photos of celebrities dressed in finery or in nothing at all, ordinary people in sidewalk cafés or on street corners, children playing in foreign lands. I could not look away from these photos, because somehow I could see beyond the subject's façade. It was as though their inner thoughts were captured there on film. It sounds absurd, but I thought I could hear those people whispering to me.

Behind one celebrity's eyes, I saw an impending divorce. In the next photo, intense fear of failure. Cancer was lurking deep within the esophagus of the third. I cannot explain how I knew these things just by looking at their portraits, but I am quite certain they were there. I felt hypnotized, as though I could, at any time, be sucked into the world captured on film by Madlyn Crane.

And then we found something that caused my own spirit to catch in my throat. Richard clicked on a heading called LOVE and there was only one photo, the black-and-white image of a child. She was jumping off a swing attached to the limb of an enormous oak tree. The photographer had captured her at just the right moment, the midair flight before hitting the ground. Her eyes were looking right into the camera—she obviously knew someone was taking her picture—and she had an enormous smile on her face, radiating the sheer thrill of being airborne. But behind those sparkling eyes and exuberant smile, I could sense something else. That little girl whispered to me: *Help me. I'm afraid.*

Then I saw the name under the photograph: HALCYON CRANE, 1974–1979.

"It's you, my dear," Richard said. We looked at each other in silence, neither knowing what else to say.

Hours later, with Richard snoring in the guest room, I padded back downstairs and opened the laptop again, its bright screen glaring in the darkness. I'm not quite sure what I was looking for—more information about her? A way to know her better somehow? What I found was this article on the *Chicago Sun Times* website:

"SOUL CAPTURER" DIES OF HEART ATTACK

Photographer Madlyn Crane died in her home on Grand Manitou Island on Thursday of an apparent heart attack, said William Archer, Ms. Crane's attorney.

In four decades as one of this nation's pre-eminent photographers, Ms. Crane shot travel pieces, newsmakers and landscapes, but she was best known for her haunting portraits. Whether she was shooting celebrities for a magazine layout, people she met on her travels, or animals, Ms. Crane had a reputation for illuminating a subject's inner being, thus earning her the nickname of "Soul Capturer," which, as it happens, was also the title of one of her books. As her fame grew, many celebrities refused to allow Ms. Crane to photograph them during times of personal strife or distress, for fear of showing too much to Ms. Crane's eerily penetrating eye.

Ms. Crane leaves no survivors.

"Apparently, she did," I said to myself. I retrieved William Archer's letter from the drawer in the kitchen where I had stuffed it and dialed the number on the letterhead. I'd only reach his voice mail at this late hour, but I wanted to call immediately, while I still had the nerve to set something in motion that I might think better of in the light of day.

"This is Hallie James," I said, to Mr. Archer's machine. "I got your package, and I'm calling to let you know I plan to travel to Grand Manitou Island on Monday. Please get in touch with me tomorrow to confirm the date."

I put the phone down and sighed in the darkness of my kitchen. And then I crept up to my empty bed, where I tossed and turned all night long. The next morning, early, the phone rang.

"Is this Miss James?"

"I can't remember the last time anyone called me that, but yes." I smiled into the receiver. "I'm Hallie."

"Hallie, I'm William Archer," he said. "I'm calling about your visit to this island next week. I was very well acquainted with Madlyn, and I want to assure you that everything you say to me will be kept in the strictest confidence."

"Thank you, but I'm not sure—" He interrupted me.

"If I may? A couple of factors are in play here that I suggest would best be discussed in person, when you arrive. Suffice it to say that one of them is Miss Crane's sizable estate and the other is the rather delicate nature of—well, if I may be blunt here—your actual existence."

"I'm not sure what you mean." I began to get a knot in my stomach. Maybe this wasn't such a good idea after all.

"Hallie, I'm aware of the fact that you're Madlyn's daughter. But nobody else on the island knows, not to my knowledge anyway. That's because certain events surrounded your . . . departure so many years ago. I was just a child myself when it happened, but the circumstances are well known here."

Well known? "Can you tell me more? I feel like I'm totally in the dark."

"It's better spoken of in person," he said quickly. "I'm only bringing it up now because of the fact that you and your father are alive—"

I interrupted, choking on the words. "My father passed away. His funeral was yesterday."

"Oh." Silence for a moment. "I'm so sorry for your loss, and for . . . well, the timing couldn't be worse. I thought it was difficult when Madlyn died before she contacted you. But your dad dying, too? This puts a whole new level of awful into the mix."

His kindness touched me. "I'm getting through it," I said, fighting back the tears. "What doesn't kill you makes you stronger; isn't that what they say?"

"I've always thought that was a load of crap," he said softly. It made me smile. "Are you sure you want to come here now? The island isn't going anywhere. We can wait."

"I think it'll do me good," I told him, understanding fully for the first time myself. "Getting away, seeing a new place. It'll take my mind off the emptiness that has settled around me here."

"Okay, then," he said. "But I need to ask one thing. Please wait until you speak with me before divulging the true nature of your visit to anyone here on the island. Believe me, it'll be easier that way. You don't want to be answering questions before you have all the facts." He went on to give me a list of practical things I should pack for my visit—sweaters, jeans, hiking boots, a warm waterproof coat—and even offered to make reservations for me on the ferry and at a local inn. "I'll have you picked up at the ferry dock as well."

And it was done. I was really going. "Thank you, Mr. Archer. I appreciate everything you're doing on my behalf."

"I'm looking forward to seeing you on Monday," he said, and I hung up the phone.

I stood there holding the receiver for a few moments, wondering what I had just talked myself into. I hadn't noticed Richard standing behind me.

"Going somewhere?" he asked, raising his eyebrows and pouring some steaming coffee into a mug.

I opened the refrigerator and handed him the skim milk. "Sugar's in the tin on the counter."

"Nice deflection, but I asked you a question." He smiled as he stirred his coffee. "You're going to Grand Manitou Island, aren't you?"

I poured myself a cup and sank into a chair at the table. "I'm flying out on Monday," I admitted.

"Are you sure that's wise right now? After all you've been through? She's not there anymore, Hallie."

"I know that. But she lived there all these years. *I* lived there, Richard; so did my dad. Maybe . . ."

I didn't know what else to say. The truth was, I wasn't quite sure why I was going.

He reached across the table and took my hand. "If you're determined to do this, I'll go with you. I can change my plans."

"It's tempting." I smiled at him, wanting what I knew I couldn't have. "But I think I need to do this alone. I have no idea who I really am, Rich. Everything I was told about my childhood has been a lie. Maybe this trip will help me find out the truth. I won't ever meet my mother, but by going to the place where she lived, I'll get to know her a little. I'll see her house and her town and where she bought her groceries. I'll walk the streets she walked and meet her friends. I know it's not much, but it's something."

He took a long sip of coffee, looking at me over the rim with concern in his eyes.

"There's another reason for me to go," I went on. "What was so terrible about our life with Madlyn Crane on Grand Manitou Island that pushed Dad to take me away and move all the way out here? There may still be some people on the island who know. That's what I'm hoping, anyway."

"Be careful what you wish for," Richard warned, wagging a finger at me. "You might not like what you unearth. Whatever the reason was, it's not going to be pleasant."

I sighed. "It might not be pleasant, but at least it will be the truth."

It sounded convincing enough, but the tightness in my stomach told me I wasn't so sure this was the right thing to do. And as I stirred my coffee, I thought I saw storm clouds forming in the cup.

· 4

After an exhausting day of travel—two hours of driving with Richard to the airport in Seattle, the long flight to Minneapolis, the white-knuckle ride on a puddle jumper to Saint Barnabas, a small mainland town across the lake from Grand Manitou, and finally the taxi to the ferry dock—I arrived with just moments to spare. As soon as the ferry shoved off, I stumbled out onto the deck to get a whiff of Great Lakes air, but the icy burst of spray hitting my cheeks made me wish that I hadn't. I held on tight to the railing as the boat dipped and tossed from side to side. As I was inching my way back toward the cabin, something in the distance caught my eye.

A wide expanse of open water lay ahead, but as the ferry turned, the island appeared, seeming to rise from beneath the surface of the lake. It looked like a great turtle's nose poking into the air above the waterline, followed by the hump of its shell. Somewhere in the dark recesses of my brain, cells that hadn't been called upon in decades sputtered and choked at the sight. Yes, I had seen this before, been here before. I couldn't quite capture the full memory, though. It hung just out of reach, like a carrot in front of a horse, drawing me forward.

"Miss?" I turned and saw a man in uniform, his gray hair blowing in the stiff wind. His weathered face spoke of years of exposure to the elements, but kindness radiated from his eyes. "Why don't you come up into the pilothouse? Your bags are safe here. The view from there is just as clear and you won't be so cold."

A very good idea. I followed him upstairs.

"We don't get many tourists this time of year," he began, as he ushered me into the cramped cabin, looking at me too hard, too long. I pulled my purse into my lap and encircled it with my arms as I settled into one of the high chairs.

"I'm not a tourist. Not exactly." He waited for me to continue. "I'm seeing William Archer on a legal matter." It was, in fact, the truth.

"Ah. Good lawyer, that one."

He stroked his beard and looked at me deeply. There was that uncomfortable feeling again. One thing I didn't want, as the only woman on this ferry in the middle of an angry lake, was to be the object of intense interest. This captain seemed nice enough, but I had no idea who he was.

"You know I won't be making a return run to the island until Friday?"

I nodded. "I've planned to stay until then."

"First time on the island?" He turned his gaze out toward the water.

"No," I replied, fidgeting in my chair. "I was there as a child, but I don't remember much about it. I'm anxious to look around. Again."

He smiled, finally. "It's a beautiful place. Pity you couldn't have seen it in summer, with everything in bloom. Tourists flock to Grand Manitou in the spring and summer, but after Halloween things die down considerably. Do you know why they call it Grand Manitou?"

"It's got to be a Native American word, right?"

He nodded. "Means *great spirit*. They believed that the Great Spirit himself, the creator, lived here. This was the gateway into his world."

"Sort of like the Mount Olympus of the Great Lakes?"

"Something like that, yes." He chuckled. Then he pointed out the window. "Look, you can see the town coming into view now."

We chugged slowly past the shoreline. Even though I had seen photographs of this place and read about it in a guidebook, I was not prepared for what I saw: Enormous Victorian-era houses with grand front porches and turreted roofs lined a high cliff that gave way to a rocky shore. Each house was more magnificent than the next, each porch larger, each yard more meticulously manicured.

"Before the turn of the last century, wealthy

39

people from Chicago and Detroit and Minneapolis built these 'shacks' as vacation homes," my de facto tour guide told me. I had the feeling he had given this speech many times before. "They came for the clean air and the cool summers."

I couldn't imagine having the kind of money it would take to build one of those grand homes at all, let alone as a summer place. "Are these houses mostly inns now?" William Archer had made arrangements for me to stay in one of the island inns. Perhaps it was one of the houses I was seeing.

"Some of them are," he told me, nodding, "but some are still in private hands."

The captain took the helm then, guiding the ferry into the dock. I prepared to gather up my bags, wondering what I would find when I set foot in my mother's world.

"Is Will meeting you at the dock, then, miss, or are you needing a ride?" the captain wanted to know. "I can arrange a cab for you before shoving off for the mainland."

"Thank you so much for the offer, but Mr. Archer is sending a car for me," I called over my shoulder, dragging my heavy bags down the ramp and onto the dock as the ferry workers scrambled to unload the rest of the cargo. I noticed that several people, along with horses pulling flat wagons, had arrived to pick up food deliveries, mail, and other supplies brought by this twice-weekly ferry. It struck me as odd: horses? Then I remembered. I had read in the guidebook that—like its counterpart, Mackinac Island—Grand Manitou did not allow motorized vehicles, with the exception of an ambulance and a fire truck or two for emergencies. Tourists parked their cars at the mainland ferry dock and got around the island either on bikes, on foot, or in horse-drawn carriages that served as taxis. Residents did the same. Even the police were on horseback.

The gray November sky hung low and the wind swirled around me, so I buttoned my jacket all the way up to the neck to ward off the chill. An unsettling emptiness permeated the air. Apart from the bustle of the ferry dock, I didn't see another soul. I looked up and down the main street but heard no sound—no cars backfiring, no radios blaring, no people talking—only the wind whispering in my ears. Used to city noises as I was, it seemed deathly quiet.

This was the town where I was born, where I lived until I was five years old, and yet nothing seemed familiar. Both sides of the street were lined with buildings, some wooden and painted in bright colors, others red brick, none more than two stories high. A slightly raised wooden sidewalk ran in front of all the buildings as far as I could see. Colorful shingles swayed in the wind, advertising the businesses, many of them no doubt closed for the season: a fudge shop, an ice-cream parlor, a bakery. Like a movie set, nothing was amiss; there was no garbage on the street, no paint peeling from the walls of any of the buildings, nothing faded or bleak, only the perfection that might result from careful stage-hands touching up the entire town between scenes. It was like Main Street at Disney World come to life—old-fashioned, idyllic, quaint.

Behind me, I heard a soft *clop, clop, clop* coming down the street, and I turned to see a horse and carriage approaching. It wasn't the open-air type you see in New York's Central Park but rather a more sensible enclosed vehicle, the likes of which you might imagine passengers using in their daily travels around the turn of the last century. Mr. Archer had said he would send a taxi for me, and here it was. Even though I knew there was no motorized traffic on the island, I stupidly had had the idea in my head that I'd be met by the kind of taxi with four wheels and an engine.

Perception and reality collided when the two chestnut-brown Clydesdales stopped in front of me and the coachman, an elderly man with a shock of white hair, said, "I assume you're Miss James. I'm here to take you to the Manitou Inn." He groaned as he clambered down from his seat to gather up my bags.

"I'm supposed to be meeting William Archer at his office."

He reached into his pocket and pulled out a small envelope, which he held out in my direction. "I'm to give you this by way of explanation," he said. I opened the envelope and read the note inside.

Dear Hallie,

Please forgive this change in plans. A last-minute urgent business matter cropped up just about the time your ferry pulled in. Rather than meeting at my office as we discussed, I've instructed Henry, the coachman, to take you to the inn.

I've taken the liberty of rescheduling our appointment for 9 a.m. tomorrow. If this doesn't work for you, please phone me from the inn and let me know a better time.

Again, please accept my apologies for any inconvenience this might cause.

Most sincerely,
William Archer

A handwritten *note?* Why hadn't he just called my cell with the change in plans? "I'll just give him a buzz to confirm," I mumbled, fishing my phone out of my purse. As I stared at the NO SERVICE message on my phone's display, I realized why Mr. Archer hadn't made the call.

Henry shrugged. He was probably thinking: *Tourist*.

I dropped the useless phone back into my purse. "I guess I'm going to the inn, then." I smiled as he held out his hand to help me up the two steps into the carriage.

"This is the first time I've ever ridden in something like this," I said to Henry, who hadn't heard me. I settled in, and with a slight shaking motion we were off. The soft sound of the hoofbeats was mesmerizing: *clop, clop, clop.* I looked out the window at the town passing by—a diner, the bank, a bar, yet another fudge shop—settled back against the carriage seat, and exhaled. A feeling of peace washed over me. I supposed it came from the lack of anything motorized—no cars, no buses, no exhaust fumes, no booming car stereos, no cell phones—to interfere with the quiet beating of my own heart.

We turned from the main street and began climbing a long hill lined with more Victorian-era houses, not quite as opulent as the mansions I saw from the ferry but certainly nice enough, each with a front porch and a well-maintained lawn. Had my mother lived in one of these houses? Had I? I tried to search the closed compartments in my brain for any hint of recognition, any flare of familiarity. I had walked these streets as a child, played here, lived here; surely there must be some imprint left, some ghostly residue of my life. Yet it was as if I were seeing it all with entirely new eyes.

Up the hill we went, finally stopping in front of a massive yellow wooden house with a porch that snaked from the front all the way around to the back. A brightly painted sign swung noisily from the eaves: MANITOU INN.

As Henry retrieved my bags, I climbed the steps toward the front door but stopped in my tracks because of the view in front of me. From the porch, I could see across the wide expanse of water in all directions, the island's rocky coast, and even the mainland on the opposite shore. In the distance, I could make out the ferry chugging along on its return trip; from this vantage point it looked like a tiny toy boat. I held my breath. I could easily imagine why wealthy people from the past built their summer homes on this spot.

"It's quite something, isn't it?" Henry was grinning broadly.

"It really is," I agreed. "I could stand here all day."

The door opened and out came a woman wearing jeans and a cream-colored fisherman's-knit sweater, bright red bifocals hanging around her neck on a silver chain. Long graying hair softened her angular face; I couldn't tell if she was about my age and prematurely gray or a phenomenal-looking sixty. The innkeeper, I assumed. I knew she was expecting me—Mr.

Archer had made arrangements for me to stay here—yet she just stood there in the doorway for a moment, eyeing me with what seemed to be suspicion mixed with surprise. I didn't quite know what to make of the cool reception, so I broke the silence between us.

"Hi!" I smiled the brightest smile I could muster, extending my hand. "I'm Hallie James. I believe I have a reservation?"

She nodded, her suspicious glance melting into a grin as she took my hand. "You sure do, Hallie. Welcome, welcome! I don't know what's wrong with me. Come in, for heaven's sake, out of this wind." She turned and called her thanks to the coachman before ushering me inside.

The house had a comforting, welcoming aura. Its shining wood floors were covered with oriental rugs; colorful oil paintings of island scenes hung on the walls; photographs lined the fireplace mantel in the living room. The overstuffed couch and love seat looked like inviting places to curl up and read. Through a doorway, I could see a study with floor-to-ceiling bookshelves.

"I'm Mira Finch," she said, leading me up the stairs to the second floor. "Your room's up here."

"I was so glad to learn that you're still open for business." I was chattering, nervously. "I understand most inns are closed this time of year."

She opened the first door at the top of the stairs. "It's true, the weather can get pretty nasty here in

46

November," she said, nodding. "I don't have any other guests, haven't for weeks. But I'm a year-round resident, so I'm happy to put you up for as long as you plan to stay. This is your room, the Mainland Suite."

"Wow," I murmured, looking at the enormous bay window. Its cushioned seat was covered with multicolored pillows; a couple of afghans were folded in the corner next to the wall. I saw the same view as from the front porch: the great expanse of choppy water below and the flickering lights of the mainland beyond. A king-sized bed held a down comforter, and a wood fire crackled in the corner fireplace. "This is absolutely beautiful."

"It'll do." Mira's smile broadened, warming somewhat. "Your keys are on the nightstand. One opens the front door—which you'll rarely find locked—the other is for your room. Coffee and some sort of breakfast—muffins, scones, eggs, whatever—will be available in the kitchen after seven o'clock, but I'm usually up earlier if you want something before then."

"Hey, please don't trouble yourself on my account," I told her. "Coffee and a little something to munch on would be great, but I'm not expecting the full treatment, it being off-season and all. You've got no other guests; I really don't want to be a bother."

Mira patted my arm; I was grateful to be melting

her somewhat icy exterior. "How about we say this: I'll make coffee in the morning. After that, the kitchen's open. I've got cereal, oatmeal, bagels, eggs. Help yourself to whatever you'd like."

"That sounds perfect," I said, lugging my bags to a settee at the foot of the bed.

I could tell she was taking a moment to decide whether or not to say something further. Finally she added, "I was just planning on sitting down for some tea when you arrived. Join me after you get settled, if you'd like."

I had imagined I would spend my first hours on this island discussing wills and mothers and deaths with Mr. Archer, but this was infinitely nicer. "I'd love that, thank you! Is it okay if I clean up a little first? I've been traveling since early this morning, and I feel the grime of several states is covering me from head to toe."

She laughed. "Take your time getting settled. I'll be downstairs whenever you're ready." And she left me alone, closing the door behind her.

I slid my pajamas out of my suitcase but left the rest of my clothes where they were. Then I took my travel kit into the bathroom, which to my delight was round. Located in one of the inn's turrets, no doubt. It contained an enormous tiled shower and a Jacuzzi, facing another window overlooking the lake. Fluffy white towels sat in a stack on the counter, along with candles, soap, shampoo, and lotions.

Instead of unpacking further, I snuggled into the window seat, pulled one of the afghans over my legs, and stared out across the water. Back home, Puget Sound was my safe haven, the barking of the seals and the lapping of the waves like a sedative to me. Any problems in my life—from high school angst to college uncertainty to my divorce to my dad's illness—were solved on the seashore, pounded out of existence by the relentless beating of the surf. I got a similar feeling here, looking out over this great lake. There were no seals or whales, but the peacefulness was the same.

I took a moment to catch my breath, and the enormity of it all hit me—I was actually on my mother's island, looking at my mother's lake! This was the place from which my father had fled with me, all those years ago.

My mind swam with a jumble of thoughts. If I had only been here a few weeks earlier, I'd have met her. If she had just called instead of sending a letter. If she had flown out to see me. If.

Tears were stinging my eyes. I went into the bathroom, peeled off my clothes, and turned on the tap. A shower would do me good. I tried not to break down, but as I stepped under the stream of water the tears began to flow. I stood there sobbing as I let the water wash away the miles between me and my home, the lies between me and my father, and the regret I felt about my mother.

Finally, I toweled off, ran a brush through my hair, pulled on a shirt and jeans, and made my way downstairs. I found Mira in the living room with a plate of cheese and crackers, veggies and dips, and some assorted meats. When she spied me coming down the stairs, she poured me a cup of tea and topped off her own.

She looked at my puffy eyes and splotchy complexion with concern. "Everything okay?"

"Long day. Long week. Long month."

"I hear you." She smiled. "I thought you'd probably be hungry after your trip so I've got a chicken in the oven, but let's dig into this for now."

She had made dinner for me? I hadn't realized how famished I was. That handful of peanuts on the plane wasn't much of a lunch. And I hadn't even thought about finding dinner on an island where most everything was closed up tight for the season.

"Thank you so much, Mira," I said, taking a sip of my tea. "I certainly didn't expect you to do anything like this, but it's wonderful and much appreciated."

"Hey, I'm an innkeeper." She grinned, clinking her cup with mine. "It's what I do. I should also give you the particulars of life on the island during the off season."

I folded myself into the armchair next to hers.

"The first thing you should know: Most shops and restaurants are closed for the season."

"So I've heard," I said, taking another sip of tea. It tasted comforting and warm. "Is anything still open?"

"There's the grocery store, the wine bar on Main Street, the diner where just about everyone congregates for breakfast and lunch, and the Lodge on the other side of the island. There's Jonah's Coffee Shop and—let's see—the library's open, too. But that's about it."

"That's more than I was expecting, actually."

Mira dug into the cheese and crackers. "So, what brings you to our little island during the gales of November?"

William Archer had given me express instructions not to discuss my circumstances with anyone. Still, after a somewhat chilly reception, Mira seemed friendly and welcoming. On the other hand, he knew I was staying at this inn; he had even made the reservation for me. If he thought I could take Mira into my confidence, he would've said so. He had alluded to a "situation" that had occurred around the time my father left with me all those years ago, something the islanders who were living here then had not forgotten. Now was not the time to find out if Mira was one of them. She was the only innkeeper still open on this island. If she threw me out for claiming to be Madlyn Crane's long-dead daughter, I'd be without a place to stay.

"I'm seeing William Archer on a legal matter."

She looked at me, a mix of interest and curiosity in her eyes. "Oh?" Clearly, she wanted to hear more. "It's really none of my business. It's the innkeeper's curse; we're naturally inquisitive."

"No, it's perfectly all right," I said to her, hesitating. "I'm here to talk with Mr. Archer about Madlyn Crane's will."

Mira stared at me for a moment and my mind raced, trying to think of a plausible way to backpedal away from an explanation.

"Oh, I'm so sorry," she said slowly. "I didn't think Madlyn had any living relatives."

I had succeeded in digging myself into a nice little hole. Should I admit who I was? Keep silent? Saying as much as I already had was clearly foolish.

"I'm not exactly—" I began, and then stopped and started again. I didn't want to tell an outright lie. Too many lies had been told already. "I really don't know much right now. I got a letter from Mr. Archer requesting me to meet with him about the will. I didn't know Madlyn Crane. I knew her work, obviously, but beyond that—"

She squinted at me. "You've never met the woman?"

"I don't remember ever meeting her, no." It was technically the truth.

She raised her eyebrows. "You've come all this way at this time of year to talk about the will of a woman you didn't know." A statement.

52

I was starting to get more than a little uncomfortable with her intrusion into my personal business. What did she care why I was here? Why was she grilling me like this? "Actually, if you *must* know, I've been dealing with quite a lot at home lately, and when I received Mr. Archer's letter I was grateful for the chance to get away for a few days."

"If you *must* know," wielded correctly, always turns the tide. I watched as her suspicion melted into concern mixed with what might have been a good dose of chagrin.

"I'm sorry," she said softly. "I understand. Everyone can use a getaway now and then, even in November."

"In any case, I'll learn more tomorrow when I see Mr. Archer. I'm curious to find out about all of this, too."

The conversation turned to other things, and we spent the rest of the evening quite amicably. After all, she had prepared dinner for me and was doing everything she could to make me feel at home. Still, I couldn't shake the feeling that had crept up my spine when I mentioned Madlyn Crane's name. It was as though Mira's suspicion and mistrust had worked its way into my body and was taking root, reminding me to be on guard.

When I finally retreated to my room I climbed beneath the thick down comforter, but I couldn't shake the cold.

I awoke with a start, a silent scream catching in my throat. Someone had touched my face; I was sure of it. I sat up fast. Was somebody here, watching me as I slept? Mira?

Moonlight streamed in from the bay window, illuminating the room with an eerie whiteness. My heart was pounding in my chest as I looked around: my bags, the television, the armoire, the window seat. Nothing seemed amiss.

I slipped out of bed and poked my head into the bathroom. Empty. So was the closet. Nobody was under my bed, either. After checking the lock on my door—bolted, the chain fastened—I exhaled, not realizing I had been holding my breath all the while.

It had been a dream, then. *Silly.*

I tried settling back down under the covers, but the adrenaline rush had pushed sleep away. I tossed and turned for an hour or so, trying to coax slumber back from wherever it had gone, but my thoughts ran wild, from my mother to William Archer's letter to Mira's suspicious eyes. The numbers on the clock glowed 4:15. I finally gave in; there would be no more sleep tonight. I slipped on my robe and padded over to the window seat, covering my legs with an afghan as I leaned back against the pillows.

There wasn't the whisper of a wave; the lake was so calm it seemed as though a thin sheet of ice were covering its surface. Moonlight sparkled on the inky water in a long column that stretched as far as I could see. There were a few lights still blinking on the mainland at this hour; most everyone else, apparently, was sensible enough to be in bed.

Curled up in the window seat, I used the water to calm my racing thoughts, breathing in and out, trying to become as still as its glassy surface. Then, not far offshore, a splash.

I squinted and saw, plain as day, an arm slowly coming up out of the water. A human arm. Then another. More splashing. Then a head, a face gasping for air. A person was in trouble out there! I jumped to my feet. But that was impossible, wasn't it? I had been sitting in the window seat for several minutes—maybe longer than that— and I hadn't seen a boat or a swimmer or . . . anything. That lake had been as still as the grave.

It didn't matter. Impossible or not, I knew what I had seen. I fumbled with the bolt on my door, flew out of my room, and pounded down the stairs. "Mira! Call nine-one-one!" I shouted, as I flung open the front door and ran outside to get a better look at what was happening. I hurried down the steps and ran to the edge of the cliff, the chill from the ground stinging my bare feet.

Mira was beside me almost instantly, portable phone in hand. "Hallie! What the hell—"

My eyes were frozen on the lake. Instead of the glassy, serene surface I had seen from my window just minutes earlier, the water was now rough and angry. Whitecaps were being whipped up by the stiff wind; the huge waves crashed violently onto the rocky shore below. *How could that be?*

"Hallie!" Mira shook me by the arm, as if to wake me from a dream. "What are you doing out here?"

I didn't respond.

"Let's get you back inside. You'll catch your death." She led me back to the house, closing the front door behind her.

"I saw—"

"What, Hallie?"

I walked over to the window. "I saw a person out there. In the lake."

"In a boat?"

"No, in the water. About a hundred yards offshore. Maybe more."

She looked at me, questioning, shaking her head. "That's impossible. You must've been dreaming."

"No, really," I insisted. "I was wide awake. I couldn't sleep, so I was sitting on the window seat in my room. And all of a sudden I saw a person out there, in the water, trying to come up

56

for air. He seemed to be drowning, Mira. I feel like we should call the police or the Coast Guard or somebody. Only . . ." My words trailed off. I was beginning to doubt what I had seen with my own eyes.

"Only, what?"

"When I was looking at the lake from my room, the surface of the water was like glass. It was completely still. And then I went outside . . ." I looked into Mira's eyes, wanting some sort of explanation for what had just occurred, some confirmation that winds blow up here in an instant. But she just shook her head.

"The gales have been blowing all night long. Haven't you heard it? The whole house has been shaking. I was worried it would keep you up."

I didn't know what to think. "But that person—"

"Hallie." She took my hand gently. "There's no way somebody could have been swimming. Even in summer you can't swim out there. The water temperature is too cold. People fall off their sailboats and get hypothermia *in August*. At this time of year? Nobody could survive for long in water that cold."

It took a moment for her words to take root in my mind. She was right, of course, it must've been a dream. Now it was my turn to apologize. "I feel like such an idiot, waking you up in the middle of the night and running outside like a crazy woman."

She smiled. "Don't sweat it. There's something about this island that does things to people. I should've mentioned it to you earlier. I think it's the combination of the horse-and-carriage thing and the rhythm of the lake itself, but people's imaginations get thrown into high gear when they're here. We get a lot of writers and artists who come specifically for inspiration.

"And it's not only that," she went on, leading me up the steps. "You may very well have seen a ghost."

I stopped. "You're kidding, right?"

"Oh, not at all." She winked at me. "I lead ghost tours around this island for visitors during high season. There is definitely something here, Hallie. The old-timers say it has something to do with ancient legends about the island being a sort of gateway to the spirit world. This place is chock-full of ghosts. I'm not surprised you picked up on it."

Back in my room, I noticed the first hint of light appearing in the eastern sky. Early as it was, I turned on the shower and stood under the hot water for a long time, trying to wash the image of that drowning person out of my mind.

After drying off, I figured I might as well dress for the day. What to wear for my meeting with a lawyer? A pair of comfortable jeans and a cotton sweater? Combined with a tweed jacket, it would have to do. I got the impression most people didn't dress formally here, anyway. I hunted in my suitcase for my hair dryer and found that the steam from the shower was still hanging in the air, like fog. It made me think of that foggy day back home, when this all began. As I ran a brush through my hair, the reflection in the bathroom mirror made me catch my breath: A hand print was on the outside of the steamy glass shower door. It was clear as daylight.

I felt exactly the same way I felt that day in the fog; fear was seeping up off the floor into my body. Did I make that hand print as I got out of the shower? Or had someone been in that steamy bathroom, standing there, watching me? I fervently hoped it was the former, but really, how often do you make a full hand print on the shower door?

I checked the bedroom. In all the excitement, I must've forgotten to flip the dead bolt when I came back to my room. Somebody could've come in here and lurked outside my shower. But who, Mira? Nobody else—that I knew of—was in the house.

· 6

I hitched a ride into town with Mira in her carriage behind two enormous Clydesdales. It was too early for my meeting, but I figured it was wise, here on the island, to take advantage of the opportunity for a ride whenever it presented itself. A chill wind wrapped around us from off the lake, and dark clouds hung low and threatening in the sky. I buttoned up my jacket and was thankful for my warm sweater.

Mira dropped me at the coffee shop on Main Street, Jonah's, armed with directions to William Archer's office. "See you later!" she called over her shoulder, as she clopped away. "Good luck with your meeting!" I looked at my watch and found I had just over an hour to kill.

I pushed open the door of the coffee shop and saw a group of people, all of them about my dad's age, sitting at a table by the window: a woman in a red fleece vest and jeans, a couple of men in flannel shirts, another woman in a fisherman's-knit sweater. Locals, obviously.

I heard their laughter and chatter as I came in, but all conversation stopped when I entered the room. Those people silenced themselves mid-laugh, mid-story, mid-sip, and every head turned in my direction. Had they been looking at me with curiosity and friendliness, it would have been one thing. But this—I felt as if I had just stumbled into a secret-society enclave. I was every inch the trespasser, thoroughly scrutinized. My skin was crawling with the force of their stares. What was their problem? Just a few weeks ago, this town had been awash with tourists. Now, suddenly, these people were stunned by the sight of a stranger in their midst?

I cleared my throat in an effort to let the man behind the counter know I was standing there. He finally saw me and broke the uncomfortable silence.

"Let me guess." He winked at me, deliberately talking loudly enough for the gang in the corner to hear. "You're in, of all places, a coffee shop, for a latte." The group got the message and reluctantly turned back to their own conversation, their eyes, mercifully, off my back.

"That's amazing." I grinned. "You must be psychic. I am indeed here for a latte. Skim. With a half shot of almond and a half shot of chocolate." Why not treat myself on such a day?

As he heated the milk for my drink, I remembered the name I saw above the door as I came in. "You must be Jonah?"

"I am indeed." He handed me the steaming mug. "And you?"

"I'm Hallie James, a stranger in these parts."

Jonah let out a laugh, which caused several heads to turn in my direction again. "Drink's on me. Welcome to the island, Hallie James."

"Are you sure?" I asked him, fishing a twenty out of my purse and brandishing it in his direction.

"Absolutely." He nodded. "Island tradition. The first out-of-season visitor of the year gets a free coffee."

Jonah was about my age, maybe a few years

younger, with shoulder-length blond hair and a sunny disposition to match. His face exuded a warmth I was grateful for.

"Thanks." I smiled, grabbed the newspaper that was sitting on the counter, and headed to a table as far as I could get from the locals.

Windows looking out onto the harbor lined the back wall of the shop. As I buried my face in the headlines, I imagined it must be quite a sight here in the summertime, sipping iced coffee while the ferries chugged into port and colorful sailboats floated languidly by. The picture it painted in my mind was so real and vivid, it was almost as though I had seen it before. That thought caught in my throat. Maybe I had! I wondered how long this coffee shop had been in business.

Roughly two minutes had passed since the last time I checked my watch. I tried to immerse myself in last week's news (the paper was old), but I couldn't quiet my racing thoughts enough to read. What would I learn at my meeting with William Archer?

The local welcome wagon pushed their chairs away from the table and began to drift out of the shop. As some of them called their goodbyes to Jonah, one woman stopped at my table, smiling. She looked as though she were baring her teeth. "I'm so sorry we all stopped and stared when you came in," she said. "It must have made you terribly uncomfortable. It's just that we don't get many tourists this time of year and—well, you looked so familiar, it took us all aback." I nodded, not knowing how to respond. She added, still smiling that oddly aggressive smile, "I'm afraid we were quite rude." She waited, then, for me to say something.

"No offense taken."

She thrust her hand in my direction. "I'm Isabel Stroud."

I took her palm in mine. "Hallie James." I managed a smile.

"So, Hallie," she began, "what brings you to Grand Manitou in the off-season?"

These are exactly the people Mr. Archer was warning me against, I thought, *those who might have some objection to me being—well, me.* "I'm here on business. I'll be here all week, actually."

"Wonderful." She was still smiling. "We'll see you around town, then."

I was sure she would. I got the distinct feeling that she and her cronies would be watching me closely, and not with a neighborly eye. As the door shut behind her, it was as though a burst of fresh air entered in her stead.

Jonah busied himself wiping down tables, saying, over his shoulder, "I'm sorry about that. It's the curse of living in a small town, I'm afraid."

"A small *island* town. After tourist season."

"Everybody's got to know your business."

Funny. Just because he'd said that, I wanted to tell him mine. "I'm here for a meeting with William Archer this morning. After that, I might have some further business to attend to, here on the island."

Jonah stopped wiping the tables. "How come Archer always finagles the meetings with pretty women? I don't get it."

My cheeks flushed. Was he actually flirting with me? It had been a long time since anyone had. He poured himself a cup of coffee and walked up to my table. "Mind if I join you?"

I wasn't sure if I wanted him to join me or not. But without waiting for my answer, he sat down in the chair opposite. "So," I said, trying to think of small talk. "I gather now's your downtime here."

Jonah nodded. "Now and through the winter. People don't like to be out on the lake when there are twenty-foot waves."

"Sissies." I took a sip of coffee. "Have you had your shop long?"

"I opened it about ten years ago," he told me. "I thought about leaving the island, finding a job on the mainland. But there's something about this place, for the right kind of person. It grabs you and won't let go."

A tingling climbed up my spine just then and I, too, felt caught. Maybe it was the way his blue eyes were shining, like steel. Maybe it was the cloud that seemed to drape itself over his sunny disposition when he said it. Was he trying to tell me something?

I didn't have time to find out, because I saw it was nearly nine o'clock. "Oh," I said. "Time for my meeting."

"I hope you'll be back soon, Hallie James," he said. All traces of whatever had clouded his face were erased by his smile, which looked familiar and safe.

"I'm sure I will." I smiled back at him, warmth flowing through me.

I pushed the door open and walked out onto Main Street, fishing the address of William Archer's office out of my purse, and began making my way down the empty street, looking into the windows of the businesses I passed. Each one was dark and closed up tight. It was like a ghost town.

And then I heard it: a whispering on the wind. A faint noise, a child's voice, singing softly, deep within my ear and yet all around me at the same time.

Say, say, oh, playmate, come out and play with me.

I whirled around to look behind me: There was nothing but the empty street.

And bring your dollies three. Climb up my apple tree.

I knew this song. I remembered it from my

childhood. I could almost see myself sitting on the ground facing a playmate, playing patty-cake, singing, clapping hands in rhythm to the words. But this wasn't the happy childhood tune I remembered. It was the same melody but morphed into a minor key. And the singing was slow and deliberate.

Slide down my rain barrel. Into my cellar door.

The cold wind was inside me now, holding fast to my throat, almost as if it were pulling the words out of my mouth. I sang along in a whisper.

And we'll be jolly friends, forevermore.

Suddenly, the song was over. I looked up and down the street, but nobody was there. I was alone. I hurried along to William Archer's office. I wanted very much to be inside with someone.

On the next block, I saw the shingle swaying back and forth in the stiff wind: ARCHER & SON, ATTORNEYS AT LAW. The slight creaking noise, coupled with what had just happened in the complete emptiness of the street, suddenly made me think I was the only person alive on the island. Everyone else here—the people in the coffee shop, Jonah, even Mira—were ghosts from another time. But of course that was a silly notion. I pushed it out of my mind as I opened the door.

The office was empty: a reception desk, several chairs, a bookshelf, but no receptionist, no other clients, and no William Archer. This constant emptiness was really beginning to unnerve me.

"Hello?" I called out. A man came walking out of a back office, carrying a cup of coffee. All of a sudden, the eerie feeling that had gripped me vanished, dissipated by the warmth of the man standing before me.

"Hallie James?"

I extended my hand. "You must be William Archer."

He took my hand and smiled. "You're right on time."

William Archer was not at all what I had expected. When I had spoken to him on the phone, the conversation was so formal that I got the impression of a buttoned-down conservative lawyer much older than myself. But in front of me stood a man in jeans and a soft plaid flannel shirt worn open over a T-shirt. He had the trim build of an athlete and seemed to be about my age. His dark wavy hair hung to his shoulders; his blue eyes were deep and bright and were, in a way, familiar to me. He looked more like an artist or an environmental activist than a lawyer.

We stood there for a minute, taking each other in, each reconciling the image we had in our minds with the reality before us.

"I'm sorry I couldn't meet you at the ferry yesterday," he said, taking a sip of his coffee.

"Quite all right," I said quickly. I could feel myself blush. *What am I, thirteen years old? Get it together, Hallie.*

"Why don't we go in here?" he gestured toward his office.

I felt the need to fill the silence that hung in the room between us—an annoying habit I wish I could break—so I resorted to meaningless small talk. "Are you the Archer or the Son?" I asked him, referring to his shingle.

"This was my dad's law practice," he explained. "I came to work with him one summer when I was just out of law school and never left. He's been retired for several years, but I haven't wanted to change the name on the door, even though it's just one Archer now."

He walked around his desk and sat down, motioning me to sit as well, and I realized it was time to get down to the reason for this meeting. I folded my hands in my lap and took a deep breath. It was like sitting in the doctor's office after a biopsy, knowing you're about to hear life-changing news. I managed a shaky smile. "I'm very nervous. You may have already figured that out."

"I know," he said, nodding and looking at me with real compassion in his eyes. "This is heavy stuff."

"Where do we start?"

"Instead of just diving into the will, let me give you a bit of background first," he began, reaching into his desk drawer. He pulled out a framed photograph. "Madlyn Crane tended to stay behind the camera, so I don't know if you've ever seen a picture of her from her younger days. I brought this from the house."

She looked nothing like the Jackie Kennedy mother I had imagined. It was not quite my own face but very close to it. Madlyn Crane had long wavy auburn hair like mine, which in this photograph was blowing in an unseen breeze. Her hazel eyes (like mine) sparkled with mischief. She was looking directly at the photographer and smiling, as though she were gazing into the eyes of someone she loved. She held a camera in one hand and had the other on her hip. A long, brightly colored scarf was wound around her neck. She wore a cream-colored sweater and shorts, and long earrings that dangled past her chin.

"You look just like her," he said softly. "It struck me when you walked in. There's no doubt in my mind now that this is all true. You're Halcyon Crane."

I tried to form a response, but the words caught in my throat. At least it explained why everyone had looked at me so oddly, from the ferry captain, to Mira, to the people in the coffee shop. Even Jonah. I was a dead ringer for a dead woman. It was a lot to take in.

"I wasn't convinced any of this was true when I got your letter," I admitted, clearing my throat. "I didn't buy into this right away. Who would?

I wasn't about to reject everything my father had ever told me about my life on the basis of one letter from a stranger."

"What convinced you?"

I told him about the photograph my mother had sent along with her letter, and the one of me on her website. I told him about my father saying her name before he died. And now, looking at this photo, there was no denying that I was this woman's daughter.

"Can you tell me a little bit about her?" I managed to ask.

As he spoke, I sat perfectly still, barely breathing, as though any movement on my part would break the spell he was weaving with his words.

"Everyone on the island knew Madlyn Crane," Mr. Archer began. "She was our most famous resident. Tourists came here specifically to catch a glimpse of her—although she didn't often make time for fans, which, I suppose, made her all the more alluring."

He told me she was a woman with a big personality, a fiery temper, strong opinions, and a generous heart.

"When she wasn't traveling the world shooting portraits of celebrities, animals in the wild, or nature scenes, she often could be found in her gallery here in town," he went on. "She displayed her own work, of course, but also the work of other local artists: painters, jewelers, and potters.

70

Fans were delighted on the rare occasions when she worked there as a sales clerk.

"Let me see, what else can I tell you about her? She loved kayaking, rowing, her dogs, and her horses. She was a third-generation islander and lived in a home built more than a century ago by her grandfather. She was proud of that house and even more proud of her heritage here on the island."

I had been longing for this kind of information all my life and now, finally hearing it, I had a difficult time gathering the words to respond. He waited quietly, understanding.

"I'm just sick that I didn't have the chance to know her," I began. "She wrote me one letter and died before I had a chance to read it. I can't get over that. What are the odds, finding a child you thought was dead and then dying yourself before . . ." I couldn't continue.

"The irony is heartbreaking," he said softly. "It's a damn shame."

We sat there awhile, neither of us saying anything.

"So, she had a heart attack? That's what I read in an obituary I found online. Is that right?" I asked finally.

William nodded. "It was a surprise to everyone on the island. Most of all to her, I imagine." He looked at me hesitantly, as though he was considering saying more.

"And?" I prodded.

"It happened in the barn. Her neighbors came over and found her when the dogs wouldn't stop howling. It took several police officers to get them—Madlyn's dogs—away from her. From her body, I mean. They didn't want to let her go."

"Loyal friends," I said, the words catching in my throat.

"Madlyn loved her animals."

"How did she find out about me?" I asked him. "She wasn't searching all these years, was she?"

William shook his head. "Everyone, including Madlyn, thought you were dead, until very recently." He pulled an envelope from his desk drawer and handed it to me. Inside, I found a newspaper clipping.

THOMAS JAMES HONORED AS TEACHER OF THE DECADE

It was a local award given to my dad by the school district just a few months before he died. Along with a short article, there was a photograph. My dad was smiling broadly for the camera, holding the plaque they'd given him. He was in the grip of the disease at that time, but he knew what was happening and was proud to be honored by his peers. I was standing next to him, also beaming.

As I held the photo in my hands and looked up at William, the question was apparently evident in my eyes.

"One of Madlyn's friends, a colleague she knew through her work, happens to live in Seattle," he explained. "She saw this article in the paper and was struck by the resemblance, which is really remarkable. So she called Madlyn and asked about it, saying that the woman in the photo looked enough like her to be her daughter. As soon as Madlyn saw it, she knew."

"But why didn't she just get on a plane? Or call me? If only she had . . ."

"She told me she hired a private investigator to do some nosing around first," he said. "She found out your father was in a nursing home and was concerned about the effect her showing up out of the blue would have on you. She wasn't quite sure how to handle such a delicate situation and decided a letter was the best approach."

I sighed and slumped a little lower in my chair.

"I know," he said, in sympathy. "I wish she had lived long enough to mail it."

I closed my eyes and covered them with my hands, afraid tears would begin. As if to pull me back from the precipice of grief that I was teetering on, William cleared his throat and said, "We should really talk about the will, Hallie. Are you ready to do that?"

"Of course," I told him. "I don't have any idea

what she might have left to me, but it will be nice to have some token of who she was."

He smiled sadly, picked up a sheet of paper that had been sitting on his desk, face down, this whole time—the will, I assumed—and said, "I'll just read this aloud."

I braced myself for what I was about to hear.

"'I, Madlyn Crane, being of sound mind and body, do hereby leave all my worldly goods to my daughter, Halcyon Crane, also known as Hallie James.'"

I gasped.

"'I do have one stipulation, however. The house is not to be sold. Hallie, you are a fourth-generation islander. You were born in that house. Your great-grandfather built it and he would want it to stay in the family as much as I do. Come and go as you wish, use my money to maintain it, but do not sell it. Raise your family here as I intended to raise mine.'"

He stopped. "There's a bit more, but it's just legal stuff. We changed her will almost immediately after she found out you were alive. She had planned to divide her estate to endow several arts foundations, but the fact of your existence changed her mind about that. Madlyn was a very family-oriented woman."

I was silent for a moment. "I can't believe she left everything to me."

"Of course you're shocked. This is so unexpected. You have just inherited a fortune from a woman you didn't even know."

"What do you mean, a fortune?"

"Madlyn was a wealthy woman," he said. "Her death has quite literally changed your life."

He handed me a stack of bank statements, investment reports, and other financial documents I didn't recognize. I looked through them, dumbly, not really knowing what I was seeing. But I do know one thing: There were a lot of zeroes. Madlyn Crane was worth millions. And now, unbelievably, so was I.

My mind was spinning. It raced from the goodbye letter I'd send to my boss, to finally being able to pay off all my creditors, to taking that trip back to Europe I'd always dreamed of. I had never in my life been financially secure, and now, in an instant, I was *wealthy*. After a moment, though, I felt ashamed. "I wish I could trade all that money for the childhood I was supposed to have had here."

William's eyes met mine. He gave me a slight smile and shrugged.

"What do I do now?" I asked him.

"You have a house and a couple of dogs waiting for you."

The enormity of that statement had not yet hit me. A house? Dogs? It didn't feel real. But then again, nothing had, from the moment I read Madlyn's letter.

"I've got the keys right here," he continued. "I thought you'd probably want to head out there after you heard they were yours." He stood up and reached for a brown leather jacket hanging on the coat rack in the corner. "I'll take you, if you'd like."

"Really? Do you have the time? I mean, what about your other clients?"

He looked around the empty room. "Everyone here can just wait until we get back." He laughed and then explained that his business, like everyone else's, slowed to a crawl when the seasonal residents packed up and went home.

"I've always meant to go south for the winter like so many people here do, my parents included," he said, pulling on his jacket, "but I never quite manage to do it. There's something about this island in winter that intrigues me. I love the solitude. It's like the whole place exists just for me."

"I've been feeling exactly the same way," I told him. "Like I've walked onto my own deserted movie set."

"You get it, then."

I nodded. But I didn't get it, not really. To me, the emptiness was more than a little unsettling, as if I were wandering alone in a graveyard. I felt it encircle me as we walked out the door and into the wind. The scent of rain was hanging in the air.

76

"My car's out back," he said, leading me around the building.

Car? As we rounded the corner, I saw what he meant. An enormous white horse—the kind of animal that I imagined had pulled fire trucks in the past—stood tied to a railing. Behind it stood a contraption that could only be described as a buggy. It had two wheels, a seat designed for two, and a canopy over the top. Looking up at the heavy gray sky, I wished for a real car—or at least an enclosed carriage like Henry's.

"This is Tinkerbelle," he said to me, reaching up to scratch the horse's nose.

It struck me funny, such a dainty name for such a massive, muscular horse. "I had a very tiny cat named Tinkerbelle once," I teased him. "It suited *her*."

He laughed, held out his hand to help me into the vehicle, and glanced upward at the rain clouds. "I hope we make it before the downpour."

I heard a rumble of thunder in the distance and hoped so, too. "How far do we have to go?"

"Only a couple of miles." He untied the horse, hopped into the driver's seat, took the reins, and made a clicking sound with his tongue. "Let's go, Belle."

And we were off. At a snail's pace. Belle was in no hurry to deliver me to my past and seemed unconcerned about the impending rain. I, on the other hand, couldn't get to the house quickly enough. "You know, I could run faster than this," I said, giving William a sidelong glance.

"You're free to lope ahead of the buggy any time the mood hits you. But don't lag behind. It can get quite unpleasant in back of a horse."

I laughed. "Hey, you must have a whole staff of people who do nothing but clean up after horses. I haven't seen any—evidence—the whole time I've been here."

"We do indeed," he said. "It's the most glamorous job on the island. We usually save it for the spoiled children of wealthy seasonal residents."

I was grateful for the bit of levity. As we got closer and closer to the house, the reality of my past life here was looming larger. I felt almost suffocated by it, but somehow the sound of Belle's hooves on the cobblestones, along with the swaying of the buggy, had a calming, almost hypnotizing effect. It was the heartbeat of this place.

"I love that sound," I murmured, referring to the hoofbeats. "It's a sound from the past, isn't it? Our ancestors heard it constantly as part of their daily lives, but now it's almost nonexistent in our world."

"It's funny you picked up on that. I always imagine what it might've been like in New York or Chicago a century ago: no cars, people coming and going in carriages, business deliveries being made by horse-drawn wagons. Hoofbeats everywhere. That sound was the constant din of traffic back then. They probably didn't even hear it or register it, because it was always there, every time they went out in the street. We've replaced it with engines and motors."

"And radios."

"And most recently the constant chatter of people on cell phones. That's my pet peeve, by the way, the privilege of listening to somebody else's conversation."

"I know. I can't stand it."

"Another reason to love the island," William said. "No cell service."

I snuck a glance at his ring finger—empty. Why? He was an eligible, presumably well-off lawyer. You'd think he'd have to beat women off with a stick. Living in Seattle, he certainly would have.

"So, William—" I began.

He interrupted. "Call me Will. Everybody else does."

"Will." I smiled, forgetting what I had intended to say. We rode in silence for a while, the swaying of the buggy and Belle's hoofbeats calming me. My eyelids felt heavy. For the first time that day, the adrenaline that had been stirred up the night before seemed to dissipate, leaving my body. Tired from too little sleep, I might have nodded off if a rumble of thunder hadn't pealed through the sky.

"We're almost there," Will said to me. "We'll make it before the rain starts. Madlyn lives just up the hill on the cliff." And then, quietly: "Lived."

It occurred to me for the first time that he was grieving for her, too. "Did you know her well?"

"Quite well, actually." He sighed. "Not only was I her lawyer, Madlyn and my mother were the best of friends. They grew up together."

Suddenly, it clicked. How could I have been such an idiot? The ease I felt with this man, roughly my age, whose mother and mine had known each other so well . . .

"Will." I looked deeply at him, trying to spark any hint of memory. "Did we know each other, before?"

He grinned broadly but stared straight ahead. "I was wondering if you'd remember."

"We were friends?"

"We played together all the time when we were kids. I practically lived at your house."

I didn't know what to say. I was five years old when my father took me away from this place— still a child, yes, but plenty old enough to remember a friend, a mother, a home. But a huge expanse of nothingness existed in my brain where those memories should've been. I felt empty, my entire childhood covered by a dark shroud. Who or what had draped it there?

"I don't remember anything, not one thing," I

said, shaking my head. "It's crazy. The only memories I have of my childhood involve me and my father in our little town north of Seattle, just the two of us. Why can't I remember this place? My mother? You? It's not like I was a baby when—"

My words evaporated in the air. We had turned into the driveway of the house where I was born, just as fat raindrops began to fall. I could swear I saw my mother, long auburn hair, fisherman's-knit sweater, colorful scarf, and all, standing on the front porch, waving.

· 7

The sky opened up and the rain fell to earth with a fury, beating down so hard it was difficult to see much past the rim of Will's buggy.

"You run up to the house, and I'll put Belle and this contraption in the stable," he directed.

I did as I was told. I jumped out of the buggy and hurried up a set of steps onto a covered front porch, where I paused to catch my breath and look around. Rain pounded down behind me, but the porch was dry. It was difficult to make out the view, in all the rain and fog, but I could tell this much: The house sat on top of a cliff overlooking the water.

My entire body was humming with electricity. This had been my home. It had not been destroyed by fire then, all those years ago, as my father had told me. My one clear memory of that time, the fire, was a lie.

Will hurried up the steps to the porch, shaking the rain off a large umbrella.

"You had an umbrella all along!"

"I found it in the stable." He laughed. "Sorry." He pointed out into the rain. "You can't tell now, but the view from this house is incredible. You can see downtown, the harbor, and the lake beyond it. I think it's the best view on the whole island, and that's saying something."

I turned, catching a glimpse of a porch swing swaying back and forth in the wind, as though an unseen rocker were admiring the view.

"Shall we go inside?" Will suggested.

"Not just yet," I said, not realizing how heavily I had been breathing until I settled onto the swing. "This is a lot to process at once. Can we sit here for a minute?"

He sat down next to me and we swayed back and forth in silence for a while. I noticed containers filled with wilting autumn plants and flowers—black-eyed Susans (my favorite), mums, and several other kinds I didn't recognize—scattered here and there on the porch. The welcome mat in front of the bright red front door said GO AWAY. That made me smile.

"After you—well . . . died"—William's eyes were on the ground—"I didn't come here for years. I couldn't."

For the second time that day, something obvious occurred to me. This man had lost a friend all those years ago and now she had reappeared, back from the dead. I wasn't the only one having a tough time with this new reality. I wasn't the only one with a lot to take in.

"What did everybody think happened to my father and me?"

"Boating accident," he said quickly. "They found your overturned kayak. The entire island put their boats in the water to search for you, but . . ." His words trailed off into a sigh.

I didn't quite know what to say. "How about we go inside?" I offered, trying to push out of my mind the image of dozens of colorful kayaks, rusting fishing boats, and elegant cruisers all searching for me. Will produced a set of keys from his pocket, unlocked the front door, and held it open as I walked through it into my home.

I found myself standing in a large square foyer, the living room on one side, the dining room on the other, and a grand wooden staircase ascending in the middle.

"Where's the welcoming committee?" Will looked left, right, and up the stairs. "Girls! Tundra! Tika!"

I heard a clatter of toenails on the wood floor, and two enormous dogs burst through the swinging door separating the dining room from what I assumed was the kitchen. They looked like huskies but were much bigger; their thick white and gray fur, bushy tails, long legs, and dark masks around steely golden eyes all hinted at ancient timberwolf ancestors. One was carrying a twisted rope bone in her mouth; the other had a stuffed rabbit. The dogs wiggled and curled around our legs, their great tails wagging, ears pinned back in greeting. Will was scratching and petting them in return, murmuring, "Good girls! Such good, good girls!"

One of them, the bigger of the two, jumped up on me, putting one saucerlike paw on my shoulder and the other on the top of my head. I was afraid to move. "They're friendly, right?"

"Down, Tundra!" Will commanded, and the dog dropped to the floor and sat in front of me. "She loves visitors. They're the highlight of her day. And yes, they're both friendly—but protective, too."

I reached down gingerly to scratch this beast behind the ears. "So these were my mother's dogs."

Will nodded. "Tundra and Tika. They're giant Alaskan malamutes. The breed is traditionally used as sled dogs, though the most work these two do is to walk from the couch to their food dishes. I've been taking care of them at home since Madlyn's death, but I brought them here this morning before going to the office. I knew you'd like to meet them at the very least, even if you don't end up keeping them. The girls belong to you now."

"They're magnificent," I murmured, staring into their fierce golden eyes.

The greeting complete, both dogs settled down, curling up next to each other on the floor. I noticed they didn't take their eyes off Will and me.

"We don't have to stand here in the foyer, you know," Will said, as he shut the front door behind us. "Take a look around."

As I wandered farther into the house, images flashed in my mind like a slide show on fast forward: A little girl dressed in white pounding up the stairs. The same girl, squealing as she slid down the banister. A glowering woman in a long black dress. Was I remembering snippets from a long-buried childhood or just imagining what might have been? I didn't know. It seemed real, but after seeing a person drowning in the water earlier and hearing that singsong tune on the street in front of Will's office, I wasn't certain I trusted my own mind.

In the living room, I ran my hand gently over the back of the sofa as I took a look around. Like those in the Manitou Inn, the floors here were made of gleaming hardwood, and the woodwork around the door frames and windows shone as though it had been freshly waxed. An overstuffed brown leather sofa sat in the middle of the room, along with a love seat and an armchair. Worn rugs were scattered about. A stone fireplace stretching all the way up to the vaulted ceiling stood in one corner, a flat-screen television in the other. Cherrywood paneling lined the walls that did not face the lake.

Photographs were everywhere—on the walls, the coffee tables, the raised stone hearth—as were framed covers of several magazines: *Time*, *National Geographic*, *Vanity Fair*. I had already seen many of the shots on Madlyn's website, but several were new to me.

I picked up a photograph here, a candle holder there, fingering the stuff of my mother's world in an attempt to leave my imprint. Dust floated in the air. The energy in the room was electric and alive, as though the house itself were watching me.

Will came over to me. "You okay?"

"I guess I'm a little overwhelmed," I admitted. The truth was, I was a lot overwhelmed. The house was bigger and more opulent than I had expected, and I was having trouble wrapping my mind around two notions: that it was now mine, and that I used to live here.

"Check out the sunporch." William pointed toward a set of sliding doors at the far end of the room. "It won't be sunny out there on a day like this, of course, but you'll get the idea."

I pushed open one of the doors into a room with

windows on three sides. It overlooked the lake to the front and the side gardens to the back. Rain was hitting the windows in gusts, mixed with a little icy sleet. Lovely. I heard the thunder again, and then a crack of lightning arced through the sky.

"Wow," I murmured, settling onto a chaise in the corner of the room. "It's great to watch a storm in here."

Along with the chaise, a couch with a muted floral print and an overstuffed striped armchair formed a sitting area, next to a small glass table and an enormous wooden rocking chair. The style could be described as the shabby chic that was popular a few years ago, but this furniture seemed just plain old. Comfortable but old. Magazines were strewn in racks, books sat on end tables. It occurred to me that this was where Madlyn spent much of her time. I could feel her—or something—alive here.

And then I heard it, as clear as crystal: *Hallie! Halcyon Crane! Have you done something with your mother's camera?* It was a female voice, a loud female voice, coming from behind me.

I spun around and onto my knees to look over the back of the chaise. Nobody was there.

"Hallie—" William poked his nose into the room and began to speak but stopped when he saw my expression. "What's the matter?"

I was breathing heavily and could feel my heart

pounding in my chest. I rubbed my hands on my jeans. "Nothing. It's just—I thought I heard something."

"The dogs?"

"No, it was a voice. I think it was my mother's voice."

He stood there for a moment, eyeing me carefully. Sizing up the lunatic, I thought. But then he said, "You know what? Maybe your memories are coming back."

Could that be? A childhood memory of this place? My first one! "I'll bet I played in here a lot as a child," I said, smiling and turning around in a circle. "I love this room."

"You did." He smiled at me. "*We* did."

I imagined a little girl, that same girl in white I had seen in my mind before, playing with toy horses in the corner. I saw her reading a picture book, sprawled out on her stomach, feet kicking up toward the sky.

"What do you say we join the dogs in the kitchen and make ourselves a cup of tea—or something stronger?" he suggested. "With this rain, we might as well settle in for a while."

"You're sure it's okay?" I felt I was trespassing, as though the real owner of the house would come barging in at any moment, demanding to know what we were doing there.

"It still hasn't sunk in. This place is yours, Hallie."

Right. I smiled. "Onward to the kitchen."

He led me back through the living room, the foyer, and the dining room into the kitchen, and I couldn't muffle the squeal of delight that escaped from my lips. Of all the rooms I had seen thus far, I liked this one the best.

The walls were painted a muted red; the windows were framed in dark wood. A long counter was topped with wooden cabinets that stretched all the way to the ceiling. An ancient armoire with glass doors displayed china and glassware, a rack of brightly colored plates stood in a row over the sink, and a small bookshelf was filled with cookbooks. A butcher-block center island was ringed with bar stools, and the mammoth stove sat sentinel beneath a set of copper pots and pans. A long rough-hewn table with chairs all around took up the end of the room by the back door and windows. A chaise sat in the far corner. What a perfect spot for curling up with a cookbook and figuring out what's for dinner!

"Madlyn had a lot of parties," Will explained, as though he were a tour guide through the mystery world my mother had inhabited. "She loved bringing people together for informal meals: professors and artists and bankers and groundskeepers, men and women from all walks of life. She liked the mix of viewpoints, I think. This kitchen got a lot of use."

I had always lived in places with cold utilitarian

kitchens, long slim rooms with metal cabinets on one side and a tiny table shoved into a corner. This kitchen had a feeling of life to it, a warmth that seemed to envelop me. It was as though the room itself were matronly and loving, ready to offer me a cup of tea or a freshly baked cookie. For the first time on the island, I felt truly at home.

"All my life I've wished for a big old kitchen," I said, but the words caught in my throat. "Exactly like this." I looked at Will. "When I was wishing for my ideal kitchen, I was actually remembering this one, wasn't I?"

"It's possible," he said, reaching up into one of the cabinets. "It makes sense that your memories are slowly taking shape, the more you see of your old surroundings." He retrieved a couple of teabags, ran some water into a teakettle, and set it on the stove. "Do you want to explore the rest of the house while the water boils?"

"I want to stay right here," I said, climbing onto one of the bar stools.

We sat there for a while, drinking tea and munching on some scones Will found in a tin on the counter, as the dogs circled and sniffed and finally settled back down. We talked a little, about nothing much in particular—where he went to law school, how I liked my home north of Seattle. Mostly we listened to the rain beat on the window-panes and the thunder growl its warnings . . .

• • •

I woke up, confused. It was nearly dark. As my eyes slowly adjusted, I could make out enough to realize that I was lying on the chaise in the sunroom, covered with an afghan. One of the dogs was on the floor next to me, her great head resting near mine. I shook the cobwebs out of my brain. Now I remembered. Will and I had come into the sunroom with our tea. I fell asleep? How idiotic.

Rain was still beating against the windows, but the thunder had subsided. Sitting up, I saw a light on in the next room. I padded through the doorway to find Will on the couch, reading.

"How long have I been out?"

"Not long. Half an hour, maybe." He closed the book, put it in his lap, and smiled at me. "We were watching the rain in the sunroom, and before I knew it . . ." He made a horrible snoring sound.

"That's really attractive." I laughed and settled into the armchair across from him.

"I assumed you succumbed to the day's events."

I rubbed my eyes. "I didn't get a whole lot of sleep last night. I nearly drifted off on the ride out here."

The rain sounded angry and heavy outside. It was just a few degrees away from snow. The thought of riding all the way back into town in Will's buggy made me feel—well, cold. "What do you do when it rains like this? For transportation, I mean?"

"If it's not too bad, I just go. But on days like this, I wait it out until the storm passes. Or I call Henry and take one of his carriages home, trailing Belle behind it. But he won't come all the way up here in this weather, unless it's an emergency."

"So what do we do now?"

Will smiled. "Popcorn and a movie? There's a DVD player and lots of selections. Maybe by the time the movie's over, the rain will have stopped long enough to get you back to the inn."

I wasn't thrilled about being trapped by a storm in the house of a dead woman with a man I barely knew. But as I snuggled deeper into the armchair, Will made a fire in the fireplace, the dogs curled up in front of me, and things soon felt friendly and companionable—as if I were home.

· 8

Riding in a horse-drawn buggy on a rainy evening has none of the turn-of-the-century charm you might expect. It was a cold damp November night, and I could see my breath in front of me as we plodded along the muddy streets.

Earlier we had watched one movie and started a second, before the rain tapered off and Will suggested we make a break for it.

The idea of staying the night had been brought up, of course. I was getting my mind around the idea that it was my house now, after all, and there were enough bedrooms and bathrooms for both of us to have our privacy. But tramping upstairs and choosing a bedroom filled with another woman's things just didn't feel right. Not to mention the fact that I had no intention of spending the night with Will, no matter how far apart our bedrooms were. So we put fresh food and water out for the dogs—Will explained he had asked a neighbor to let them out in the morning—locked up the place, ran out to the stable, and hitched up Belle. Five minutes into the cold, damp ride, I regretted it but didn't say so.

"Hey." A thought popped into my brain. "In the will, my mother said she had horses, too. Where are they?"

"Next door at the Wilsons'," he said, gesturing down the lane. "Charlie and Alice are happy to take care of them until you decide what to do."

I wasn't sure what that would be, especially in regard to the animals. I loved Tundra and Tika already, but I couldn't take them back home with me on the plane.

"That begs the question: What are your plans?" Will asked, as we clopped along down the soggy road.

"I haven't really decided. I'm definitely not going to sell the house; my mother's wishes were crystal clear on that point. Beyond that? I don't know."

My options were, for once in my life, wide open. I knew one thing: Quitting my job would be my first order of business in the morning. I'd call my boss to deliver the bad news. Or maybe just send him an e-mail. Yes, that was better. It made me a little sad to admit that quitting my job was the first thing I would do after being told I had inherited a house and a large sum of money. I had devoted more than a decade to a career I could jettison without a backward glance. I wondered what I might have done with my life instead, where my passions might have led me, if I hadn't worked simply to make money.

Then a rather unpleasant thought occurred to me. I had intended to make this a brief trip to the island—one week, tops—but when it came right down to it, I didn't really have a reason to rush home. My dad was gone. I had friends, sure, but truthfully, since moving back to the States after my divorce, I'd had some trouble reconnecting with many of my oldest ones. I'd been gone for nearly a decade, and during that time most of them had begun to build families of their own. They were busy ferrying children to music lessons and soccer games, while I found myself suddenly single and alone. Our lives had gone on different tracks.

Richard, who in many ways was still my closest

friend despite everything, was back in England by now, so there was nobody, not even a pet, whose life was hanging on my return. It seemed unbearably sad, sitting there in Will's damp buggy, that I could have reached a certain age without accumulating any tethers.

I decided, right then and there: "I'm going to stay awhile, at least for a couple of weeks." Madlyn's house—my house now—was a tether, after all. I was tied to this place, if not by a living person then by her memory, and the memories of all the people who had lived here before. Including me.

"That's great." Will smiled sideways at me. "It's been nice getting to know you again today. I'm glad you're not going to hurry up and leave."

I was glad too, suddenly.

"Since you'll be staying a bit, we should talk about the issue of telling everyone who you are," he said.

Ah, yes. I had forgotten, for the moment, that he had specifically warned me about revealing the fact that I was Madlyn Crane's long-dead daughter. What had he said in that first phone call? There was a "situation" concerning the disappearance of my father and me, something islanders still remembered.

"I ran into a group of locals at the coffee shop today who gave me a less-than-royal welcome," I admitted. "It was freaky. They looked at me as though I were a ghost."

Will nodded his head. "Considering the resemblance, can you blame them? There's something else, though. I've been wondering all day about how to bring this subject up. I should've said something earlier, when we were at the house, but I didn't know how."

The air between us thickened. "People aren't going to welcome me with open arms," I said. "I get that."

Will shook his head. "It's not that, not at all. They'll welcome you just fine. It's just . . ." He hesitated. "I'm having trouble finding the right words."

"You're starting to scare me a little, Will. What could be so bad?"

He stared straight ahead. "I think islanders are going to have some trouble digesting the notion that not so much *you* but your *father* was alive all these years."

"You mean, because he . . ." My words were falling apart before I had a chance to say them. I tried again. "Because he took me away from my mother? I know she was a well-loved person here. They'll be—what—outraged on her behalf? If that's what it is, I can understand it, I guess. I agree with them, actually."

Will shook his head. "No, that's not it. Not all of it. I mean, people will certainly feel that way, sure. But what I'm talking about is something else."

Silence, then. I felt a very sharp pain in the pit of my stomach that made me want to jump out of that buggy and run the other way. I almost did it, but I had nowhere to run. I had to sit and listen to whatever horrible thing Will had to tell me.

"What kind of father was your dad?" he asked me finally.

"The best father anyone ever had," I said, perhaps a bit too defensively. "Okay, all right. I know he *abducted* me. I have no idea why he did what he did, but I'm sure he had his reasons. And I'll tell you this: He gave me an idyllic childhood. He worked hard to be both mother and father to me. I loved him more than you can imagine and, not incidentally, so did everyone he ever met in our town. He was a teacher at the high school. Three hundred people came to his funeral. I have enough casseroles and banana bread in my freezer from the wake to feed me for a year."

Tears stung my eyes at the thought of my dad. Suddenly, I missed him so much. I had been focusing on my mother during this whole trip and had forgotten how alone my dad's death—and, indeed, his illness—had left me. I turned my face away from Will.

"I'm sorry, Hallie," he said. "I'm glad to hear you had such a great father, I really am. And, for the record, I never quite believed what people were saying about him. It just seemed wrong to me."

"What people were *saying?* It was thirty years ago. How could it possibly still matter to people now? I mean, come on. Thirty years is a long time to hold a grudge."

"Not about the murder of a child."

"But I'm *not* dead, Will. Everyone will see—"

"Not you, Hallie," he said softly. "Somebody else. Another child died just before you left the island. She died at your house. You obviously don't remember any of it."

For the rest of my life, I will be able to feel the physical impact those words had on my body. My senses went into overdrive. I became aware of, and felt swallowed by, the intense darkness outside the buggy. I heard the footfalls of an animal creeping its way through the nearby marsh. I could smell the dusty perspiration of the horse in front of us, mixed with the mossy, rainy air. And my whole body was tingling with dread.

I managed to croak out, "What did you say?"

Will sat staring straight ahead, holding Belle's reins and shaking his head. "This is really hard. Even for a lawyer."

I couldn't respond. I was just hoping he would go on anyway. Thankfully, he did.

"Better you hear it from me, right? Better you know everything."

I nodded, staring at him, wide-eyed.

He took a deep breath and cleared his throat. "Okay. I'm just going to say it. A girl died—was murdered—at your house, and all the evidence pointed to your father's having done it."

That's impossible! It's patently false. My dad didn't even like to kill spiders, for God's sake; he'd never kill a person, let alone a child.

He went on. "She fell from a third-floor window."

An image began to form in my mind. A girl with long braids. A white dress. An open window. I was leaning out of it, looking down at the ground. I saw a body there, below. I didn't tell Will about these images, or memories, or whatever they were. I said, "She fell? An accident, obviously. Why did people think it was murder?"

"The police found signs of a struggle in the room she fell from: lamps knocked over, the dresser pushed onto its side, things in disarray. The girl's dress was ripped. And they found your dad's fingerprints on the window and frame and his footprints around the body. And—" He stopped abruptly.

"What?"

"There were marks on her neck consistent with strangulation."

I digested that remark in silence. It was impossible, all of it. My father might have faked our deaths, he might have abducted me and moved me halfway across the country, but he was no child killer.

"People think my father killed this girl?" I couldn't believe I was even saying the words. "That's ridiculous." I was talking louder than I meant to. "Is that what she died of, then? Strangulation? Or did the fall kill her? Because there's no way my father would strangle a child and throw her out a window. It had to have been an accident."

"The fall killed her."

I stared at him silently. He went on. "The police were about to arrest your dad when you two . . . went missing."

I knew by his expression that there was more to the story, but I wasn't sure I wanted to hear it.

"Most people here on the island thought he killed himself *and* you," he said finally. "The way they saw it, his suicide was an admission of guilt."

"Who was the girl?" I managed to say.

"Her name was Julie Sutton," Will said quietly. "She was playing with you at your house that day."

I could feel my lungs expanding, but I couldn't get any air. *Julie Sutton.* The sound of her name created a deep black hole in my mind. I knew I should know her, remember her, but the hole swallowed up any memories that might have been there.

"She was a friend of mine?" I whispered.

Will nodded. "And mine."

"Were you there, too?"

He shook his head. "I was on the mainland with my parents that day, or I certainly would have been with you."

"But . . ." I couldn't formulate words for what I was feeling. *A child killed at my house? A friend of mine? I was there?* I managed to say it: "Did I see it?"

"I don't know," he said. "Nobody knew exactly what happened, where you were or where your dad was. But everyone assumed that, yeah, you witnessed the murder."

I shook my head in disbelief. It couldn't be true. It just couldn't. Not my dad.

"Her parents still live here on the island," Will continued. "They, like everyone else here, blame your father for Julie's death. So now you can see why people aren't going to be exactly thrilled to learn he escaped justice for his crime and went on to live the rest of his life in a little town north of Seattle instead of in prison."

We rode in silence for a few minutes. I thought of one Halloween when my dad dressed up like a cowboy to take me, Annie Oakley, trick-or-treating. I thought of the concern in his eyes on the humid night I showed up on his doorstep, suitcases in hand, after I left Richard. I thought of his vacant stare the last time I saw him. And then I thought of my mother, living on this island all these years with neighbors who believed her husband was a murderer.

"How did they treat her? My mother, I mean. After we were gone."

"Truthfully, Hallie, I don't know," Will said to me. "I was just a kid myself. But she stayed, didn't she? It probably has a lot to do with her long family history here. She was an islander. If I had to guess what happened, I'd say that people came around to believing she was just as much a victim as you were."

My stomach contracted suddenly. "Stop!" I cried. "I have to get out. I'm going to be sick."

As Will pulled on Belle's reins, I leaped out of that ridiculous contraption onto the muddy road and ran, blindly, into the dark. After a few steps, I leaned over and vomited, my body shaking with the force of it.

And then Will was there, offering a handkerchief, saying a string of what I presumed to be kind words, but I couldn't hear him. I sank onto the wet grass. My body physically couldn't handle the possibility that my father might have killed that girl and then fled to escape prosecution. I thought my chest might actually rip open, that I might break in two. This is what it is to die of shock, I thought. I'm going to have a heart attack right here.

But I didn't, of course. Will led me back to the buggy and helped me climb in. "Let's get you back to the inn," he said.

I didn't want to go back to Mira's prying questions. I knew she'd be curious about my meeting with Will that day. But I didn't want to go back to Madlyn's house, either. I didn't want to be anywhere on this island. Maybe my coming here was a mistake. I wanted to be the woman I was before this all began. I wanted to be Hallie James, daughter of Thomas James, the best father in the whole world.

· 9

He did take me back to the inn, of course. I had no other place to go.

"I'm sorry about all this, Hallie," he said, as we pulled up outside the inn. I nodded. I hadn't spoken during the rest of the ride home. "For the record, I never believed your father killed that girl. I knew your dad. I don't think he had it in him."

I didn't know what I believed. I had been searching for a reason for my father's taking me away from here, and now, by God, I had one. It made a disgusting sort of sense. And yet it just didn't connect with the man I knew.

I climbed out of the buggy and stumbled on shaky legs. Within an instant, Will was at my side. "Let me help you inside, at least," he said, wrapping a strong arm around my waist.

I leaned into him and put my head on his shoulder, allowing him to take me up the steps toward the front door.

"Have dinner with me tomorrow?" he asked. "And call me in the morning? Or come by the office. I really want to know that you've gotten through the night."

"Okay," I whispered, and tried to manufacture a smile. I don't think it came off too well.

Will enveloped me in his arms, then, and I sighed into his embrace, closing my eyes and resting my face on his chest. He smelled of rain and kindness. "This is going to be okay," he promised. "You're in a hell of a spot here. People will be shocked, sure. But I'll be by your side, standing between you and anyone on this island who tries to say one word against your father."

I sighed again. Had I ever had as good a friend as this man I barely knew?

"I mean it, Hallie, I want to hear from you in the morning," he said, and went off in his buggy, after waiting on the porch until I was safely inside.

Through what I fully believe was an act of God, Mira was not at home, so I did not have to face the questions I knew she would ask. I found a note saying she had gone out for the evening. The house was blissfully empty. Even nicer than that, a roast was warming in the oven. *Help yourself! See you at breakfast!* God bless her. I was starving. It was just after six o'clock, but it seemed much later. It occurred to me that I hadn't eaten much since breakfast, only the scones and popcorn that we had had at Madlyn's, which had ended up on the ground. I still had a metallic taste in my mouth. Suddenly, dinner sounded like a wonderful idea.

I went to the kitchen, made a sandwich from the roast beef in the oven, and took a bag of salad out of the fridge. Blue cheese dressing, perfect. Then I found a tray. I didn't want a chance meeting with the returning innkeeper, so I decided to eat in my room. I teetered my way up the stairs, hoping I wouldn't drop anything.

I settled the tray down on my bed and switched on the TV, wanting some mindless companionship with my meal. After I had eaten, I drew a bath and slipped into the steaming water. I was enormously grateful to be able to retreat into the tub that particular night. I've always found a long hot bath to be the cure for almost any problem—or at least a way to release its stress.

But it wasn't long before the tears came yet again. Would I ever stop crying? At the same time, I felt as though every cell in my body were screaming in response to what I had learned. *My dad? My sweet dad?*

I cried for the gentle, level-headed, sensible man whose rock-solid love and support built the foundation for the woman I grew up to be. I cried for all the nights he tucked me into bed with a kiss on the forehead and a wish that I would have sweet dreams. I cried for the man who didn't hide his tears but, instead, wrapped me in his arms, both of us grieving, when we had to put our old dog to sleep. I cried for the shell of a man he became because of his disease, the birds outside the window his only enjoyment.

Could this man also have been a murderer? Could he have murdered the girl they found outside our window that day? What possible reason would my dad—or anyone—have to kill a child? I also felt a pang of disloyalty. My father had taken me and fled this island thirty years ago, and now here I was, stirring up everything he spent his life laying to rest. Maybe I shouldn't be here at all.

I knew one thing: I was immeasurably grateful to Will for warning me, before I came to the island, not to blurt out the fact that I was the long-dead Halcyon Crane. God knows how that ferry captain might have reacted to the news; certainly he was around when the incident happened. And what about Mira? She was, I estimated, a decade or more older than I and, by her own account, a longtime islander. She must remember the murder or at least have heard of it. What would people do when they learned the truth? What would they think of me?

I toyed with the idea of leaving the island right away, on the next ferry. I would go home to my safe warm house on Puget Sound without facing these people. But then I remembered: It wasn't possible, no matter how much I wanted to run away. I had two whole days to endure on this island before the ferry would come.

I slipped under the surface of the water and floated there awhile, holding my breath. It felt good to be weightless, the rush of the water filling my ears.

Then I heard something: laughter. I opened my eyes and saw the face of a little girl looking down at me. The girl in the white dress. With long braids. The same girl I had imagined seeing earlier at Madlyn's house. She was standing over the tub, watching me. Her mouth didn't move, but I heard the singing all the same: *Say, say, oh, playmate. Come out and play with me.*

I shot up out of the water, sputtering, to find— nobody. I hurried out of the tub, wrapped a towel around me, and padded out into the main room. No one was there. No one had been there. No little girl in a white dress.

My entire body was quivering. Was this girl a figment of my imagination? Was she Julie Sutton, the girl who had died? Was I remembering her?

I pulled on my pajamas, climbed into bed, and found I could not stop shaking. I switched on the television, wanting to fill the room with voices, and laughter, and ridiculous situations.

I don't remember turning off the television, but I must've done that because I drifted off to sleep. I dreamed of the ferry ride I had taken the day before, only I wasn't alone on deck as I watched the island emerge out of the water. My father came up behind me and wrapped me in his arms.

"Hi, Peanut," he said softly.

"Dad!" I cried, hugging him, and only then did I realize that it wasn't my adult self, there on deck, but myself as a child. He picked me up, and I wrapped my legs around his waist monkey-style, the way small children do.

"I don't want you to go back there, Hallie," my father said to me. "It's not safe for you."

"But I'm already here, Daddy."

"Look," he said, pointing across the water. I turned my head toward the island, which was coming closer and closer. What I saw horrified me: hundreds, maybe thousands, of writhing beings, some in the water, some on land. I believed they were ghosts or spirits of some kind, moving in slow motion, all of them looking at me with empty eyes. They were trying to speak, but their mouths were dark hollow shells.

My father spoke. "You see now, Hallie. This is why I took you away."

I woke with a start, sweating, my legs caught between the damp, twisted sheets. It was only one o'clock. I had another six hours to get through until daylight.

10

I opened my eyes to see the sun streaming in through the windows. Glancing at the clock, I bolted awake. Almost ten-thirty! How could I have slept so late?

As I showered and made my way downstairs, I pondered my dilemma. The way I saw it, I had only two choices: I could hide here, staying out of everyone's way until the next ferry, sell the house, and never come back to the island again. Or I could do what my father hadn't done all those years ago: stay and fight.

I found Mira in her office, a tiny room just off the kitchen. I popped my head inside and said hello.

"Hey, Sleeping Beauty!"

"Yeah." I sighed. "I had a rough day. And night."

She looked up from the papers in front of her, lowering the pen poised in her hand. "Hallie, is everything okay?" Her expression was so kind. I wondered how it would change when I told her what I had to say.

"Well," I began, "I got some strange and upsetting news yesterday."

Mira stood up. "Why don't I get you some coffee and a muffin and you can tell me all about it."

My heart was beating so hard in my throat that I was certain it looked like an enormous Adam's apple. And my stomach was beginning to churn. I hoped I wouldn't have a repeat performance of last night's unpleasantness.

Mira had arranged a full pot of coffee, a jug of milk, a few muffins, and two cups on a tray. "Why don't you come into the sunroom?" She beckoned, sitting down in a wicker armchair while I took the rocker across from her.

As she poured the coffee, adding milk to mine, I leaped directly into the fray. "Madlyn Crane left everything she owned to me."

Mira choked on the sip of coffee she had just taken. "But I thought you said you didn't know her."

"I didn't," I said evenly. "But she knew me." Mira was clearly not understanding, so I went on. "I just found out I'm her daughter."

Mira stared at me, confusion all over her face, weighing her disbelief against my uncanny resemblance to my mother.

"Madlyn had another daughter?" she said. "I never knew that. I don't think anyone here knew that."

Another daughter. Mira, apparently, was not the brightest bulb. What did she think, Madlyn had two daughters, both named Hallie?

"I don't know anything about *another* daughter," I said slowly. "Mira, my name is

Hallie James. But islanders would know me as Halcyon Crane." My former real name echoed like an incantation inside of my head: Halcyon Crane. Me.

Her face was crimson. "But Halcyon was killed thirty years ago."

"And yet here I am. Believe me when I tell you I'm just as surprised as you are."

"But"—she was searching for words—"the accident. Halcyon survived?" Mira's mind was obviously spinning. "How? I was at her funeral."

I shook my head. "There was no accident. Apparently the whole thing was deliberate. I grew up in Bellingham, Washington, a small town north of Seattle. I lived there all these years with my dad. I grew up thinking my mother was dead, never knowing she was actually very much alive here on the island."

"Bellingham." I could see Mira's mind was racing. She was getting it. "You're Halcyon. Madlyn and Noah's daughter."

Noah. The sound hit me like a thunderbolt. It had never occurred to me that Thomas James wasn't my father's real name, but of course it wasn't. I nodded. "That's right." And then I told her about the morning Madlyn's letter arrived in my mailbox and turned my entire world upside down. "I didn't believe it myself for a while," I said to her. "But she sent photos. Apparently it's all true."

Silence.

"She didn't say anything to me," Mira mused finally, sipping her coffee. "Nothing at all. I wonder how in the world she found you. It's not like she was looking for an abducted child all these years. Everyone thought you were dead."

"A friend of hers who lives in Seattle saw a picture of me and my father in a local newspaper," I explained. "The resemblance was striking enough for her to mention it to Madlyn."

Mira nodded, taking it all in.

"What eats at me most is the timing," I admitted. "I grieved for my mother all my life, and she was right here all the time. She finds me and, *bang,* she's gone. We were so close to finally seeing each other again, and now I'll never know her."

Mira reached over and took my hand. "I could see the resemblance the moment you walked in the door, of course. I thought you were a relative, a cousin maybe . . ." She shook her head. "He escaped. We all thought he was dead. The Suttons—what you must've endured all those years at the hands of that monster. I'm so sorry, Hallie."

I was tempted to play the wounded child card. It was convenient, her feeling sorry for me, but I couldn't betray my dad for the sake of convenience. "He was no monster, Mira. I loved him more than anything. He was a perfect father."

The sympathy in Mira's eyes turned cold. "Perfect father? That's quite a description, considering the man is a murderer who took you away from your mother and made sure everyone thought you were dead."

"Mira, please. You don't know anything about the life I had with my father. He was a good man. I know he was. We were very close."

"Hallie, you have no idea what that man did."

"I know exactly what he did—and what he didn't do," I told her. "I heard about that girl's death for the first time yesterday. And my father *didn't* murder her."

"You don't know that. The police——"

Was this how it was going to go with every islander? Was I going to have to defend my dad's memory in what was tantamount to a street brawl?

"I don't care what the police said. The man who raised me didn't kill anybody."

Mira sniffed. "Tell that to the Suttons."

"I will!" I said indignantly. "I *will* tell that to the Suttons! Bring them on, Mira! I'm sorry their daughter is dead, but my dad didn't kill her. I was there. It was an accident."

Mira's eyes widened. "You saw what happened? We all suspected as much! That's why he killed you—or pretended to."

"I don't remember it." I looked down at my hands, trying to regain my composure. "I wish I

113

could. I don't remember anything about my life here on the island, not one thing. Yes, it looks pretty bad. He took me away from here under false pretenses. He changed our names. I know that now. The only thing I have to go on is what I actually remember—the best father a girl could ever have."

"You can talk all you want about his being a great father, but it's not up to you or me," she said. "This is a police matter, Hallie. There's no statute of limitations on murder. When the police learn he's been alive all these years—"

Then it hit me. She didn't know my dad was dead. "The police aren't going to reopen this case, Mira," I told her softly. "My dad's gone. Remember I said I was having a hard time back home? It was because he died—the day after I got the letter from Madlyn."

"Noah's dead?" Mira's eyes darted back and forth, as if she were looking for something she'd never find. "I . . . this is a lot to digest in one sit-ting. Noah was alive all these years, but now he's dead? You thought your mother was dead all these years, but she was alive—and now *she's* dead? What you've been through!"

"Yeah, it's been . . . devastating. I guess that's the only way to describe it."

"Hallie, I'm so sorry. I didn't mean to imply anything or to insult his memory. What you've endured these past few weeks I wouldn't wish on anyone. It's just that we've believed, all this time—"

My head was starting to pound. I ran a hand through my hair. "Thank you for that, Mira. But I know what you've believed, and it's not true. It can't be."

"Okay, then," she conceded. "If it's not true, if he didn't kill that poor girl, why did he leave? What other reason could there be?"

"That's what I need to find out. If he was not guilty of murder, and yet all the evidence pointed to him and the police were bearing down on him, it would've been cause enough to run. Or it might have been something else."

"Another woman, maybe?" Mira offered.

"I don't think so," I said slowly. "There was no woman in our lives. My dad never even dated anybody, all those years. When I was in high school, I used to encourage him to see the single mothers of my friends, but he never would. He used to say he had had one true love in his life and that was all he ever needed."

"If that was so, why would he take her child away from her?" she said icily.

Mira had a point. And suddenly I knew, without a doubt, what I was going to do.

"Well, I certainly have the time and the resources to find out," I told her, standing up with an air of finality. "Mira, thank you for your hospitality. I'd appreciate it if you'd put my bill together so I can settle up. Madlyn's house is mine now, and I'm going to move in. Today."

Mira nodded. "If you need any help along the way, Hallie, please don't hesitate to call on me. I want to know the truth about what happened just as much as you do."

I hugged her tight. "Thank you, Mira. I promise I will."

She pulled back and grabbed my hands, squeezing them hard. "Listen. Somebody's going to have to break this news to the Suttons. It's going to devastate them."

The thought of confronting the Suttons made me physically ill. "Mira, would you do it? I don't even know these people. It would be better coming from someone they know and love."

She nodded. "I'll make sure they hear today."

After paying my bill, I arranged with Henry to take my bags to my new house and hurried down the hill toward town at a quick walk. I hadn't had any real exercise since I reached the island. The day was blue and brisk following yesterday's rainstorm, but I didn't mind the cold. It felt like a cool washcloth to the face after an intense bout of crying. I tried to distract myself by imagining what the harbor must look like in summer, filled with ferries and sailboats and yachts. But all I could think of was a father and daughter fleeing together to a new life, while the parents of another daughter grieved in unimaginable horror.

I reached town to discover it was deserted, as usual. Should I go to Will's office? The coffee shop? The harbor? Will put an end to my wondering by poking his head out of his office door.

"Hey!" he called to me. "I saw you coming down the hill. How about some coffee?"

"Sure," I called back, and he emerged onto the street, closing his door behind him.

"How did you sleep?" he asked me.

"Not well," I said, taking off my sunglasses to reveal puffy dark-ringed eyes. "This morning wasn't any better. I told Mira the truth and got an earful in response."

"I'll bet you did." Will flashed me a grin as he opened the door to the coffee shop and we slipped inside, out of the chill. "I want to hear all about it. But first, how do you like your latte?"

"Skim, with a half shot of chocolate and a half shot of almond," Jonah piped up. I looked up to see him standing behind the counter.

"I like a man who remembers how I drink my coffee."

Will looked at Jonah and then at me. "Did I miss something? You guys know each other?"

"I was in here yesterday," I explained quickly.

"How did your meeting with this clown go?" Jonah asked, nodding toward Will as he slid my coffee across the counter.

I grinned. "It went as well as a meeting with a lawyer can go, I suppose."

Jonah chuckled. "One of the gals who was in here yesterday saw you two headed out toward Madlyn Crane's place." He leaned in, giving me a conspiratorial wink.

"Yup, that's where we went." I took a deep breath and continued. "You might as well know. The house belongs to me now, Jonah. She left it to me in her will, among other things."

Jonah squinted at me for a moment. "I knew it!" he exclaimed, slapping a hand on the counter. "I saw the resemblance when you came in yesterday; we all did. But I wasn't sure—"

"Hey, let's give the lady a break from the questioning," Will interjected. "She has a lot to take in right now, and she's not up to another inquisition this morning."

Jonah gave him a sidelong glance. "What do you mean, *another* inquisition?"

"She's staying at the Manitou Inn." Will smiled, and a knowing look came over Jonah's face. Apparently, Mira's reputation as a busybody was well known.

"Enough said," Jonah conceded. "I won't keep you. You guys grab a seat and enjoy that coffee."

We sank into a pair of armchairs by the fire, and in hushed tones I told Will about my confrontation with Mira, my decision to move to the house, and my determination to get to the bottom

118

of what really happened there all those years ago.

"This mystery about the murder, I just can't let it be. I have to try to clear my dad's name." I paused. "But there's something else I want to find out, too, something that's like a thread running through everything."

"What's that?"

"I know nothing of my family history. My great-grandfather built the house I now own, and I don't know the first thing about him, or about anyone else who ever lived there over the years. I want to know them. I want to know what I'm really made of. The good, the bad, and the ugly."

Will chuckled. "Good and bad, maybe. Ugly? Never."

I felt my cheeks heat up. "Will, seriously."

"Seriously, I suspect you'll find a little of all three." Will leaned back in his chair and took a sip of coffee. "That's how family histories usually go. I'm sure you'll find it all at the house. There'll be boxes of old photos and other family memorabilia stashed somewhere."

I nodded. "Henry has already taken my bags over there. After I get settled, I'll dive into the mystery of Julie Sutton's death. Do you think the local police still have their records of the case?" I really had no idea what I'd do with those records, if I even got a chance to see them. The chances of finding any new information after thirty years were slim to none. Still. It was a place to start.

"I'm sure they've got them in some dusty file cabinet somewhere," Will said, finishing his coffee with a slurp. "Listen, I have to get back to the office. How about dinner tonight?"

On the one hand, the thought of being alone in Madlyn's house for the whole evening was less than appealing. But on the other, I didn't want to give Will the wrong idea.

Seeing the hesitation in my eyes, he prodded. "There's a great place on the other side of the island. A girl's gotta eat."

I caved. "Sounds good to me." What could it hurt?

As I gathered up my purse to leave, Jonah called from behind the counter. "Did I hear you right, you're staying awhile?"

"I am indeed," I told him, smiling broadly. "I'm moving into the house today."

He threw a bag of coffee beans my way. "Madlyn was a tea drinker."

I caught the bag with a smile. "Maybe you can come over to help me drink this one day soon."

"I'd like that," he said.

Will threw him a look as he guided me out to the street. "I'd drive you up myself, but I've got some calls to make in a few minutes and they might take a while." He glanced at his watch. "I'll call Henry to come and get you. He usually makes his way downtown around this time anyway."

I walked with Will toward his office and was

about to ask him what time he'd pick me up for dinner when I heard the familiar sound of hoofbeats.

"Henry! Right on cue." Will waved him over. I noticed my bags were tied on top of the carriage. "This lady needs to go up to the Crane house."

Henry pulled his horses to a stop and Will held out his hand to help me up into the carriage. "How's six o'clock for dinner?"

"Great." I smiled and clambered up to my seat, and Henry headed off. We were only a few blocks into the ride when he stopped the carriage, hopped down, and poked his head in the window. "I thought you might want to stop at the grocery store to get some provisions. I'll wait here for you."

It hadn't even occurred to me to get groceries. "Thanks. I won't be too long, Henry," I said, as I hurried into the store.

I wasn't quite sure what I needed. Yogurt, eggs, and some fruit. Peanut butter, English muffins, milk. I whipped through the store's deli section, picking up sliced turkey, cheese, and tortillas. I threw a bag of lettuce and some blue cheese dressing into my cart, along with a pound of hamburger, buns, and a couple of low-calorie French bread pizzas. Potato chips and onion dip. Four bottles of wine—*What the hell, I'm under stress*—and I was good to go. I could pick up more provisions later.

The feel of a hand tugging on my sleeve caused

me to whirl around in surprise. It was a woman in her early seventies, with curly gray hair and kind brown eyes.

"Is it true?" she asked.

"I'm not quite sure what you mean, ma'am," I said to her quietly. "But if you're asking if I'm the daughter of Noah and Madlyn Crane, the answer is yes. My name is Hallie James."

She shook her head violently, the kindness in her eyes replaced by a simmering fury. "Tell me, Halcyon, how has *your* life been these past thirty years?"

The man behind the deli counter looked up. "You okay there, Mrs. Sutton?"

Mrs. Sutton! I bit my lip and braced for the impact. "I'm . . . I'm so sorry for your loss, Mrs. Sutton," I stammered, "but—"

"But what?" She cut me off. "What could you possibly be intending to say to me?"

I suppose I was intending to say that my father hadn't killed her daughter. But standing there with this sad old woman, her eyes brimming with bitter tears of rage and grief for her long-dead daughter, I was speechless.

"Was my daughter afraid when your father tried to strangle her? Did she cry out for me when he pushed her through that window?" She gripped my arm with her bony hands. I looked up and down the aisle for help, but the shopkeeper had disappeared.

"I'm sorry, Mrs. Sutton, but I can't remember anything about what happened," I told her quickly, trying in vain to free my arm from her grasp. "The first I had ever heard about your daughter's death was yesterday. And for that matter, the first I had ever heard about this island and my whole life here was just a week before that. I believed, all my life, that my mother died in a fire in Seattle when I was five years old; that's all I ever knew." I said all this in one breath, hoping she would realize I wasn't to blame for her loss.

"Well, I know different," she spat back at me, her voice growing louder. "I know my daughter never went to a dance. She never had a boyfriend. She never went to a prom. She never fell in love and got married. She never had children. And all the while, you were alive, doing all those things, raised by the man who killed her."

She was tightening her grip on my arm, a fierce look in her eyes. I had to get away from her immediately. I couldn't bear to hear her grief. More than that, I felt she was a real danger to me. The woman was in a rage; there was no telling what she might do. I finally broke free of her grasp and, abandoning my cart, ran from the store. I heard her calling after me, "How dare you come back to this island? How *dare* you?"

"Thanks so much for waiting," I managed to choke out as I got back into the carriage, my whole body shaking from the force of the encounter I had just experienced.

"No trouble at all, Halcyon." Henry nodded as he gently snapped the reins, easing the carriage into motion. He didn't ask about my lack of groceries; blessedly, he didn't ask about anything at all as we clopped our way home.

When we reached the house, he took my bags from the carriage and carried them to the front door. "She was a good girl, Madlyn was. Her father and I were friends, back then. He was our local veterinarian, you know."

I smiled into Henry's caring face. "No, I didn't know that. I don't know much about my family history, I'm afraid."

"That'll change, I have a feeling," Henry said. "It's a miracle, you being back here. She grieved for you every day of her life. It's a pity she couldn't have seen what a lovely woman you've become."

Tears welled up and I turned my head with an embarrassed blink. "Thank you." I nodded at him, fumbling with the keys.

"If you need anything, just holler," he said, patting my arm. "I'm just a phone call away."

"You're going to be sorry you said that."

"No, indeed. Night or day."

I waved to him from the porch and then turned inside, pushing my bags in front of me. To hell with the Suttons. At long last, I was finally home.

11

Tundra and Tika greeted me like a returning hero—tails wagging, ears back, bodies wiggling round and round—but their enthusiasm did little to abate my uneasiness as I eyed the grand staircase of my childhood home, wondering how I was going to put one foot in front of the other and climb into the unknown. I hadn't ventured up to the second and third floors last night. Why hadn't I explored the whole house with Will by my side?

I got the distinct feeling I didn't belong here, as if I were a trespassing teenager in danger of being caught by the ill-tempered homeowner at any moment. This was my house now, I reminded myself. Madlyn wanted me to have it. *She wanted me here.* I went from room to room on the main floor, repeating it aloud—"This is my house now; this is my house now"—as if to explain my presence to anyone who might be listening.

I stood at the foot of the stairs awhile, looking at the gleaming wood and the soft maroon of the rug running up the center. *Just do it, already.* I took a deep breath and climbed the stairs, chanting *I belong here* with each step. When I reached the top, I found myself in a long hallway containing several doors, all of them closed.

I opened the first door gingerly, and then poked

my head into each room in turn. Guest bedrooms, mostly. A guest bath at the end of the hall. The second floor of the house had the same feel as the first—cozy, warm, welcoming. Handmade quilts covered the beds; photos (I assumed they were taken by Madlyn) hung on the walls. Why had I felt so uneasy about coming up here?

I kept hoping my memories would come rushing back, that the act of opening a door would somehow unlock my long-forgotten childhood. Surely I would recognize what had been my own room? But nothing looked familiar. I was seeing it all with new eyes.

Two last doors stood at the end of the hallway. I opened the nearer door and, to my astonishment, found a woman standing beside the bed. I saw her only for a second or two, because I screamed and slammed the door.

In movies you see women shrieking at the top of their lungs all the time, but I always doubted I would—or could—make a noise like that if a truly terrifying circumstance ever arose. Wrong. I screamed like a banshee when I saw that woman in the bedroom and reeled backward, after slamming the door, my back colliding with the opposite wall.

I stood there trembling, trying to catch my breath. I had assumed the dogs were my only companions in the house, so I was completely taken aback by finding someone there. In combination with her rather unsettling appearance, it made for quite a fright. She was wearing a long black dress and sensible shoes, and her wispy gray hair was twisted into a severe bun on top of her head. Her skin was as white as alabaster.

She opened the bedroom door and scowled at me. "May I help you?"

"I—I—"

"I'm Iris Malone, Mrs. Crane's housekeeper," she said. "I'm here to go through her things."

Oh, of course. I was starting to get my wind back.

"And you are . . . ?" she wanted to know. This woman had a haughty air about her, as though she, and not I, belonged there. Technically, I suppose she was correct in that assumption. She was the housekeeper, so it made sense if she felt a certain ownership of the place. And I was a stranger. I might have been anybody—a fan, a looter, or worse—for all she knew.

Still. Those *things* she was going through had been my mother's, and now they belonged to me. I went from frightened idiot to indignant heir in a matter of seconds.

I straightened up. "I guess you haven't heard."

She squinted at me in response.

"There's no need for you to go through Mrs. Crane's things," I proclaimed. "I'm Halcyon Crane, Madlyn's daughter. I believe it's my place to do that."

Watching Iris's face blanch in that moment, I saw that it really is possible for a person to turn a whiter shade of pale. She walked over to me and raised one claw, and for an instant I thought she was going to slap me or scratch my face or God knows what. But she didn't. Placing her hand on my cheek with what I could only assume was as much warmth as she could summon, which wasn't much, she croaked, "So it's true."

I nodded, as much to free my cheek from the touch of her talons as to confirm her statement. "I was just as surprised to learn this as you are."

I don't know if she heard me. She was staring at my face and stroking my hair, her eyes unfocused and hazy, as though she were somewhere else, in another place and time.

"It *is* you, Hallie," she murmured. "We thought you were dead."

Iris wrapped her arms around me, pulling me close. Her embrace felt cold, as though she were trying to transmit her chill into my body. She smelled of decaying roses and dirt. I pulled away after a moment, a little too forcefully, perhaps. This seemed to bring her back into the moment. She shook her head and looked at me with clear pale-blue eyes.

"Yes, it is really me. I'm Hallie, and very much alive. I've met with Madlyn's attorney, who read her will. She has left the house and everything in it to me, her daughter. So, please, I'd like to be the one to go through her things."

"Of course," Iris said, nodding in that efficient yet deferential manner I had always imagined in household servants of the very rich. We stood there for a moment, looking at each other. A standoff, of sorts. I wasn't sure what to do next.

"So. What they're saying is true?" Iris wanted to know.

"If you're talking about the fact that my father has also been alive all these years, the answer is yes. If you hadn't heard the details, we were living in Washington State, where I was a copy editor at the local newspaper and my dad taught math at the high school. He died a few weeks ago." For good measure, I added, "Until very recently, I had no idea that my mother was alive. I had been told she died in a fire when I was a child."

Iris clucked. "And you believed that?"

"Of course I believed it." Who was she to question me about my life? "Now, if you'll excuse me, Iris—"

"Your mother was a wonderful woman," Iris said, with fury in her eyes, as if she thought I needed convincing on that point. She fiddled with her apron, and I could see the tears she was trying desperately to conceal. She withdrew a balled-up Kleenex from her sleeve and dabbed at her eyes.

It was a gesture so fragile and vulnerable that my anger began to subside.

"Did you work for her very long?" I asked her.

"I was here before she was born, and I was here the day she died," she said proudly. "I took care of Mrs. Crane for her entire life, and this house for longer than that."

I caught my breath. "You knew me when I was a child."

Iris nodded, and a slight smile slowly cracked across her face. "I was here when you were born and I was here when she got the news that you and your father were dead. I was sitting beside her at your memorial service."

She seemed almost gleeful. I felt an urgent need to get out of the hallway.

"Why don't we go downstairs and have some tea, and you can tell me all about it?" I said, hurrying toward the stairs.

"Oh, no. I couldn't. I should take my leave," she said, and she began to shuffle toward the stairs, one pained, measured step after another.

Guilt crept in. Here was this old hen who had taken care of my mother all her life. Iris was obviously grieving the loss of her employer and, indeed, her whole way of life. I looked at her, standing there in her shabby black dress, holding the tissue every old woman seems to have up her sleeve. What I really wanted was for this creepy old bat to climb on her broomstick and leave me to my house and its secrets. But my mother had employed her all these years. (And yet, oddly enough, left her nothing in her will. I didn't know what to make of that.) I wondered if Iris had enough money set aside to make ends meet, or if my mother's death would put her in the breadline.

We reached the bottom of the stairs, where my bags were sitting in the corner. Iris looked at them pointedly. "You're here to stay?"

"I don't know," I told her. "For the immediate future, yes. I'm going to stay for a few weeks. Long-term, I'm not sure. I don't have any concrete plans."

"I'll come a few times each week to help out while you're here, then." This was not a question but a statement. "I'll tend to the laundry and the cleaning, and do some cooking as well."

"That's really not necess—"

"It's no trouble at all," she said quickly. Maybe she really did need the money. Or at least something to do, a reason to get up in the morning.

I caved. "Great. I'll be glad to have your help, and I'll pay you whatever my mother paid you. I'm sure there are records around here somewhere?"

Iris nodded slowly as we walked into the kitchen. "It occurs to me, Miss Crane, that given your particular circumstances growing up, you must know little to nothing about your mother and her—your—family. If you'd like, I can fill in the details for you. I've been here through it all."

I looked at her carefully; her clear blue eyes blinked back. "You're absolutely right! The truth is, I'm desperate to learn about my mother and her ancestors. The only thing I really know about Madlyn Crane is what I've read about her work."

At this, Iris smiled. "I'll be happy to tell you all I can."

I hadn't been sure how I was going to learn my family's history. Pictures and records existed, names and important dates. But here was somebody who could tell me about the people themselves. "Hearing those stories will mean the world to me, Iris."

She smiled a self-satisfied smile. "I'll take my leave of you now, miss, so you can settle in," she said, with an air of finality. But as she made her way toward the door, she turned one last time. "Is there anything I can do for you now, before I go?" Her eyes were oddly expectant, almost childlike.

"I can't think of anything, no," I said.

"All right, then. Expect me back on Monday morning." With that, she left through the kitchen door.

It was as though she took the gloom with her and left a fresh breeze in its place. Suddenly, I was parched. I looked into the refrigerator for something to drink and found a single bottle of water. I was mid-gulp when I realized with a shudder that my dead mother had purchased it.

I left the bottle on the counter, grabbed my bags, and headed back upstairs to the master suite where I had discovered Iris. There I found an enormous main room with a fireplace tucked into one corner. On the wall across from the king-sized bed (cherrywood headboard: antique, I assumed) hung a flat-screen television. A nice mix of old and new. It was, in a word, awesome, and I don't use that word lightly. It was a perfect place for me, an Eden. I didn't need any other part of the house; I could've lived right there. I'd had apartments that weren't as big, and none, certainly had been as beautiful. Books were piled on the nightstand: a couple of recent best sellers, a nonfiction work about the discovery of a long-lost book of the Bible, and a crossword puzzle dictionary. I picked them up, one by one, and smiled. Her bedtime reading told me the most I had learned about my mother since I had been here.

A big bay window, bigger than the one at the Manitou Inn, looked out onto the lake. It seemed to be a feature of many of the houses here; the islanders apparently loved their views. Next, I poked my head into the bathroom. I was delighted to see a huge claw-foot tub under one of the windows—a nice view from the bath—and a tiled shower in one corner. This was an old house, but obviously Madlyn had renovated it. *I could get used to this.*

The bedroom opened up to another room, a study. Bookshelves lined the walls; another fireplace stood in a corner; photos in frames were everywhere. Two big overstuffed leather chairs with ottomans stood in front of the fireplace, with a comfy chaise on the opposite wall.

Back in the bedroom, I opened a door to find a walk-in closet, with clothes hanging from long racks on both walls. My mother's clothes. I embraced an armful of blouses and buried my face in the fabrics; they smelled like lilac and herbs and lavender. Behind my closed eyes, I saw my mother's face, smiling. *I love you, Hallie girl.* A memory of her at last. At the realization of this, I slumped down to the floor. I missed her so intensely right at that moment, there among her things.

"Why couldn't you have stayed alive long enough for me to get here?" I asked her, out loud. I sat there awhile, in my mother's closet, until it was time to get myself together and start unpacking.

I pushed some of my mother's things aside to make room for my clothes. Seeing my shirts there, hanging side by side with hers, gave me a feeling of belonging that nothing else had. There we were, my mother and I, together. Her house was my house now, and I felt it, through and through.

I looked at the clock in her bedroom, surprised. Nearly five o'clock already. Will would be here in less than an hour. I wanted to shower and change, so I went looking for towels. I didn't have to look far; there was a linen closet in the bathroom where I found everything I needed: fluffy white towels, shampoo (my favorite brand), body wash, and even a few extra Puffs. I smiled. My mother and I shared the same tastes.

I undressed, placing my necklace and earrings on the vanity, and hopped into the shower; the steaming water promised renewal and optimism. Afterward, I pulled on a white robe that was hanging on the back of the door. Using her things and wearing her robe made me feel so close to my mother. Maybe I could find something of hers to wear for my dinner with Will.

I wasn't sure if the restaurant where we were going was casual or fancy, but I knew one thing: We'd be riding in an open-air carriage to get there. No short skirts or high-heeled pumps tonight.

I stood there awhile staring into the closet. I didn't want to give Will the wrong impression—this wasn't a date, it was a friendly dinner. How could I convey that, exactly? I found a long black stretchy cotton dress with a scoop neckline—casual enough so I wouldn't look like I was dressed for a prom if Will was in jeans, yet dressy enough if he showed up in a suit. I had a pair of black flats in my suitcase that would go perfectly with the dress.

I pulled on the dress and scrutinized myself in the mirror. It hugged in all the right places and camouflaged the trouble spots. As I stood there gazing at my reflection, a second vision of myself swam into view behind me. The mirror itself was vibrating and swaying, as though someone had thrown a rock into the glassy surface of a pool, and I saw another me, wearing the same black dress, brushing the same hair. Me, but not me. Older. I took a sharp breath. Was I seeing my mother's reflection in her own mirror?

I was afraid to breathe or move or do anything to disturb the image of my mother standing behind me. I watched as, in slow motion, she raised her arms and wrapped them around my shoulders. I felt her gently stroking my hair. After a lifetime of wishing for it, it was finally happening. My mother was embracing me. Hoping to feel what the image in the mirror reflected, I closed my eyes. When I opened them again, she was gone. I turned around and looked behind me, not sure she had been there at all. How could she have been? No, I reasoned, it was just a fantasy, brought about by standing in my mother's house, wearing my mother's dress, staring in my mother's mirror.

I shook my head to bring me back into the moment. Will would be here soon, and I had to finish getting ready. All I needed now was my jewelry. The necklace was on the vanity where I had left it, but when I went to put on the earrings they were gone.

That's odd. I looked on the floor—maybe they had fallen off the vanity?—but found nothing there. Maybe I had put them into my purse? They weren't there either. I wondered if they had fallen down the sink, but no, the drain was closed. That reminded me: I needed to brush my teeth. I retrieved my toothbrush from my suitcase, came back into the bathroom, and was lifting the brush to my teeth when I saw the earrings. They were on the vanity, just where I had left them.

What was going on? Those earrings were not on the vanity a moment ago. Or were they?

I didn't have long to ponder this mystery, because the doorbell and the barking dogs told me Will had arrived. I slipped my earrings into place, grabbed my purse, and headed down the stairs.

"Hey," he said, as I opened the door. "You look great!"

He looked great, too, in jeans (I was glad I wasn't too dressy), a striped shirt, and a soft brown leather jacket. The bunch of black-eyed Susans in his hand made my stomach do a quick flip.

I flashed a teasing grin. "Did you pull these from the flowerpots on the porch?"

"No, I stopped at the cemetery and took them off a grave."

I couldn't help laughing. "Wherever you found them, thank you. Black-eyed Susans are my favorite." I buried my nose in the deep yellow petals.

A short while later we were in the buggy clopping toward our dinner reservation. Will turned off the main road and headed into the forest, explaining that the restaurant was on the other side of the island, where I hadn't yet been.

"We're about to go through an ancient stand of trees," Will explained, as we jostled along. "The native people who first lived on this island thought these trees were enchanted, that at any time one or all of them could come to life, reach out, and—" He made a grabbing gesture with his hand and chuckled.

Although the night sky was filled with stars, the darkness was inky and dense around us. Tufts of fog drifted here and there like ghosts flitting through the trees. I looked nervously from one side of the carriage to the other. It felt as if a set of eyes was out there, in the woods, watching. Maybe even in the trees themselves. This island's native residents weren't so silly in thinking these woods were enchanted.

I tried to make light of it. "I'm getting a definite Ichabod Crane feeling—" I started, but I choked on the word *Crane*. That I shared the name of a character who had been decapitated in woods like these on an autumn night did nothing to assuage the gnawing in my stomach.

"It does feel a little strange out here at night, I'll give you that." Will chuckled, clearly amused at my nervousness. "Especially since we're about to go by the oldest cemetery on the island." He looked at me wide-eyed, in mock surprise.

"Oh, right." I stifled the urge to pinch him.

"I'm not kidding." He grinned, pointing to the left. There I saw an old wrought-iron fence, decaying gravestones, and dead leaves swirling around like restless spirits.

"I actually sort of like cemeteries, especially very old ones." I chattered away loudly to fill up the dread that was hanging in the air. "Graveyards give a sense of tangible history to a place, names of people, dates when they were born and died."

"Oh, I agree completely. This one is very cool in just that way. You can find gravestones from three hundred years ago. It's amazing."

I was hoping he wasn't intending to give me a tour right then. "Maybe we'll come back some-time during the light of day." I smiled. "High noon. Bright sunshine."

"You know," he mused, "I had an experience in that cemetery not too long ago that I'll never forget."

"Are you going to tell me a ghost story now to

139

further terrify me? I'll pinch you if you do. Hard."

Will laughed. "It's not a ghost story," he said, and then, thinking for a moment, changed his mind. "Well, it might be. Do you still want to hear it?"

"Okay. Yes . . . yes!"

"All right. I was riding my bike along the path that climbs the hill near here, and I got the urge to go into the cemetery and take a look at all those old gravestones," he began. "I hadn't been in there since I was a kid. I was looking around, and I came upon an old, white, crumbling stone. It looked ancient. I read the names: Persephone, Patience, and Penelope Hill. Triplets, apparently. They were born on the same day in 1905 and died on the same day in 1913."

A tendril of chill slithered its way up my spine.

"Of course, I was struck by the fact that they died on the same day and thought about the family that had to bury their three young children," he went on. "But the thing that really got to me? Somebody had been there recently, within a day or so, and placed fresh flowers on the grave."

I shuddered. "That is the creepiest thing I've heard, on a day of hearing very creepy things."

"You haven't heard the creepiest part yet," he continued. "Does the name Hill mean anything to you?"

"No. Should it?"

"It's your family name. On Madlyn's side. Your house? Built by Hills."

I crossed my arms over my chest in a kind of hug. "Was it my mother, tending those graves? It speaks to the enduring nature of grief, doesn't it? I mean, somebody is still thinking about those long-dead girls, even though they couldn't possibly have known them while they were alive."

The forest opened up and revealed a massive Tudor-style building and barn, quite unlike any of the breezy wooden Cape Cod houses that dominated the other side of the island. This looked solid and masculine and regal, like something you might find deep within the forest of a Grimm's fairy tale. We pulled up to the barn, where an attendant loped out to take Belle's reins. I saw the barn was full of similar carriages and horses. Will helped me down, and we walked toward the house.

"Wow," I said, looking around. "This is something."

"I thought you'd like it." He smiled. "It was built as a hunting lodge by an industrialist from Germany in the late seventeen hundreds. It was passed down through the generations but stood empty for almost a century until the current owner bought it and restored it. Now it's an inn and restaurant. The best on the island, to my way of thinking."

We walked through enormous double doors and into a hallway lined with dark wood paneling. A candle chandelier, similar to the one at Madlyn's house, blazed in the foyer, bathing the room in soft flickering light. A bar stood to the left, where several men were enjoying what I assumed were predinner cocktails.

A maître d' wearing a tuxedo greeted us. "Mr. Archer, Miss Crane, so nice to see you both." How lovely to be greeted by name. Will must've told him who I was when he made the reservation. The maître d' smiled over his shoulder and led us into the main dining room. "Right this way."

A massive stone fireplace dominated one wall. Above it hung a boar's head, complete with tusks. Long dark wooden beams lined the ceiling. Candle chandeliers similar to the one in the foyer, along with candles on the tables, provided the only light. The walls were a deep red, and there were several stained-glass windows, although, without sunlight streaming through them, I couldn't see the scenes they depicted.

I was surprised to see every table was occupied; I hadn't thought that so many people were even on the island at this time of year. With everyone talking and laughing, the room should've been very noisy, but the chatter was muted by the high ceiling to a dull, seemingly faraway roar.

Everyone looks so happy, I thought, as the host

held a chair for me to sit down. People would catch my eye, one after another, and nod or smile my way. If word about my return had reached these folks, they were certainly not upset about it. The flickering candlelight made the air in the room seem hazy and swirling, made people's faces look slightly out of focus, as though I were looking at them through the lens of an old spyglass.

"What looks good to you?" Will's voice brought me back from my dreamy reverie. "Steaks are good here."

They were. Over dinner, our conversation meandered this way and that, from island life to national politics to favorite movies. We shared our important stories, some funny and some heartbreaking. I told him of my year traveling in Europe and my marriage; he told me of his college days and the time he nearly drowned in a rip current just off the island.

I could feel the air between us changing, morphing into something tangible and electric and real. In an earlier time in my life, this would have been the moment I thought I was falling in love with the man sitting across from me. But I was more cautious now.

When we finished our meals, the waiter brought the check. "Why don't you go to the bar for some hot cognacs to go while I get the buggy?" Will suggested. "That'll take the chill out of a cold ride home."

Hot cognacs *to go*. What a fabulous concept. "A capital idea, Mr. Archer." I smiled and headed to the bar as he walked out the door.

When, cognacs in hand, I pushed my way outside into the night, I was met by a faceful of chill. Will was standing alongside Belle, waiting to help me up. I climbed in and he draped a thick woolen blanket over my lap before jumping up himself. I handed him one of the cups and took a sip of my own, the warm spiciness lighting me up from inside.

"This is one of the benefits of a horse and carriage," he said, as we touched paper cups in a toast. "You can have your nightcap on the drive home."

When Will pulled Belle to a stop in front of the house, I was glad I had left so many lights on— the warm yellow glow from the windows looked inviting and homey.

"Thanks for a lovely time," I said, gathering up my purse and pushing the blanket off my knees.

"Thank *you*," he said softly, reaching up and grasping a lock of my hair, twirling it lightly before letting it fall back into place as he leaned in to kiss me.

I stiffened and pulled back, jumping out of the buggy just in time and calling a hasty farewell as I ran up the steps.

12

I've brought you a housewarming gift!" Mira announced the next afternoon. She stood on the porch, holding a wicker picnic basket. "Welcome to the island!"

"Thanks so much, Mira!" I exclaimed, as I took the basket from her arms. It was heavier than I had imagined. "This is really thoughtful."

We stood in the doorway for a moment, smiling awkwardly, and then I said, "Come in, come in!"

We trooped into the kitchen, where I turned the heat on under the kettle and opened the basket. I found it lined with a red-and-white checked table-cloth and filled with gourmet items: fancy mixes for scones and soup and cardamom bread, island-made jams and salsa, a crock of lemon curd—even a bottle of red wine.

It was a very kind thing for Mira to do, to search out these various treats, put them in a basket, and haul it over here, especially consid-ering that our last encounter had been rather chilly.

I handed Mira a cup of tea and she held it aloft in the air between us. "To your new beginning!"

A new beginning. That's exactly what this was for me, wasn't it? I hadn't thought of it that way before. I was so wrapped up in death I had failed to appreciate that I was beginning to build a life, albeit a small one, here on the island. And it wasn't half bad.

"Why don't we go into the sunroom with our tea?" I suggested.

"This is such a gorgeous place," she mused on our way from the kitchen. "It's been years since I was here."

I was sure that was, at least partially, the reason for her visit—to get a look inside Madlyn's home. She also would want to find out if I had made any plans. What was I going to do with the house, turn it into an inn? Live in it? I imagine she wondered about all these things. Still, I didn't care. It was nice to have a visitor, even a gossipy one.

We spent the next hour or so chatting as she told me some island particulars: Thursday was garbage day, the wine bar on Main Street was closed on Sundays, Henry didn't like to drive people to the other side of the island anymore so I shouldn't ask. I told her I wasn't sure about my long-term future, but for the short term I intended to stay.

"Excellent news! It'll be wonderful to have another interesting Crane woman on the island." She grinned.

She left with the promise to meet me for lunch sometime the next week. After her visit, I felt warm inside. I wasn't a stranger on the island anymore. I knew people and they knew me. I would have garbage to put out next Thursday!

Little by little, despite the uncertainty surrounding my departure from here thirty years
ago, and the ugliness of my encounters with the
group of islanders at the coffee shop and with
Julie Sutton's mother in the grocery store, I was
starting to belong.

The phone rang, startling me out of my reveric.
It was the first time the phone had rung since I'd
been there, and in the few seconds it took me to
cross the room and pick it up I thought of a
myriad of practical things I had so far neglected
to do. Bills, for example. I didn't even know if
Madlyn heated with oil or propane or electricity.
I made a mental note to put the utilities in my
name and make sure they were paid up. I didn't
want to wake up one morning with no lights or
heat.

"Hello?" I wondered who might be calling me.
I had already talked to Will that morning when he
stopped by to tell me he was off to the mainland
to tend to some business for a client, and Mira
had just left. So who was this?

"Hello, Hallie James. This is Jonah, from the
coffee shop."

A grin spread across my face. "Hello, Jonah
from the coffee shop."

"I know this is awfully short notice, but I'm just
getting ready to close up here, and I started
thinking how nice it would be to meet you for
drinks at the wine bar on Main Street."

Getting out of the house suddenly seemed like a very good idea. "Sounds like fun."

"Excellent. Meet me in an hour?"

After giving the dogs a jaunt around the property and filling their food dishes, I grabbed my jacket and an umbrella, in case of rain, and set off down the hill. I wasn't sure about Jonah's mode of transportation, but I hoped he could take me home after our drinks. Barring that, I figured I could call Henry.

I got into town just as rain began to fall and hurried into the wine bar, shaking off my umbrella in the doorway. I found a cozy room with booths along the windowed wall facing the street and tables scattered in the center. Black leather-covered bar stools stood in front of an enormous, elaborately carved wooden bar (it looked ancient) accented by a mirror running all the way along the back wall and various bottles stacked to the ceiling, which itself was painted with an ornate mural depicting what I assumed to be life on the island in the early days. Small sconces along the walls gave a soft yellow light, and votive candles flickered on every table and the bar, bathing the room in a cozy glow. Two men I hadn't seen before were sitting at one end of the bar, and when I came in, one turned to me and smiled. Other than those two, I saw no one.

I settled onto a stool at the opposite end of the bar, relieved at the relative solitude of the place.

Outside, sleet was hitting the glass in icy bursts. Just then, the door opened and a wave of chilly air rushed into the room along with the stunningly handsome Jonah.

"Hey," he said to me, smiling as he ran a hand through his sandy-blond hair. "Beautiful day out there. I nearly got blown down the street by the wind."

I smiled back at him. "Winnie-the-Pooh would call this a blustery day."

"Ah, but that was on a Windsday," he replied, his eyes shining as he led me over to a booth by the window.

"Pinot, Jonah?" the bartender called out.

Jonah looked at me, raising his eyebrows. That sounded good to me, so I nodded in response. "Make it a bottle, Cal," Jonah replied.

The wine was warm and syrupy, and I felt myself relax as it slid down my throat.

"So, who are you, Hallie James? Where did you come from?"

"Don't you know?" I teased. "I thought everyone on the island was talking about me."

"Well, sure. I know you're Madlyn's daughter, and I've heard what everyone has been saying about you and your father. But that doesn't really tell me anything, does it? You lived half a lifetime between leaving this island and returning to it. That's what I want to hear about."

I wanted to leap across the table and hug this

man. What a fabulous thing for him to say. If only more people on the island felt that way.

"So, tell me about Hallie James," he continued. "What was her life like on the wild West Coast?"

We talked all the way through that bottle of pinot and a second one, punctuated by some hot artichoke dip and crusty French bread. I told him about my childhood in Bellingham and what kind of man my father had been. I told him what it was like growing up the daughter of a single dad, and about my beloved seals, whose barking on the rocks of Puget Sound lulled me to sleep. Jonah seemed as interested as though I were telling him the most fascinating story he'd ever heard. It was intoxicating, I must admit.

"How did your dad die, if you don't mind my asking?" he said, leaning toward me and resting his chin on one hand.

"Early-onset Alzheimer's," I said, looking down at my glass. "It took him quickly, within two years. I suppose that's merciful. The funny thing is, I'm mourning his death, of course, but I'd been grieving ever since I had to put him into a nursing home. And even before that, when the signs of the disease were first appearing. My dad was gone a long time ago."

"You must've felt very lonely during those years," Jonah said softly.

"Yeah, I did. I went to see him in the nursing home every day after work"—I sighed, remembering how painful it was to visit a father who no longer knew me—"but that wasn't my dad, not really."

"He was lucky to have such a devoted daughter," Jonah said. But something about the way he said it didn't match the kind words. His face was unchanged and his eyes were still shining, but . . . I can't really explain it. Maybe it was the wine, or maybe I was being paranoid, but his statement sounded the least little bit like an accusation. My father had a devoted daughter and—what, Julie Sutton's father didn't? That's what it sounded like to me. I had to shrug it off because it didn't make any sense. Jonah seemed to be about my age. He certainly wouldn't be one of the islanders holding a grudge against my dad. Nevertheless, a cloud hung in the air between us for a moment and then dissipated as our conversation turned to other matters.

We left the bar much later. Jonah asked if I'd like to come back to his place for coffee—he lived above his shop on the main street, I learned—but it didn't seem like a good idea to me. I had drunk too much wine with too little food, always a recipe for bad decision-making.

"I think I had better just head home," I told him, hanging on to his arm for support as we walked unsteadily down the street. It had stopped sleeting and the wind had died down, but it was still chilly and damp. I pulled my jacket closed around me. "Can we call Henry from your place?"

Jonah shook his head. "Henry's in bed now, I'm afraid. In the high season there are carriages everywhere at all hours, but now that it's just Henry driving, people need to get where they're going early unless they have their own transportation."

Well, this was very unwelcome news. I had no way to get home. Since Jonah lived downtown, he didn't need to have his own horse and carriage. Will was on the mainland, and I hated to bother Mira at this hour. That meant I was out of options.

"I guess I'll just walk home," I told him, gazing up at the dark hill, an uneasy feeling settling around me. "It's really not that far. And I could use the air."

"I'll walk with you, then," he said. But that didn't seem like a sensible idea either. He'd have to walk two miles up the hill and two miles back down just to see me home.

"I'm a big girl," I told him. "I'll make it back to the house just fine."

He argued a bit but relented when I reminded him of his early wake-up call, and we parted as I headed out of town. I liked Jonah a lot, despite the fact that I got a strange vibe from him. I couldn't quite figure him out, but I knew one thing: There was no chemistry between us. Not anything like what I felt when I was with Will.

No, Jonah and I were destined to be friends and nothing more.

It took a while for my eyes to adjust to the darkness after I was out of range of the Main Street lights. I put one foot in front of the other—it's only two miles, I told myself—and just kept moving forward despite the fact that I was becoming more and more uneasy. No stars were visible in the cloudy sky, no moon illuminated the landscape. It was inky black as far as I could see. The dark night seemed to press in around me from all sides.

As I walked along, I was thinking about my date with Jonah. Something hadn't occurred to me when we were sitting in the bar, but it did now, as I trudged through the cool air. Jonah had asked a lot of questions, but he didn't answer many. I had told him my entire life story, but I had learned almost nothing about him. I had been so wrapped up in talking about myself, I hadn't noticed he didn't share anything about his own life. Was that a good or a bad thing? It was the exact opposite of most men I knew, including my ex-husband, who adored nothing better than talking about himself. *Richard.* I made a mental note to call and tell him everything that had transpired. He had made me promise to do so, but I had forgotten.

I was so wrapped up in my own thoughts that I didn't hear the carriage until it was nearly upon me. I turned to see a black horse pulling a two-seater buggy similar to Will's. It was coming up behind me awfully fast; I had just enough time to scramble into the ditch on the side of the road as it thundered by. The driver, a man I vaguely recognized but couldn't quite place, pulled the horse to a stop several yards away from me. I thought he was stopping to make sure I was all right or even to give me a ride. But he wasn't. He turned to me and said, in a low growl, "You shouldn't be walking alone on this road late at night, Halcyon. It's dangerous. Anything might happen out here." And then he went on his way.

I was speechless. What the hell kind of thing was that to say? No offer of a ride? Thanks for nothing! I stood there, watching that carriage roll on into the darkness ahead. *Did that just happen? Did this man actually threaten me?*

I could understand how people here might still be harboring anger and resentment against my father, but what did this guy have against *me?* I was five years old when it all went down, for heaven's sake. I knew I'd be facing some ugliness when people found out the truth about who I was—the incident in the grocery store with Mrs. Sutton was a prime example of that—but I had no idea that someone would actually *threaten* me. I wished Will weren't away on business.

There was nothing left to do, of course, but continue on home. I saw my house, not far away,

154

light shimmering from the downstairs windows. Suddenly I wanted very much to be safe inside. I ran, breathless, until I reached the front door. I slammed it shut, leaned against it, and locked it safely behind me. I checked all the doors and windows before calling the dogs to accompany me to my bedroom, and I locked that door, too, for good measure. But I still couldn't get the man's threatening words out of my mind.

The next morning, walking the dogs, I decided to go into town. I wanted to talk to Jonah—maybe he knew the man I'd encountered last night or had seen the carriage leaving town—but I didn't want to go alone. As if reading my thoughts, the girls positioned themselves on either side of me as we headed down the hill, and curled up next to the coffee shop door as I burst through it, finding the place empty but for Jonah. I told him the whole story in one long stream.

Jonah put up his hands as if to hold back the tide of my words. "Slow down, Hallie. What man? Who was it?"

"I don't know." I was pacing back and forth in front of the counter. "He looked vaguely familiar, but I couldn't quite place him. He was driving a black horse and a two-seater buggy."

Jonah thought for a moment, squinting as if to get a clear picture in his mind's eye. "I'm sorry. I can't imagine who that might be."

"I'm wondering if I should go to the police," I said to him, rubbing my forehead.

"And say what? That somebody you can't identify tried to run you down?"

He was just standing there, rational and sensible and calm, while I paced like a caged wolf. "I shouldn't tell the police about this? I mean, I think this guy was threatening me."

He shook his head. "All I'm saying is, there's got to be a rational explanation for what happened. You may feel like everyone is gossiping about you, and you know what? That's true. You're the best story to hit this island in decades. But it's going to die down soon, trust me. And no matter how much people are talking right now, nobody on this island would threaten you, Hallie. Not one soul. I know everyone who lives here."

"You sound just like my father," I muttered, rubbing my forehead. "Always a rational explanation for things."

He smiled and reached across the counter to take my hand. "There usually is. It was a dark road, after all. Maybe the guy was startled because he didn't see you until it was almost too late."

He had a point, I had to admit. Maybe Jonah was right. Maybe I had misinterpreted the whole thing. I was suddenly embarrassed by the scene I had just made and grateful that nobody but Jonah was in the shop to see it.

"You know what? You're right. I *am* thinking that everyone is whispering about me, and paranoia is obviously setting in. Let's just forget it, can we?" I asked him.

"Don't worry about it," Jonah said, idly wiping down the counter. "You had a fright last night, that's all."

"I'm going to let you get back to work," I said, pushing my way out the door. On my way back up the hill with the dogs, walking the route that had seemed so malevolent and frightening last night but that was now made benign by the light of day, I let it go. There was no reason for that man, or anyone else, to be threatening me. I had done nothing—that I knew of.

After a quiet weekend spent reading and settling in, Monday dawned gray and blustery. I took the dogs for a quick trip outside, then headed with them upstairs, where I crept back into bed and watched the sleet hitting the windowpanes in icy bursts. It felt good to laze about, warm and snug under the covers, flanked by two enormous dogs, on such a nasty morning. I might have lain there all day if I hadn't remembered that Iris was on her way. I threw back the covers, hopped into the shower, and, to my own astonishment, found myself actually looking forward to seeing her. Maybe we could sit down over coffee and she could tell me about my mother or about my childhood here. It would be a welcome change from the town gossip and the ghostly encounters that had been my lot so far.

Dressed, I went down the back stairs to the kitchen, where the smell of brewing coffee told me Iris had already arrived.

"Morning, miss." She smiled. "I've made scones, started the laundry, and picked up the living room."

Already? How long had she been here? It was a bit odd, knowing she had let herself in and was scurrying around the house while I was sleeping or showering.

But I shrugged it off; it was her job. Besides, one look at the fresh coffee and the plate of warm scones, and I was charmed by the idea of having a housekeeper.

"Thank you for all of this, Iris." I yawned and poured a cup of coffee. "It's wonderful, it really is. Care to join me for some coffee and a scone?"

"Perhaps after I finish my work, miss," she said curtly. "I still have the windows to do."

While Iris shuffled about, dusting, cleaning the windows with vinegar, sweeping, finishing the wash, and rubbing down the woodwork with Murphy's Oil Soap, I hung around feeling guilty. It goes without saying that I had not had the luxury of a housekeeper growing up. Now here I was, an able-bodied young woman, sitting around on my ever-widening rear end while poor decrepit Iris slaved away in her long black dress and sensible shoes. More than once I tried to give her a hand, but I was rebuffed in the iciest of tones.

"This is my job, miss. I've been taking care of this house for more years than you've been alive. Let me do things my own way."

Fine. I retreated to the master suite. Iris could clean house all day long if she wanted. I didn't have to watch her.

I started a fire in the bedroom fireplace and spent the morning curled up in the window seat with a good book, watching the sleet continue to fall on the angry water. It was exactly the sort of morning I love best, nothing to do but indulge myself, the blustery weather preventing me from doing anything productive like exercise or gardening.

The phone rang. "I found out who your mystery man is," Jonah told me.

"You mean the guy in the carriage who tried to run me down?"

"John Stroud. And he wasn't trying to run you down. He was one of the men here the other morning when you came in. And he was here this morning, talking about what happened. He didn't see you in the dark until it was almost too late. You gave him quite a fright, apparently. His blood pressure went through the roof."

"*I* gave *him* a fright?"

"He asked me to tell you how sorry he was."

"I'll bet."

"Anyway, Hallie, the mystery is solved. He wasn't deliberately trying to hurt you. It was an honest mistake. Just drop it and move on."

I wished the islanders would do the same. Would they hate me forever, or was I perceiving their disapproval because of the guilt I felt about somehow being a party to Julie Sutton's death? Did I feel it on my father's behalf?

I didn't mention any of these thoughts to Jonah. Instead, we made small talk for a bit before he ended the conversation with an invitation for me to stop by the shop soon. "I'll buy you a latte," he said, before hanging up.

I heard a crackling coming from the other side of the room and then a voice. "Miss? Lunch is served." I looked around in the direction of the voice and noticed a small intercom on the wall. I hurried over to it and pressed one of the buttons. "Um, thank you?" I said into it, too loudly. "I'll be right down."

As I slipped down the back stairs, I could smell something wonderful wafting from the kitchen. I found a thick stew simmering on the stove and Iris taking a fresh loaf of crusty bread out of the oven. One place was set at the table.

"Won't you join me?" I asked her as I sat down. "You must be hungry after all of your work this morning."

"I've already eaten, miss," she said to me, ladling the stew into a small earthenware crock and setting it, with a basket containing several slices of fresh hot bread and a butter dish, in front of me. "This lunch is for you. But I will join you for a cup of tea. It occurs to me that you might like to hear about your family now. I'm the only one left alive to tell you their story. If you don't hear it from me, you won't hear it. And they—the stories of your people—will be lost forever."

As sleet continued to hit the windowpanes behind us, and I lifted a steaming spoonful of stew from its crock, Iris began to tell me a tale.

PART TWO

13

When Hannah and Simeon Hill, your great-grandparents, came to this island, it was just after the turn of the last century and they were newly married. Hannah was nothing more than a girl, just seventeen years old; Simeon was thirty, thirty-five, perhaps. Maybe more. They're both buried in the cemetery on the other side of the island. Have you seen it?"

"I have indeed. We drove by it the other day."

Iris went on. "Good. You can find the exact birth and death dates on their headstones, but he was a good deal older than his bride. By the time they married, Simeon was already quite a wealthy man. He had started a logging company with his brothers a decade earlier and now he owned the company outright. Much of what you have inherited was initially earned by Simeon Hill and invested wisely over time."

I looked around the magnificent kitchen and gave silent thanks for my great-grandfather's industrious nature. Iris took a sip of her tea and continued, her eyes hazy and unfocused, staring off into nothingness as she spoke.

"Simeon brought his new bride here to this island, which had been an important fur trading outpost for more than a hundred years. By 1900, most of the trappers had gone and Grand Manitou was fast becoming a playground for the wealthy from Chicago and Minneapolis and elsewhere. Simeon had been here several times on business, fell in love with the island, and built a fine house for his young wife."

"What was the island like back then?" I asked.

"Much the same as it is now," Iris replied. "Grand homes, wealthy people, horses and carriages. Not much has changed in a hundred years. The island is charmed in that way. Time passes here, of course, but not like it does elsewhere."

She cleared her throat, took a long sip of tea, and continued.

"By all accounts, Simeon and Hannah had a good marriage, despite the difference in their ages. It is widely known how devoted they were to each other. He was very handsome—tall, dark-haired, eyes as inky as the lake on a November day—and although Hannah was no great beauty, she possessed a certain air about her that drew people in. It was youth and exuberance, certainly, but she also had the most magnificent head of hair on the island—thick, wavy, and auburn just like your mother's—and she usually wore it long and free instead of piled on top of her head as was the style for most women of the day."

Iris turned her eyes toward mine, squinting. "Can you see them, child? Can you see Hannah and Simeon?"

Could I *see* them? What was that supposed to

mean? "I can imagine them, yes," I said, not knowing exactly what she was after.

"Good, good." Iris nodded. "Happy as they were, they didn't have the one thing that would make their family complete: a child. One year passed with no children, then another, and another, and soon tongues began to wag around town, with women providing all sorts of advice for poor Hannah.

" 'Eat more salty foods,' a woman whispered to her after church one Sunday.

" 'Make sure to go to him when the moon is full,' said another.

"None of these silly remedies had any effect at all, of course, and Hannah was becoming desperate. She knew Simeon was eager to sire a new generation of Hills, a family to take over the house and the business someday. But as more and more time passed with no baby, Hannah grew afraid that Simeon would find another way to produce heirs to the family fortune—a new wife.

"She had seen it herself, right there on the island. Three years earlier she had watched in horror as Sandra Harrington boarded the ferry, bags in hand, a veil covering her face. She never returned. A few months later her husband brought a new young wife to live in the house he had built for Sandra, and they set about the business of starting a family."

"That's horrible!" I said, imagining the humiliation of poor barren Sandra, sent away.

"Believe me, worse has happened to women who couldn't produce heirs." Iris clucked. "Sandra was lucky to wind up with a generous stipend to live on instead of a mysterious death."

I shuddered. "Why couldn't they just adopt?"

"Oh, child, that wasn't done in those days. Wealthy men wanted blood heirs and were not forgiving to women who could not produce them. Hannah wasn't about to let that happen to her— she loved her husband too much—so she decided to take drastic measures."

Iris's tone became low and conspiratorial, as though she were telling me something she shouldn't. "One afternoon when Simeon was away on the mainland, Hannah went to the other side of the island and knocked on the door of a local medicine woman, Martine Bertrand, a French Canadian who had come here fifty years earlier with her fur trader husband.

"According to local legend, Martine was a witch." Iris's eyes sparkled. "The Witch of Summer Glen, the children used to call her. Deep within the cedar forest on the other side of the island is a clearing with a small creek running through it that became known as Summer Glen. This fur trader, Jacques Bertrand, built a small cottage there for himself and his wife. But that was long, long ago, fifty years before Hannah

168

herself came to the island. Martine was now an old woman who had been living alone in Summer Glen for decades.

"Plenty of tales exist about her, local legends made more exciting over time, no doubt. Children would sneak through the woods to get a look at the old woman, despite their terror that she would spirit them away. They say she was a vindictive, evil old witch, casting spells against the high society that had turned her rustic island home into an enclave for the wealthy."

"A witch, Iris? Come on. You're not about to tell me you think she actually was a witch."

Iris smiled. "Of course not, child. All those rumors are nothing but hysterical nonsense. Martine was a healer, a medicine woman, someone who knew how to make potions and poultices with ingredients she found in the earth and the water. She possessed much knowledge, ancient knowledge. Though nobody would readily admit it, and certainly wouldn't talk about it outright, many of the society ladies would steal across the island, wearing cloaks to disguise themselves, and knock on Martine's back door. Some sought love potions for indifferent men, others a cure for a recurring cough. Some wanted the right combination of herbs to break a child's fever; others wanted teas that would ease female complaints. Martine always gave them what they were looking for and never asked for anything in return—no payment, no acknowledgment on the street, not even a kind word.

"Rumor had it, however, that Martine exacted her own price. They say she sometimes laced her potions with malevolence and magic, curing and cursing at the same time. A man would recover from fever only to find his voice mysteriously gone. An always sickly child would become hale and hearty enough to play outside, only to die in a fall from the first tree he ever climbed."

"But that can't be true," I murmured, feeling physically cold at the thought of my great-grandmother going to such a woman for help. This story was beginning to sound suspiciously dark and gloomy. Was it true or was Iris embellishing a local legend?

"I don't know whether to believe those stories or not." Iris eyed me suspiciously, as if reading my thoughts. "I only know what happened to Hannah.

"When all else had failed, when doctors could do nothing but encourage her to pray, and when hope of ever having a child was seeping away, Hannah wrapped her crimson cloak around her, stole out to the stable, saddled her horse—your great-grandmother was an accomplished horse-woman in her day—rode to Summer Glen, and knocked on Martine's back door."

Iris's eyes were deep and dark now, filled with excitement and thrill. "Martine was waiting in the kitchen. She ushered her visitor inside—the doorway was so small your great-grandmother had to stoop to make her way under the lintel.Hannah found herself in a tiny kitchen, dominated by a big cast-iron pot bubbling away on the stove.

" 'So you have finally come to Summer Glen, Hannah Hill,' the old woman said to her. 'What is it you want of me?'

" 'Please,' Hannah begged in a low whisper. 'All I want is to give my husband a child.'

" 'Is that all you want? You want no more than that?'

"Hannah bowed her head. 'Please. I've come to you because of what people say, and I believe you have the power to give me what I seek. I want to be able to give my husband a child.'

" 'You do not need me for that,' Martine said to her. 'You are fully capable of giving your husband a child. It is he who cannot give a child to you.'

"Hannah was speechless.

" 'But I can help you help him.' Martine smiled slyly and crossed the room. She returned, holding a small cloth bag. She opened it and Hannah saw it contained dried leaves and herbs she could not identify.

" 'Your husband is a tea drinker, yes?' she asked. Hannah nodded. Simeon liked freshly brewed tea in the mornings and afternoons, a habit he had picked up from his British mother.

" 'Mix a spoonful of this with his tea leaves for three mornings,' Martine instructed. 'He will not be able to smell it or taste it. On the third evening, go to him and you will conceive.'

"Hannah looked at this stooped, gnarled old woman, black shawl around her shoulders, bag of magical herbs in her hand, and suddenly had doubts. Should she be doing this? Wasn't this against God and nature?

" 'Is this—witchcraft?' Hannah wanted to know.

"The old woman smiled. 'That depends. I know certain secrets about making cures from what I find here in the glen. If you want to call that witchcraft, so be it. I call it the knowledge to use what God has given us on this earth.'

"Hannah nodded, somewhat calmed by Martine's words. Gingerly, she took the bag from the old woman's hand. 'Are you sure this will not harm my husband in any way?'

" 'The only thing these herbs will do for your husband is make it possible for him to father children—not just once but from now until his dying day,' Martine said forcefully. 'The tea will change him forever; he will be fertile like any other man. You will bear as many children as you desire. But it will not otherwise harm or damage or change your husband. On that you have my promise.'

" 'I've wished for a child for so long,' Hannah murmured, eyeing the contents of the bag.

172

"'Be careful what you wish for,' Martine warned. 'And listen well to me, Hannah Hill. I said this tea will not harm your husband, and it will not, but you must know this: He is not meant to father children. His line should end with him. By using these herbs, you are calling forth certain *powers* to deliver children to you, against what nature itself has intended. This cannot be undone.'

"'Yes.' Hannah nodded anxiously. 'That's why I've come.'

"'But you must understand.' Martine tried again. 'Any child conceived this way, out of—as you call it—witchcraft, can be unpredictable. You might get a demon or an angel or something in between; there is no way of knowing. *Children conceived out of witchcraft are witches them-selves, as are their children and their children's children.* Whether they are good or evil depends on their spirit. I cannot control the type of spirit that might come through. Your children, their children, and their children—all will be similarly cursed or gifted.'"

"More talk about witches, Iris?" I said. "This is sounding like the stuff of Grimm's tales."

"And yet it's the story of your own family." She looked me square in the face. "Best listen, child."

I nodded, drawing my arms around me as though I had felt a sudden chill. "I'm sorry. Please go on."

173

"Hannah listened to what Martine was telling her about cursed or gifted children, but there, in that tiny kitchen, she reasoned that the same uncertainty would surround any child. No mother knew what kind of child she would have, sweet or rebellious, blond or brunette, strong or sickly. That was up to God, or so Hannah believed. Martine was really saying the same thing, wasn't she? In her desperation, Hannah thought so. Hesitating only for a moment, she put the cloth bag in her pocket and got back on her horse.

"Over the next three days, Hannah brewed the herbs and leaves with her husband's morning tea, and, just as Martine predicted, on the third day she did indeed conceive a child. Hannah knew it the moment it occurred, with a jolt that felt to her like an explosion deep within her body. And nine months later, Hannah and Simeon were the parents of triplet girls, Penelope, Persephone, and Patience."

"I heard about them!" I told Iris. "Will Archer found their graves. They died so young. What happened to them?"

Iris smiled ruefully and shook her head. "This is where the story gets a little bit haunting," she said slowly, sipping her tea. "You know what people said about Martine, how she always exacted her price for the cures she doled out? Well, in this case, it was true.

"Simeon and Hannah loved their daughters

174

fiercely, but, truth be told, something about the girls just wasn't right. From a very young age, they were devilish and mischievous, pinching one another in their cribs, pushing one another down the stairs, deliberately frightening their mother by pretending one or another of them was dead."

A shudder crept up my spine.

"They were not like other children of the time, who were, for the most part, obedient and quiet. You never knew what those triplets might do. They gave Hannah and Simeon quite a time of it.

"They loved playing hide-and-seek in the house and around the grounds, and poor Hannah was forever looking for them." At this, Iris actually chuckled. It was a gurgling, choking sound I didn't care to hear again.

"It wasn't just the disobedience," Iris continued, shaking her head. "It was also their strangeness. It seemed as though the girls were not separate people at all. They never went anywhere alone. They spoke in the same monotone voice, came when you called any one of them, and would stand in front of you with identical looks on their faces. I know it sounds like a fantastic tale, but it seemed as though the girls shared one soul. Of course that could not have been the case."

"Of course," I mumbled.

"One more thing you should know about them," Iris went on, her eyes shining. "They were almost transparent. Their skin was papery thin, so thin you could see blue rivulets of blood rushing through their veins just beneath the surface. Their eyes were the palest of blue, so pale it was nearly not a color at all. And their hair was stark white. It was as though Hannah had given birth to a trio of ghosts."

"Will said the girls died young."

"There was a freak storm when they were eight years old. The townspeople were certain Martine had caused it, but that was, of course, hysteria on their part. Storms brew up out of lake and water wind here on the island when you least expect them. This one happened on an early November day, a beautiful day. The girls were playing outside, right there on the cliff. Hannah was in this very kitchen making supper when the storm descended. Nobody knew it was coming. That's how it was with storms and tornadoes and floods back in those days, with no modern weather forecasting."

My mind sputtered, caught in a hazy fog of remembering. "Are you talking about the 1913 storm? I've heard about that somewhere."

Iris nodded. "It was one of the worst disasters ever to happen here—or anywhere else on the Great Lakes, for that matter." She gathered her thoughts and went on. "It was a relatively mild day, typical of early November, the type of day that lures sailors and fishermen onto the lakes

176

with the promise of calm seas and balmy temperatures, only to turn ugly and murderous once the poor souls are too far from land to return.

"This was the time of year in which the leaves had long since fallen, their abandoned branches now spindly and gnarled, exposed and vulnerable—as, in a way, were the residents themselves—to the wind and snow that would surely come. But that particular day, no snow was on the ground, the sun was high and bright in the sky, and the winds were calm."

"It sounds like the weather now," I offered.

"Exactly like now. People relished those rare November days, riding their bicycles one last time before the snowfall, hanging wash on the line to capture the air's fresh scent, opening their windows to coax that freshness inside the house before closing them for six months of winter.

"That's why Hannah Hill had no objection when her young daughters begged to go outside after school instead of doing their chores. Let the children play out of doors while they can, Hannah decided, glad to have them out of her hair for a few hours. Her husband was scheduled to return from a trip to the mainland that afternoon, and she wanted to make everything right in the house for his arrival.

"It was so balmy, the girls didn't take their coats when they ran off to the cliff, some hundred yards away. Hannah, meanwhile, cleaned and fluffed the living room and turned her attention to dinner. During the off-season, she and her husband gave the servants a liberal amount of free time to visit family on the mainland, and this was one of those days. Hannah was managing on her own—unlike many women of her station, she was a capable cook and housekeeper—and enjoyed the quiet pursuits of making just the right dinner for Simeon and creating a lovely atmosphere for him to find when he returned home. These were acts of love for Hannah.

"She was making a meat pie, a favorite dish of her husband's, wanting him to find a kitchen smelling of care and attention when he got home. She had no idea, as she chopped the onions, potatoes, and carrots, that her life was about to take a horrifying turn. It always happens that way, doesn't it? Destruction descends at a moment's notice, without any warning, when one is caught up in the business of everyday living."

I nodded, thinking of the day this life-altering journey began for me.

"She didn't notice, being inside the warm kitchen with the stove blazing, that the temperature outside had dropped dramatically. Had she realized what was happening, she might have called her daughters in. The four of them might have huddled together by the fire, perfectly safe in the fortress of a home her husband had built, until the storm passed.

"Certainly, if Hannah had had any inkling that a storm had been killing people on the lakes for four full days already—and was rapidly moving eastward, toward the island—she would have acted differently. But as it was, the Hill triplets were playing their favorite game, hide-and-seek, on the cliff while their mother made dinner.

"As two of them hid and called out clues to the searcher, the storm was marching through the Great Lakes, ravaging whatever it touched. Ten-foot snowdrifts engulfed entire towns; hurricane-force winds shattered windows and tore up cobblestones. People lucky enough to be in their houses were trapped there. Those caught unawares on their way home were never seen again.

"The snow and wind were only the half of it, however. This was early November, and none of the lakes had yet frozen, so enormous icy waves, taller than three-story buildings, slammed into shore, destroying docks and piers and seawalls."

I pulled my legs under me. "I can't imagine a storm that fierce."

Iris shook her head. "It was nature's fury unleashed, child, nothing less. Imagine being out on the water with those waves engulfing ships and freezing them solid. Dozens of freighters went down in a single day, not to mention all the small fishing boats and other vessels that were lost. Hundreds upon hundreds of people died, including three little girls who were playing outside when this murderous storm finally reached Grand Manitou Island."

I had been holding my breath for this entire story. I was so cold I felt I, too, was being caught unawares in that dreadful weather.

"The death of the Hill triplets wasn't as simple as just freezing to death, which in the end, of course, they did. Before the girls knew what was happening, the storm was upon them. The temperature dropped dramatically and the wind came. Had they gone inside right away, they would have survived. They would have grown up, married, had children, and finally died. But that didn't happen.

"Persephone spotted it first: a steamer, out of control, being pounded like a toy boat against the rocks just offshore. The horrifying realization hit the girls: Their father was returning home that afternoon, on board that steamer.

"Despite the cold, despite the wind, the three sisters scrambled down a path on the rocky cliffside to the shore; in their young, naïve minds, they believed they could do something to help their father. They were yelling *Papa! Papa!* but their words were swallowed up by the wind and carried away, and they could only watch in abject terror as wave after icy wave bombarded the steamer, encasing it—and all the men aboard—in a solid layer of ice.

"As bad as it was for their father on that steamer, the girls had worse trouble. They were standing on the shoreline, just steps from the water, when the snow bore down on them.

"An ordinary blizzard on the Great Lakes is an awesome and frightening thing, but this was wrath tenfold. Carried on the back of the punishing gale-force wind, the snow began streaming sideways so hard and fast that the girls could not keep their eyes open against its force. It was a complete whiteout—even if they could have opened those pale blue eyes, they would not have seen anything beyond their own noses.

"They stumbled, cold, frightened, frantic, holding onto one another, toward the cliff, but they had no idea where to find the path up to the house. They couldn't make out anything, held as they were in the grip of that blinding white monster. So they huddled together against the rocky cliff, hoping someone would come to their aid.

"But no one came. It didn't take long before the massive waves that had blown the steamer into the rocks reached land—and the three girls. Wave after wave hit the poor sisters, and within minutes they were frozen solid in a block of ice, wrapped in one another's arms.

"Meanwhile, up at the house, a frantic mother was looking for her daughters. Hannah had been working at the stove when she happened to glance out the kitchen window and, in horror, realized that a blizzard had descended upon them. She grabbed her shawl and ran outside into the storm, screaming her daughters' names: 'Persephone! Penelope! Patience!'

"More and more panicked as the minutes passed, she too was soon blinded and confused by the storm. Which way back to the house? Where were the girls? She couldn't see more than an inch in front of her, the snow beating down so hard and fast that it sliced tiny wounds into her exposed face and arms. She had trouble remaining upright in the punishing wind, so she bent low, yet she kept on. She would not leave her girls out there, alone, in the storm. Tears froze on her face, creating a hideous, icy mask of grief."

My own eyes had welled with tears, and as I reached for my napkin to blot them away, Iris handed me an old lace handkerchief. Like her, it smelled of decaying roses and dust. "I know, child," she said, with a softness on her face that I hadn't before seen. "I know." She waited until I had blown my nose and dried my eyes and then continued her tale.

"Hannah Hill didn't know it, but she was walking directly toward the cliff. She would've stumbled to her death if she hadn't heard voices, soft and low, on the wind behind her. She held her breath and listened.

"'You're going the wrong way!' The voices

seemed to be saying. 'You're cold! You're ice cold!' And then laughter.

"Was it the children playing hide-and-seek? Hannah turned and began walking blindly in the direction of the voices. 'Girls? Where are you?'

"She heard, 'Warmer! You're getting warmer!'

"'Girls! Stop this game and come inside!'

"'Warmer, Mama, warmer!' And so Hannah kept going, against the wind, one foot in front of the other, following the sound of those voices— 'You're hot! You're burning up!'—until one foot bumped into a stone step. Hannah was astonished to find herself standing at her own back door. She hadn't been able to see the house until she was upon it.

"Hannah stood there for a long while, listening in vain for the voices; she heard only the howling of the wind. Had the voices been there at all? Surely no child could have been playing out in that storm.

"She thought she might rest a moment before heading out to look for her daughters once again. She went inside, closed the door, and lay down on the floor in front of the fire, her face and arms bleeding from the razor-thin cuts made by the icy snow. She would just put her head down for a moment, she thought, and then resume the search. She was so tired."

"Oh, no," I whispered. "Don't tell me—"

Iris nodded. "Yes, child. This is no children's

story. It's as real as it gets. Poor Hannah woke up the next day, after the storm had passed. The residents of Grand Manitou Island, including Hannah Hill, knew it was time to look for the dead and do what they could for the living. As they emerged from their homes, they saw a world completely covered in ice. Bright sunshine glinted off shining trees, porches, and fences. Three feet of snow had fallen, drifting to cover second-story windows in some places. It might have seemed beautiful, had it not been so deadly. Hannah tried to make her way from her house to the cliff but could not manage to slog through all that snow. Digging out would have to be the work of hardier souls, those with snowshoes and shovels and spirits that were not in mourning. She went back into her house and slumped in a chair by the fire, waiting for someone to come.

"It was a good thing she was not the one to find the bodies of her daughters, frozen together, their terrified expressions still clearly visible through the inch-thick layer of ice that encased them. But they weren't the only souls frozen to death that day.

"For nearly a week after the storm, Manitou residents watched in horror as the frozen, deathly still bodies of sailors, having perished on steamers and freighters and fishing boats, floated ashore, one after another, in a ghostly parade of the dead."

I thought about the dream I'd had about my father and knew then where all those lost souls had come from. "And Simeon? Did he survive?"

Iris nodded. "Miraculously enough, he did. Everyone on board his steamer lived to tell the tale. The waves had run the boat aground on an enormous rock, so it didn't sink despite the fact that much of it was torn to shreds. The passengers had huddled together in the pilothouse. After the storm subsided they tried to break out through the doors and windows, using anything they could find. But it was no use. A thick layer of ice covered everything. They were entombed.

"Luckily for them, rescue was on the way. The next day, men from the island made their way to the steamer in fishing boats and were astonished to find everyone alive, trapped within. The rescuers went back to the island, grabbed every pickax and shovel they could find, and returned to the steamer, working furiously to break the icy shell.

"Simeon's gratitude for surviving the storm was short-lived. He came home to find his beloved daughters dead and his wife in a state of catatonic grief. Nature's fury had taken more from him than his own life.

"Time passed, and Hannah slowly came back to herself. She and her husband were resilient and not unaccustomed to death, so they leaned on each other for comfort and support, and in time, they put the enormous pain of their loss behind them. Their lives went on. Simeon and Hannah had a son a few years later.

"But that is not the end of this sad tale. Curiously enough, until the day she died, Hannah Hill was never again caught unawares by a storm as she was on that horrible day."

"What do you mean, Iris? How?"

"Whenever a storm was brewing, whether it was an emotional storm, as when, many years later, Simeon died of a heart attack one afternoon on the golf course, or a dangerous physical storm like the one that took her daughters' lives, Hannah would hear small voices whispering to her, warning her of impending doom."

"How can you possibly know all this, Iris? Did you hear the story from my mother?"

Pridefully, she sat a little straighter. "Child, I was the one who told these stories to your mother and to her father before her. I was here. My mother was Hannah and Simeon's housekeeper. We lived here, on the third floor of this house. I knew the girls and I saw it all. And everything that came after."

"You knew the girls?" I was stunned.

"Of course! I played with them. I was just a girl myself."

Somehow, it was not difficult to imagine the creepy Iris playing with those three bedeviled girls.

"So where were you when the storm hit?"

"I was on the mainland that day, with my mother," she explained. "It was her day off and we went to shop as we oftentimes did. We were stranded in the hotel; the snowdrifts were so high we couldn't see out of the second-floor windows! If I hadn't gone with her, I surely would've been playing with the girls outside that day. My life was spared."

I gazed out the window. I had no idea how much time had passed while Iris was telling her tale, but it seemed to me that the gray day was spilling into a gray evening.

Iris cleared her throat and stood up from the table. "That's enough for one day, I believe," she said. She took her cup and saucer to the sink, gave them a quick wash, and dried them with a towel. "I'll take my leave now, miss, and be back on Wednesday. Perhaps you'd like to pick up where we left off, once I've finished my work. There's much more to tell, and much more for you to see."

"You're a wonderful storyteller," I said to her.

Iris puffed up a little at this compliment, clearly pleased. With that, she pulled on her overcoat and rain bonnet and made her way to the back door. I felt bad about her going out into the rain on her own. I would have offered her a lift home—if I had had the means to give her one.

"Shall I walk with you, Iris? Make sure you get

home okay?" I asked, but she just shook her head.

"No need, miss. I've been walking these lanes since long before you were born. I know my way well enough."

I went with her to the door, where I gingerly hugged her brittle frame. "Thank you, Iris. You don't know what it has meant to me, finally hearing about my family."

"Oh, I think I do, child." She smiled. "I think I do." I watched as she made her way down the path toward the driveway and slipped out of sight, into the gloom. Then I closed the door, but I couldn't get rid of the damp feeling that had seeped in from outside.

· 14

Later, as I sat by the fire, I stared into the flames and thought about the story Iris had told me. It was, literally, the first family story I had ever heard. My father never told me anything about his family and he certainly never told me anything about my mother's. Now I had a history—ancestors with names and lives and, in this case, tragedies—Hannah and Simeon Hill, my great-grandparents. As I looked around the room, I thought, *They built this house, began to raise one family here, lost it, and then somehow finished raising another.* And here I was, a woman with the same genes, the same heritage, the same lineage, living here still. Despite the icy reception I had received from some of the townspeople, I at last had a solid feeling of belonging.

Day slipped into night and I crept under the covers of my bed, ready for sleep, when two thoughts seeped into my brain, thoughts strange enough to make me sit upright with a jolt.

Iris said she was a child when the girls died, that she knew them. But they died in 1913. *Just how old was Iris?*

As I was calming down from that idea—okay, she was old as the hills, so what?—the second thought occurred to me. I heard, as clearly as if I had been standing in a corner of the room when they were first uttered, the words Martine said to Hannah the day she went to seek out a fertility potion:

By using these herbs, you are calling forth certain powers to deliver a child to you. . . . This cannot be undone. Any child conceived this way, out of—as you call it—witchcraft, can be unpredictable. You might get a demon or an angel or something in between; there is no way of knowing.

I had been thinking of Martine as nothing more than a woman who knew enough about the earth and plants and herbs to make poultices and cures for sicknesses and maladies. Women with that type of knowledge were branded as witches back then. But the warning from Martine, and the fact

189

that the girls had indeed been an eerie lot, made me wonder exactly what was in that bag of herbs.

Then Martine's next lines came to mind: *Children conceived out of witchcraft are witches themselves. As are their children and their children's children.*

I took a quick breath. That meant me.

· 15

I awoke with a start. Somebody had touched my face, I was sure of it. I thought in my grogginess: *Iris?* It couldn't be. Why would Iris be creeping about in my house in the middle of the night? Still, my eyes adjusted to the darkness and peered this way and that, half expecting to see her face, white and ashen, at my bedside. I looked at the clock: 3:15 a.m. This was silly, I thought. Iris wouldn't be here in the dead of night.

I was about to close my eyes and fade back into sleep when I realized I had felt the same thing, the same delicate brushing against my face, several nights earlier at the inn. Was that same someone—or something—here in my room now?

I sat up in bed, flipped on the bedside lamp, and looked around. Nothing was amiss that I could see. There was the sweater I had thrown on the chair when I put on my pajamas; there was the book I had been reading before I fell asleep. No ghouls were hiding under the bed, no ghosts floating in the corners of the room.

Still, it wouldn't hurt to give the whole suite a once-over. I swung my legs over the side of the bed, tucked my feet into my slippers, and padded across the floor to the sitting room. I turned on the light and saw that all was just as I had left it: the afghan on the armchair, the water glass on the side table.

Bathroom? I looked in the tub and poked my head into the shower. Nothing but a spider scurrying toward the drain. I was thinking about opening the bedroom door and looking up and down the hallway for good measure, but I decided against it. I was in a little fortress here, safe and protected in my small suite of rooms. There was no need to open up the door and invite the rest of this enormous house into the mix. If I did that, I'd have to explore every room in order to feel secure enough to sleep.

I lay down on my bed, convinced I had been dreaming. I was just closing my eyes when the singing began.

Say, say, oh, playmate.

My eyes shot open. Did I really hear what I thought I heard? It was the same song in the same strange minor key that I had heard a few days before. My heart was beating hard and fast in my chest as I gathered the courage to look once again around my room. I did not want to see Iris there—

or someone worse—singing that eerie song in the darkness.

Nobody was there, thank goodness. I was alone in the room. I exhaled.

Come out and play with me.

Oh, no, no. Stop that singing! I don't want to hear more singing. It sounded far away, as though coming from outside. Oh, Lord. Is somebody outside my window, singing? In the middle of the night? How long it would take for this person to find his or her way inside the house? How many paces would it take me to get to the kitchen, where I could at least grab a knife or even a large fork to protect myself? Was this night going to end with me fighting for my life?

And bring your dollies three.

Like hell I will. I flipped off my bedside light, gathered my courage, and walked over to the window. The bright moon was illuminating the grounds and shining on the water. A multitude of stars filled the sky, and slight wispy clouds floated this way and that. The leafless trees stood sentinel on the cliff, their limbs inky and black.

Nobody was there. Only trees and rocks and the lake, just as they should be. I was midway through my sigh of relief when there it was again.

Climb up my apple tree.

I squinted to get a clearer view of the grounds below, trying to spot whoever or whatever was doing this.

There, from behind one gnarled tree branch, I saw something floating through the air. Held aloft by the wind, it danced and swayed in the darkness, its white surface illuminated by the moon's light: a single silk ribbon. All the breath flew from my body in the instant I saw that ribbon, and I sat down hard on the window seat, my heart pounding, my mind grasping at several thoughts at once. And then she stepped out from behind the tree: a girl, with long fair braids, one of them missing a ribbon. She was looking directly up at me, smiling.

I was still as the grave. I could not believe what I was seeing: a little girl, there in my yard, in the middle of the night. My eyes fixed on her smiling face, I watched her open her mouth to speak. As her lips began to move, I heard a small voice whispering directly into my ear, as though she were standing right behind me.

And we'll be jolly friends, forevermore.

I made a noise that emanated from the core of my being, a sound so fierce and terrible and deep that, as I think of it now, it might really have had the power to curdle the blood of any unfortunate soul who happened to be within earshot. As I screamed once, twice, and a third time, I jumped up and whirled around in a circle, first one way, then back again, to make sure nothing was lurking behind me.

Breathing heavily, telling myself, *That didn't just happen, that did* not *just happen,* I ran across the room and turned on the overhead light, bright as day. Then I crept back to the windows and, one after another after another, I pulled down every shade. If she was still out there, I could not see her. And she could not see me.

Now what, call the police? And tell them I had been frightened by a little girl playing with a ribbon? That I had seen a ghost? I'd look like a complete idiot.

I could call Will, Jonah, or Mira, but I didn't think anyone would appreciate being awakened at three in the morning for a nonemergency. Especially not Jonah, who had to get up in a couple of hours himself. I didn't want to jeopardize my seedling friendships with any of them by hysterical calls in the middle of the night. I had already puzzled Mira with my nighttime outburst at the inn, I had already seemed paranoid when I made a scene in Jonah's about the man and his carriage almost running me down as I walked home a few nights earlier. I was rapidly becoming the crazy lady who thinks everyone, living or dead, is out to get her. Despite how frightened I was, I didn't want to further that reputation. I was completely on my own.

Shaking, I crawled back into bed. Why couldn't the dogs be sleeping with me instead of downstairs? I grabbed the remote. Thank goodness for cable. I flipped through the channels until I found an old rerun of a sitcom I used to enjoy. Perfect.

● ● ●

A couple of hours later, I was flipping through the channels again—a World War II documentary, a Weather Channel storm story, a testimonial for a weight-loss drug (mildly intriguing)—when I paused on what looked like a movie. There was something familiar and comforting about the scene: blue sky, laundry flapping on the line, a child rolling in the green grass.

But then the child winced as though she were in pain. "Ouch!" she squealed. "Stop it!" She got up and ran from the clothesline. "Leave me alone!" Crying, she fell backward, as though she had been pushed. "Stop it! I don't like you!"

"Hey, Peanut," a voice called as a man walked into view. "What's the matter with my girl?" He scooped the child into his arms and comforted her, cooing, "It's all right now, honey. It's all right. I'm here now." As they walked out of sight, the girl gazed over the man's shoulder and stuck out her tongue.

The camera panned to the object of the girl's derision: a child. Dressed in white. Long braids tied with white ribbons.

Mid-scream, I realized that I was awake. I had fallen asleep, obviously, and was dreaming about the girl I had seen outside my window. After rubbing my eyes, I caught sight of the time. Nearly eight-thirty. Bright morning sunshine bathed my room in light.

I lay there for a moment deciding whether to get up or slip back into sleep, but when it hit me I shot upright in bed. The windows. I had closed those shades last night; I was sure of it. Now they were open, just as they had been when I went to bed the first time. And the television was turned off, as were the lights.

I tucked my feet into my slippers, hopped out of bed, and gingerly opened the bedroom door, looking up and down the hallway before venturing into it. I made my way down the back stairs to the kitchen, where, to my astonishment, I found fresh coffee brewing. A basket of hot muffins sat on the counter. At my place at the kitchen table, some yogurt and a bowl filled with fruit.

Iris, of course. Had she opened my shades and turned off my television? It was the only explanation—or so it seemed. I went from room to room searching for her, calling her name. However unsettling as Iris was, she was at least a human companion. After the night I had just endured, I needed one. But Iris was nowhere to be found. She had made coffee and breakfast for me and then departed. At least, I hoped it had been Iris. With shaking hands, I poured some coffee and flipped on the morning news. *My house. My coffee.* No ghost was going to scare me away.

My father had taught me to be a practical thinker, but reason couldn't explain away a little girl in a white dress outside my window in the middle of the night, whispering into my ear a strange and unsettling childhood song. Either someone was playing an elaborate hoax on me—but who? to what end?—or something truly otherworldly was happening.

With a sinking feeling, I told myself I knew exactly who that little girl was. Iris was the only person alive who could tell me what the triplets looked like, but she wasn't scheduled to come back to the house until Thursday, and I had no idea how to get in touch with her. But she *had* been to the house and made breakfast today, hadn't she? Maybe she'd come back tomorrow to do the same.

I topped off my coffee and wandered into the living room. Madlyn must have had photos—somewhere—of her relatives and ancestors, especially considering the fact that the Hills had lived in this house for three generations. Old family photos, perhaps an album, had to exist.

I dug around the living room for a while and found a couple of albums, but they mostly consisted of recent photos. Madlyn and friends, Madlyn and celebrities, Madlyn and politicians. I spent a few hours going through them, enthralled by being privy, just a little bit, to my mother's world. I even found a shot of my mother with her arm around a young Will, his tall gawky build suggesting he was about fourteen. Will.

I felt a tightening deep inside. What had he thought of me pulling away from that kiss? I certainly didn't want to alienate him—I needed all the friends I could get on this island—but having sprinted up to the house after what he probably considered a date, I knew I'd have to make the first move if we were to get together again. Maybe he was back from his business on the mainland and we could have lunch. I picked up the phone and dialed his office.

"Hello to you, Miss Crane," he said, surprising me by answering his phone himself. Obviously he had caller ID.

"Don't you have a receptionist?" I laughed, ridiculously happy to hear his voice. It felt good to be talking out loud—to anyone—after the night I'd had.

"The job's open for the season if you want it," he said. "But of course, you're a lady of leisure these days."

"I'll have you know I've been hard at work this morning," I told him.

"Have you now?"

"I have indeed. Care to know what I've been working on?"

"I'm dying to know."

"Lunch plans. Got any?"

"Let me just check my schedule." I heard a great shuffling of papers and then: "You're in luck. By an astonishing coincidence, I have no lunch plans for today. Or any day for the next five months, with the possible exception of a dental appointment in January that I'm already planning to cancel."

"I'm so glad you'll be able to squeeze me in."

"Where would you like to eat? We have all of two choices."

"Actually, I was thinking you could come here for lunch," I told him. "I thought maybe we could have a picnic on the grounds since it's such a nice day." I had cold chicken and salad makings as well as the rest of Iris's bread, cheese, a little fruit, and some wine. And the picnic basket from Mira.

"Hey, what a good idea," Will said. "I'll stop by the deli at the grocery store and bring a little something. And I know a perfect spot for a picnic on the grounds of the house. You know it, too, but you probably don't remember it."

"I do?" Nothing came to mind. "I mean, I don't?"

"I'll refresh your memory when I get there. About noon?"

"Sounds great." I looked at the clock. It was nearing eleven already. I raced upstairs and hopped into the shower.

I wrapped myself and my hair in a couple of thick towels and trotted to the closet, where I began to go through my clothes for just the right outfit. I settled on jeans and a cream fisherman's-knit sweater. I found a long colorful scarf in the closet and wound it around my neck. After drying my hair and putting on some makeup, I gave myself a final once-over in the mirror. Ready as I would ever be.

Only then did I realize I was hearing the quiet drone of the television in the background. I poked my head out of the bathroom and, sure enough, a morning talk show was in full swing.

All the lights were on, too. And the shades were closed. Just as I had left things last night. *Okaaay.* When I woke up this morning, the TV and lights were off and the shades open. Weren't they?

I stood there for a moment, taking in the scene. Somebody—or something—was messing with my head. This was a child's trick. If it had happened in the middle of the night I would've been terrified, but now, in the light of day, it just made me angry.

"Very funny, girls," I shouted into the empty room. "You're not scaring me, if that's what you're trying to do. You're annoying me."

I stalked out of the room, slammed the door, and started down the hallway, stopping short when I heard giggling coming from my room. My breath caught in my throat. Maybe I wasn't so fearless after all. I ran down the stairs and into the kitchen, not daring to look back over my shoulder. I hurriedly threw together the picnic lunch and hovered near the door and the dogs until I saw Will loping up the drive.

Soon enough, we were sitting together, nibbling on cold chicken salad and sipping white wine as he relayed an account of his past few days, tending to the needs of an extremely fussy and wealthy client.

"That reminds me," I started. "I've been meaning to ask. How did you get back from the mainland? I thought the ferry didn't come back until Friday."

Will nodded. "Exactly right. The only way to get back and forth this time of year is on a private boat, which is what I did. My client sent his for me."

I yawned—not from the conversation but because of the wine in the middle of the day—and looked around. Will had led me to a part of the estate I had never seen. I hadn't done much exploring on the grounds since I had been here—too much of the house itself to explore, I supposed. Through the gardens and a stand of trees, a clearing opened. It was high on the cliff overlooking the water, but the view here was wider than the view from the house. We could see down the shoreline for miles.

I had spread a plastic tarp on the ground first, then a thick blanket, then the lightweight red-and-white tablecloth Mira had given me. And we settled in. It was a bright blue day, crisp enough for a jacket but comfortable in the sun. The dogs lay on the cliff beside us, noses held aloft in the slight breeze.

"And what have you been doing for the past few days?" Will asked.

"Before I tell you, I have a question." I grinned at him over the rim of my wineglass. "What are your feelings about ghosts?"

"You mean, do I believe in them in a literal sense?"

"Well, yes."

"I'm not sure." He took a sip of his wine. "It doesn't seem to be beyond the realm of possibility, but I've never experienced a ghostly encounter personally. Although people say this island is full of them. Why?"

I was already wishing I hadn't brought it up. But the frightening experiences I was having were wearing on me and I couldn't afford to hide in my denial any longer. I had to tell someone. "Strange things have been happening to me ever since I got here," I began. "Truthfully, they started happening before I got here."

He sat up straight and folded his arms. "What kind of things?"

Taking a long sip of wine, I told him the whole story. I told him about my experience at the inn, first seeing the person drowning, then the hand print, then the vision of a girl hovering over me while I bathed. I told him about my jewelry disappearing and appearing the night we went to the restaurant on the other side of the island. Finally, I told him about the girl outside my window.

"She was singing," I told him. "Do you want to know what she sang?"

He smiled. " 'Muskrat Love'?"

I can't explain why—maybe it was a function of how nervous it made me to tell Will about the ghosts, maybe it was because it put that whole horrible incident the night before into an absurd light—but the image of that creepy little ghost girl singing "Muskrat Love" struck me as so funny that I put my head down on the blanket and exploded into laughter. It was one of those unexplainable, unstoppable, breathless bouts of laugh-until-you-cry that keeps feeding on itself. When I could finally catch my breath, I kicked at Will and said, "She was not singing 'Muskrat Love.' "

"What was it, then?"

I sang, minor key and all, softly into his ear. *"Say, say, oh, playmate. Come out and play with me."*

"Whoa!" Will shivered, displaying goose bumps on one arm. "That officially gave me chills. Listen, are you sure you saw what you thought you saw last night? Are you sure you weren't sleeping?"

"Reasonably sure," I said. "So, Mr. Attorney, what's the rational real-world explanation for all the things that have happened to me in the past few days?"

"I don't know what to tell you." Will sighed. "I'd love to be able to say that the little girl who was outside your window last night is a well-known prankster here on the island who makes a career out of scaring newcomers."

"But you can't tell me that, can you?"

Will shook his head. "No, I can't."

"I know this sounds crazy, but I'm wondering if she's one of those dead triplets you told me about. I've been learning about my family history, and I know they died in a blizzard right here on the property. Do you think—"

"I really don't know what to think, Hallie," he interjected. "The only sort of real-world explanation I can offer is the possibility that your imagination is working overtime. We had the conversation about the triplets the night we went to the restaurant. Maybe it planted a seed in your mind. You had the encounter with this girl last night, right? You'd been asleep. Maybe it was all a dream. Can you be sure it wasn't?"

"Well, no," I admitted. "The thing is, though, I saw the same girl at the inn before we went to the restaurant. Before I even knew about the triplets."

Will nodded. "Right."

I went on. "And what about the fact that I closed the shades and turned *on* the lights and the TV last night, but when I woke up this morning, the shades were open and the lights and TV were *off?*"

He smiled. "That proves it was a dream, though, doesn't it?"

"You'd think so," I told him, excited now. "Except that when I got out of the shower this morning, I found the shades drawn again and the lights and the TV turned back on."

I sat there, looking at him expectantly. When he didn't say anything for a moment, I filled up the silence. "This is the part where you think I'm just fabricating and all of this is in my head, isn't it? You're wondering if you can creep away from the crazy woman slowly and safely."

Will laughed. "I wasn't wondering that, actually. I was wondering what in the hell is going on."

"I can't think of any other explanation. Can you? Other than me being insane."

"Yes, there's that." He laughed. "The old schizophrenia flaring up again. Off your meds?"

I pinched his arm in response.

We chuckled for a few moments, and then he said, "Okay. Let's say you've got a bona fide ghost at the house. What now?"

"I'm not quite sure," I confessed. "If I was watching this in a movie, I'd be screaming at me to get out."

"Yeah, the whole little-girl-ghost thing is about as ghoulish as you can get," Will mused.

We both lay on our backs, looking up at the sky, which was rapidly turning gray.

"So what now?" he asked again.

I sighed. "If only I knew."

Giant drops of rain began to fall. As we threw the picnic mess back into the basket, a deep rumble of thunder echoed over the hill and we were drenched by the time we burst through the kitchen door, laughing and out of breath. Before I knew what was happening, Will's arms were around me, his mouth on mine. His lips tasted like wine and rain and possibility, and for a moment I almost let myself get carried away in the romance of the moment. But something inside me went cold. All I wanted was to be free of his touch.

I put my hands on his chest and pressed myself back toward the wall, shaking my head. "No, Will."

He looked at me, confusion clouding his eyes. "Hallie," he began.

"I'm sorry," I said weakly, staring at the ground.

"No, *I'm* sorry," he murmured. "I didn't mean . . . Look, I thought—" His words hung in the air. I didn't catch them, I didn't offer a safety net, and I could almost hear the thud as they fell to the ground.

"I should leave," he said softly, turning his eyes to the door. He didn't look at me again. He just walked out of the house and into the storm without a backward glance, and I let him go.

I stood there for a moment, wondering what I had just done.

It rained for the rest of the afternoon. I tried to fill up the time with reading and watching TV and playing with the dogs, but my mind was on Will. The look in his eyes before he left was devastating.

I tried to call him several times but only reached voice mail. Then I took the phone into the living room, made a quick calculation about the time difference, sank into one of the armchairs, and dialed Richard, half a world away.

"Well, it's about bloody time," he said gruffly, and instantly I was filled with the warmth of his humor and his caring. "I've been worried sick about you. Tell me *everything*."

And so I did. I told him about the house and the dogs and Iris, Jonah, and Mira and the island itself. I told him about inheriting everything from my mother, and what little I knew about her. I told him about Iris, laughing about her dour demeanor. I told him about the singsong tune I kept hearing and about my strange experiences here in the house and at the inn. And I told him about Julie Sutton.

"It all sounds quite Gothic," he said. "A huge old house, stuck on an island in bad weather, an unsolved murder, mysterious encounters with ghosts and rude townspeople, even the eerie old maid."

I agreed, laughing. "It does sound rather

Gothic. The house is just gorgeous, Rich. You'll have to come someday soon."

A silence, then. I could hear the tiny clink of his spoon against the side of a china teacup. "Hallie." He was still stirring, which he always did to fill time when he wasn't quite sure how to phrase what he wanted to say. "What aren't you telling me? I know there's something you're not saying."

I hesitated for a moment before admitting it. "Okay," I said quickly. "I met someone and I think I just screwed it up."

"Ah. That's the real reason for your call. All this ghost talk was just the preamble."

I felt a twinge of guilt. I should've called him sooner, as I had promised. "I really need somebody to talk to, Rich. Somebody who knows me. Somebody who isn't weirded out by how much I look like a dead woman. To everyone here, I'm just this freak who died thirty years ago."

He chuckled at this. "You really do fit in there among the skulking maids and haunted houses, don't you?"

"Finally, a place where I belong." I laughed, too.

"All right, freaky girl. Go ahead. Tell me about him. Who is he and what did you do?"

"He's a lawyer here on the island," I began. "We were friends when we were kids."

"That's starting off very well. Go on."

"We've spent a lot of time together; he was my mother's lawyer. He's the one who contacted me initially. We get along great. It's like we've known each other forever. He's easy to talk to, and . . ."

"And?"

"Well, he's everything I've ever looked for in a guy," I admitted, both to Richard and to myself. "He's smart, thoughtful, funny, and we like to do the same things. I don't know. He's a real catch. Plus, he's gorgeous."

"Oh. Well, then, I can see why you threw him out, or whatever you did. He sounds perfectly hideous."

A smile crept across my face. "That's the thing. There's nothing wrong with him. It's just—when he tried to kiss me, I froze."

"What do you mean, froze?"

"I mean, I froze. I couldn't respond to him."

"Why ever not?"

I thought about this for a moment. "I'm not sure. We were having such a great time on our picnic. And then it started to rain. We ran into the house—"

"It sounds quite romantic, Hallie."

"It was. It's just . . ."

"What? The right setting, the wrong guy? No chemistry?"

I shook my head. "No, that's not it, not exactly. There's plenty of chemistry between us."

I heard Richard stirring his tea again. "What happened then?"

Poor Will's face swam into my mind. "He seemed really confused and embarrassed and muttered an apology. And then he left. I haven't talked to him since."

More stirring. "I'm going to ask you a question now. You're not going to like it, but I'm going to ask it anyway."

My stomach tightened up. Richard has a way of cutting right to the chase, and he is not known for his gentleness in doing so.

He went on. "What are you afraid of?"

"I'm not sure what you mean by that."

"Well, come on, Hallie. Gorgeous guy. You get along great. He's got no discernible flaws, and you've got chemistry between you. You're both single. Why not give it a go? I mean, really. What's the worst that could happen?"

All of a sudden I realized why I had wanted to talk to Richard. "Well, he could be the love of my life, marry me, and then discover I'm not his type."

Richard sighed. "I wish I were there right now to throw my arms around you, tell you how sorry I am, and make you believe that it's never going to happen to you again."

"I wish you were here, too. I wish a lot of things."

Richard cleared his throat. "I have to ask. Have you dated *anyone* since we broke up?"

"Not really," I admitted. "I've been on a few dates, but—"

He cut me off. "Listen, Hallie. You've got to get back out there. You are a terrific woman, the best I've ever met. You're drop-dead gorgeous, and now you are a woman of means. You deserve to be happy, my darling. You can't cut yourself off from love because of me, you just can't. I cannot have wrecked you. I'd never forgive myself."

"But I believed you," I said. "I trusted you, and then my world came crashing down."

"You're right. That's exactly what happened. But the thing is, Hallie, that wall of protection you've built around yourself isn't going to bring you happiness. It might bring safety, but it's awfully cold and lonely living alone in a fortress. You have to dare to take a risk. You have to risk having your heart broken, again and again and again. That's the only way you'll find happiness, my love. It's the only way."

· 17

I tossed and turned all night, Richard's words rattling through my brain. Was he right? Had I really built a fortress around myself?

The next morning, I called Will at the office. Still no answer. Obviously, he was avoiding me. Had I destroyed whatever had been happening between us before it even had a chance to start? I toyed with the idea of marching into town to find him, but the rain hadn't let up overnight. It was still pouring outside.

No Iris this morning either, and even the dogs had retreated to parts unknown. I was on my own. I sank into one of the kitchen chairs next to the window, looked out onto the rainy yard, and sighed.

Hours passed. I rattled around the house trying to occupy myself; I watched a DVD, read a bit, but always kept coming back to the kitchen window. Staring out seemed to make the most sense; it seemed like the right thing to do. I desperately wanted to talk to Will, but I wasn't sure what I would say.

Finally, I saw a figure coming up the drive, and a moment later Will burst through the back door, his clothes soaking wet. "Hallie, I—" he started, the rest of his thought hanging in midair.

"I know," I said, crossing the room in an instant. I brushed a wet tendril of hair off his forehead. "I'm sorry. I've been through so much lately, and I reacted badly."

He grasped my arms in his hands, finally finding his voice. "I understand you've been through the wringer, but you've got to understand something. I'm not your ex-husband. And I'm not your father. What you see is what you get; I'm as uncomplicated as that. I have no secrets, no hidden life, no agenda. It's just me, a man who is scared to death because he's fallen in love with you and you don't seem to be on the same trip."

My heart began pounding. I wanted nothing more than to run out of the door, away from the edge of the cliff. But I didn't do that. With Richard's advice ringing in my ears, I leaped off the precipice, not caring how hard I might hit the ground. I wound my arms around Will's neck and pressed my mouth to his, tasting wind and rain and forever. With thunder growling outside and the lights flickering on and off, we made our way up the back stairs to my bedroom and fell into each other's arms.

Later, Will wrapped himself in a robe and went downstairs to the kitchen to retrieve our wine. We lay in bed together, talking about our dreams, our disappointments, our important stories. But truly, nothing in my past seemed as important as what was happening between us right then.

"I'm sorry about yesterday," I finally said, twisting the sheet between my hands.

Will reached up and brushed a strand of hair from my eyes. "I know it's hard for you to trust me," he said gently. "But I'll never let you down like they did."

I looked deeply into his eyes and knew I was hearing the truth.

"By the way," he asked, as he rolled onto his

back and stretched. "When did you have time to make dinner?"

I wasn't sure what he meant. "I didn't."

"Somebody did. There's a pot of something on the stove. I noticed it when I went down to the kitchen to get the wine."

We both pulled on robes and investigated. It was true, there was a big pot of barbecued boneless spareribs simmering on the stove, along with cornbread muffins in the oven. Suddenly, I was famished.

"It looks fabulous," he murmured.

After I had set the table and served us both big plates of ribs, I explained. "Must've been Iris."

"This is the second time you've mentioned her. Who's Iris?" Will wanted to know. It struck me as funny that, on an island this small, he didn't already know her.

"The housekeeper," I explained. "I found her going through Madlyn's things the first day I moved in. She told me she had been keeping house here for decades. Her mother worked here before her, when the first Hills built the house."

"Oh, right," Will said slowly. "I vaguely remember Iris. I haven't seen her in years. But of course I haven't been to the house in years. Madlyn and I would do all our business in my office." He thought a moment. "Iris was old thirty years ago, or she looked old, at any rate. She must be—what—pushing eighty now?"

"More than that, I think," I told him. "She told me she knew the triplets, used to play with them as a child. But that was ninety years ago."

"And she still comes here to clean?"

"She cleans like a tornado." I laughed. "Look at this place, it's spotless. She cooks, too, as you can see."

Will squinted at me. "Don't you think it's time Iris retired, slave mistress?"

"Believe me, I've tried to rip that dust mop from her hands on more than one occasion. I feel guilty every time she's here, working like a dog while I sit around watching soap operas. But she won't let me help and gets offended when I tell her to take it easy."

"She's proud."

"Yes, that's it. She feels a sense of ownership of this place, and rightly so. She grew up here."

We sat in silence for a moment.

"You've got to meet her sometime. I'm telling you, Iris is the eeriest human being alive."

"How so?"

"It's her manner," I mused. "She seems to have taken her persona right out of a Vincent Price film. Dour, ashen-faced. She wears a long black dress and winds her white hair into a tight bun on top of her head. And she comes and goes whenever she wants. I'll get up in the morning and discover she's been creeping around while I slept. She was down here in the kitchen today while we were—upstairs."

Will laughed. "She sounds lovely."

"Hey, at least she leaves food in her wake," I said.

When we had finished eating, we went back upstairs, watched a Woody Allen movie, and then snuggled down in my bed. I slept better in Will's arms than I had during my entire stay on this island: no ghostly visits, no scary dreams, nothing that went bump in the night—except each other.

• 18

The next morning I was sitting at the kitchen table drinking coffee with Will when the phone rang. It was a call for him, oddly enough. He had given my number to his answering service, apparently, and now real life—a client from the mainland—was intruding on our love affair. I had imagined we'd spend the day together.

"Duty calls," he said, kissing me goodbye. "I wasn't expecting this conference call, but I've got to get to the office."

I pouted. "That's what they all say."

He stopped and scooped me into his arms. "Dinner tonight?"

"I'll cook," I said. "I'll make my famous Cornish pasty. You'll love it."

"I knew you'd force me into eating English

216

food sooner or later." He grinned as he made his way out the door.

A short while later I was climbing out of the shower and heard a soft whirring; someone was vacuuming downstairs. I pulled on my clothes and went down to greet Iris.

She scowled at me. "You've had an overnight guest."

I wasn't sure if she was simply making conversation, in her strange and uneasy way, or if she was passing judgment on the fact that Will had spent the night. In any case, what business was it of hers?

"Yes," I said, a bit too loudly, over the vacuum. "Will Archer. I hope to see a lot more of him."

"Your choice, of course," Iris muttered darkly, and went back to her vacuuming.

I was about to deliver a sermon about minding one's own business when I thought better of it. Perhaps I could coax Iris to sit down with me again today. Maybe she'd tell me another story about the past. I could've sworn I saw a slight smile creep across her face as I walked past her toward the sunroom, as though she knew what power she held.

I whistled for the dogs, and we walked down the hill to the grocery store, to stock up for dinner tonight and for the coming weekend. It felt good to get out of the house and into the bright blue day. The dogs ran ahead, playing and barking and then circling back. They never strayed too far.

I'd learned that the grocery store had a delivery service for residents who didn't have the means to get the bags back to their homes. Just pick out your groceries, pay for them, and they arrive on your doorstep within the hour. I was immensely grateful for this as I walked leisurely through the aisles, finding the ingredients for Cornish pasty and wild rice soup and throwing in some cheeses, fruit, crackers, and wine as well.

When I finished shopping, I went outside and whistled for the dogs. To my horror, there on the other side of the street stood Julie Sutton's parents. I was not up for another confrontation with these people, so I tried to slink around the building into the alley, but then I heard my name called. "Halcyon! Please wait!" *Damn it all.* I turned to find that they were walking across the street in my direction, so I steadied myself and braced for a fight.

I didn't get one.

"Halcyon, I'm Frank Sutton," Julie's father said to me, extending his hand. "I believe you met my wife, June, the other day."

I nodded, wondering where this was going. "That's right."

"I'm just sick about the way I treated you," June Sutton said, her eyes brimming with tears. "I had no right to talk to you the way I did, and I want you to know I'm sorry."

I squeezed her hands. "I can't imagine what you went through back then. I can only tell you that I didn't know anything about it until I got here to the island."

"I know," June said. "I shouldn't have taken it out on you. It's just that, after all these years—"

I could see she was close to losing it again, so I spoke up. "Please, think nothing of it. We'll put it behind us and start fresh."

The Suttons nodded, each suffering the particular hell that only parents who have lost a child can know, and we went our separate ways. I was more determined than ever to learn the truth about what had happened to their daughter, once and for all.

I walked up and down the streets of town, one destination on my mind. Finally, two blocks off Main Street in an old three-story brick building, I found what I was seeking: the police station.

I took a deep breath and pushed open the door to find a man seated at a desk immersed in paperwork. He looked up as I walked in. "Ah . . . I'd like to inquire about the possibility of gaining access to the police files dealing with a closed case."

He squinted at me. I wasn't sure if he knew who I was or not. "Which case?"

"Well, it's something that happened here on the island thirty years ago, and—"

He cut me off. "You're Halcyon Crane." He was not smiling.

I nodded, putting my hands on the counter. "That's right. I'd like to see the file of the Julie Sutton investigation, please."

"The Sutton *murder*," he corrected me.

"Her death." I could feel tension in the air between us, as though the very mention of the case was making this man angry.

He shook his head. "No can do, I'm afraid."

I knew I couldn't just waltz into the police station and emerge with the file, so I was prepared to fight. "Aren't police records of closed cases, especially ones this old, a matter of public record?" I wasn't sure about this, but I thought I'd seen it on a *Law & Order* episode.

He nodded. "You're right. Closed cases *are* a matter of public record. But this case isn't closed."

"But"—I was confused—"it happened thirty years ago and the suspect is dead. Maybe you hadn't heard that my father died a few weeks ago."

"Dead or alive, his status has no bearing on the case," the policeman told me. "It's an open investigation."

"I don't understand. Are you investigating another suspect?"

The policeman shook his head. "In this state, all murder cases are considered open until they're solved. We haven't looked into this case since your father's death—since he went *missing* thirty years ago. But that doesn't mean the case is solved."

"So there's no way for me to get a look at the file."

"Unfortunately, no." And he went back to his work, or pretended to. Defeated, I gathered up my purse and went outside into the sunshine.

"Lost the battle but not the war," I muttered to myself as I walked up the street.

Back at the house, I saw Iris had already set out some leftovers for lunch—ribs, bread, and a steaming cup of stew from the day before. She was at the stove when the dogs and I burst in through the back door.

"Won't you join me for lunch, Iris?"

"No, miss, I've already eaten. This lunch is for you." She also handed me a cup of tea, steam filling the air in front of me. It was a scent I didn't recognize—a strange herbal concoction of earthy smells: moss, leaves, and autumn. "Your mother's special blend." Iris smiled, remembering, as she sat down at the kitchen table beside me, and I knew it was time for her to continue her story.

"I told you that Hannah recovered from the loss of her girls with strength and courage," Iris began, "but that's not entirely the case. She did go on with her life, and she and Simeon did have another child: your grandfather, Charles Hill. He lived and died in this house. But that's a story for another day."

I took a big bite of the ribs, chewing slowly as she continued.

"Hannah went on with her life after the girls died, it's true, but it was not without suffering and not without foolishness. She was destroyed by the loss of her daughters, as any mother would be. But the difference between Hannah and any other mother was that Hannah knew she had conceived those babies only with the help of the Witch of Summer Glen."

I felt that familiar chill creeping up my spine. Iris's eyes grew dark and cloudy.

"For weeks after the girls' deaths, Hannah was consumed by a sort of madness. She was convinced that the children, while not actually alive—she had been at their funeral, everyone on the island had attended—were still hovering near her. Unexplainable things would happen around the house: a clock falling from the fireplace mantel, glasses shattering, doors opening and closing of their own volition. Hannah came to believe that the girls were causing these things to happen, and she concluded, to her horror, that her precious daughters were someplace between life and their heavenly reward. The girls hadn't made it to heaven, Hannah believed, and she was frantic for their safety."

"What did Simeon think about all of this?" I interrupted.

"Simeon?" She sneered. "He was a good man,

to be sure, but an extraordinarily practical one. He put no stock in the otherworldly. Clocks falling, glass shattering, doors opening and closing—these things could be easily explained. This was, and is, a drafty house.

"He had no idea, remember, that Hannah had visited the witch Martine in order to conceive those babies and that his daughters were the direct result of a spell. So he humored his wife. A bereaved mother must be permitted ample time to grieve, after all, no matter what form that grief takes.

"Privately, however, he visited with the minister on the island—a devout missionary with no tolerance for anyone who did not conform to the line of strict church doctrine. He also consulted her doctor, who quietly suggested medication or even committal if Hannah's hysteria didn't resolve itself in short order. So Simeon held his breath and waited, watching his wife closely as he talked to her in the most gentle of tones.

"One afternoon when Simeon had gone to work, she saddled up her horse and rode to the other side of the island. She had questions, and she knew only one person who could answer them."

"Martine."

Iris nodded. "Although it had been nearly nine years since she had last seen her, the witch was waiting. Hannah told Martine the whole tragic story: her daughters had perished in the blizzard but had somehow managed to guide their mother to safety, sparing her their tragic fate.

" 'I am convinced they are still with me, there in the house,' Hannah said to the witch.

" 'How do you know this?' Martine asked, absently handing Hannah a cup of tea.

" 'I can feel it,' Hannah answered, drinking it. 'I feel their presence near me. And things have happened around the house. Glasses break. A clock fell. Doors open and close.'

" 'But they have not contacted you? They have not spoken to you since the day they died?'

" 'No,' Hannah admitted, 'but I am sure they are with me.'

"Hannah began to feel hazy and random, as though her thoughts weren't her own. The edges of reality began to blur, the world disappeared, and she saw nothing except the old witch's face.

" 'What do you want of me, Hannah Hill?'

" 'I want to communicate with my daughters,' Hannah replied. 'I want to tell them I'm all right. I want to know that they're all right.'

" 'Summoning the spirits of the dead is not a thing to be done lightly,' Martine warned. 'Summoning the spirits of the dead who were given life through witchcraft is all the more dangerous.'

" 'Why is that?'

" 'By calling them to you, you're asking them to stay in this world. Are you prepared for that?'

" 'They're my daughters,' Hannah insisted, her head heavy and dull. 'Are they all right? Do they need me to do something for them? I want to know. I need to know.'

" 'Are you certain?' Martine asked.

" 'Yes,' Hannah murmured.

" 'So be it. I will come to you when your husband is away. Together we will summon the girls, and you will have what you desire.' "

As I listened to this part of the tale, something nagged at me. "Iris," I interrupted. "How do you know all these things? How can you possibly know the conversations that took place between Hannah and Martine?"

Iris looked annoyed by the question. "Just listen, Halcyon. It will all become clear in time. Do not interrupt."

I settled back into my chair, murmuring, "Sorry," while Iris cleared her throat, took a sip of tea, and prepared to continue.

"Hannah thanked Martine and left. It was only when she was away from the house, deep in the cool air of the woods, that she realized she had not asked Martine for what she *really* wanted: help in seeing that her girls would get their reward in heaven. No matter. Martine had said she would be able to talk to the girls. She would sort it all out then.

"The minutes dissolved into hours and seeped into days as Hannah anxiously awaited Martine's visit. Every day Simeon left the house for work, Hannah would sit expectantly in the kitchen, at this very table, staring out to the road beyond the house."

Iris pointed an arthritic finger toward the windows behind me. I fidgeted in my seat, imagining my great-grandmother sitting just where I was sitting, waiting for a witch who would contact her dead daughters. I thought of my own ghostly visitors, if that's indeed what they were, and shivered. I sipped my tea, hoping to feel its warmth inside.

"Finally, the day came," Iris continued. "Martine, disguised in a hooded cloak, appeared at Hannah's back door. She was carrying a small velvet bag.

"'You are sure no one else is here?' Martine asked her, looking around the room furtively. Hannah nodded. But she was not correct. Hannah did not know I was here, along with a young cousin of mine from the mainland. My mother was here as well, doing the wash in the laundry house, which at one time stood where Madlyn's garden is today."

I looked out the window and saw the ghostly outline of a crude wooden building. Iris's mother was carrying loads of white sheets out of its door toward the clothesline. I shook my head. *Am I really seeing what I think I'm seeing?*

Iris interrupted my vision. "Look deeply, child. Deep within yourself."

"I don't understand what you mean."

"You will." Iris smiled. "The visions will solidify. Soon I'll become little more than a narrator for what you're seeing with your own eyes. After that, you won't need me at all."

"Iris, you're not making any sense."

"You'll soon see." Then she continued the story. "I suppose Mrs. Hill was too wrapped up in her desire to talk to her daughters again to have thought about the maid and *her* daughter. My cousin Jane and I were playing outside in the big stand of cedar trees when we saw Martine coming up the drive.

"Of course, when we saw her we ran to the house immediately to get a better look. We had heard tales of the Witch of Summer Glen, but we had been much too afraid to cross the island to spy on her as the other children did. Now, here she was, coming up my very own drive!

"My cousin and I looked through the window and watched as Martine opened the small crimson velvet bag and began setting items from it on the kitchen table: a lace cloth, candles, dried herbs. Then she said, 'I need one personal item from each of the girls.'

"Hannah left the kitchen and returned a few moments later with three satin ribbons. " 'They wore these in their hair,' she murmured, clutching the ribbons as though they were sacred talismans."

My breath caught in my throat at this. Satin ribbons?

"Martine nodded her approval silently and gathered the ribbons in the center of the table. She placed the candles around them. Into the flame of one of the lit candles, she sprinkled an herb of some kind, which produced a crimson-colored smoke and a dark musky scent so strong it reached even to our young noses, outside the window. And then Martine began to speak in a language I did not understand. She was saying strange-sounding words, over and over and over—an incantation. She seemed to have slipped into some sort of altered state, a trance, because her eyes began to roll back into her head, exposing the whiteness around them.

"I looked at Hannah, and she was still as the grave. She seemed hypnotized. She was staring into space, not looking at Martine, not looking at us through the window, just staring.

"I, too, began to feel a sort of pull toward oblivion. I tried to move but could not, trapped as I was, right there, at the window, watching this witch cast a spell that would summon the dead.

"Suddenly I understood the words Martine was saying. She had begun to chant the girls' names, over and over again. Persephone, Patience, Penelope; Persephone, Patience, Penelope. She was calling on their spirits to return."

As Iris chanted the girls' names, I felt as

though I became the little child outside the window, peeking in at the scene. Through the hazy windowpane I saw Martine's grizzled face, Hannah's blank stare, the kitchen transformed into how it had been a century earlier—no microwave in the corner, no stainless-steel fridge—just two women sitting at the kitchen table, summoning the dead.

"Persephone, Patience, Penelope," Iris went on, her face contorting into the sort of trancelike mask Martine's face had worn.

I felt the ribbon on my cheek. I wanted to cry out for Iris to stop. Was she was summoning those children just as Martine had done almost a century ago? I didn't want to find out. I tried to tell Iris to stop whatever she was doing, but I couldn't move; I couldn't speak; I was trapped in the web Iris was weaving with her words.

Now the scene shifted. I was no longer the girl outside the window but Hannah. Vaguely, somewhere in the distance, I could see Iris sitting next to me, eyes rolled back in her head, chanting an incantation to three dead children. The clearer, more tangible image before me was that of Martine sitting across the table. I was seeing what my great-grandmother had seen, here in the kitchen, nearly ninety years ago.

A crash from the living room caused the vision to dissipate like steam rising from a teacup. I shook my head to clear my confusion as the kitchen door flew open and slammed closed, again and again and again. This brought Iris out of whatever spell she was weaving as well, and she looked at me with clear, dark eyes.

I jumped up from the table. "What do you think you're doing?" I demanded to know, looking around wildly. Several glasses had fallen from the shelves and shattered on the counter. Thankfully, the doors had quieted down of their own accord.

Iris just smiled and shook her head. "I'm merely trying to finish the story. There is much more to tell."

"I'm not at all sure I want to know the rest, to tell you the truth," I said, holding fast to the back of my chair. "I mean, look around. Did all those glasses just fling themselves off the shelf?"

"I'll clean them up as soon as we're finished," she said.

"That's not the point. Were you trying to summon those girls, just like Martine did?"

She looked at me and said, in a voice not entirely her own, "I do not need to summon Penelope, Patience, and Persephone. They are here. When the witch summoned them that day, she called them to this house from beyond and they have been here ever since."

I sat down hard. It was true, then.

"There is more to the story, child, more you must hear."

I nodded weakly, and Iris went on.

"As Martine chanted the girls' names, glasses began to break, doors began to open and close, and Hannah, when she was able to break free of the spell Martine was wrapping around the table, sprang to her feet and cried, 'Girls! Girls! It's your mother!'

"But the girls weren't bothering with their mother that day. As I said, these girls were not normal children of the day. They were mischievous to the point of viciousness, even in life. It was as though they didn't have souls at all. Nary a conscience among them.

"Martine and Hannah did not see my cousin and me, crouched and shivering with fear beneath the kitchen window, but Persephone, Patience, and Penelope did. They homed in on my cousin, the poor thing. I'm still not sure why they left me alone; perhaps because I had been their playmate in life.

"I heard them giggling and whispering as they descended upon my poor cousin Jane. They pushed and jostled and kicked her. They pinched her and tripped her. I should have intervened, should have done something to help, but I was just as terrified as Jane was. I cowered behind a bush and watched as Jane ran screaming from her invisible tormentors. The last I saw, she was tumbling over the cliff."

I sat there staring at Iris in stunned silence for a

moment. "What do you mean, the last you saw of her?"

"I mean Jane died that day, Halcyon. They found her body in the exact spot where the girls had died a few months earlier."

· 19

"I think I know why my father took me away from here," I told Will later that night over dinner.

When he arrived on my doorstep a few hours after Iris had left, I flew into his arms. I had been terrified the rest of the afternoon in the house alone. Hearing the story about Hannah, Martine, and the girls—and poor Jane!—had pushed *me* over some kind of precipice. This had gone beyond a few odd ghostly encounters that would make interesting dinner party conversation. Now I felt as though I had been drawn into a nightmare. I had suddenly become the unlucky sap who happens upon the children of the corn, the traveler whose car breaks down in a town filled with vampires.

I stayed with the dogs in the kitchen until Will got there, not wishing to venture into other parts of the house, areas where three evil little girls could be lurking. I busied myself making dinner. The dogs sensed my uneasiness and kept close, curled up next to me all the while.

Now I was serving Will a slice of Cornish pasty and telling him everything—how Hannah and Martine had summoned the spirits of the girls, how Iris had been watching from the window and saw the whole thing unfold, how poor Jane had been driven to her death by the three spirits.

"That's an incredible story." Will shook his head. "I wonder if any of it's true."

I held my soup spoon in midair. "You think Iris was making it up? Why would she do that?"

Will backpedaled. "I'm not saying she fabricated anything, but it all happened a long, long time ago, when Iris was just a child. An old witch, spells, incantations, summoning dead children—you have to admit, Hallie, that it sounds like a legend. Something straight out of a child's imagination."

"I'd love to believe Iris's story was just her imagination working overtime, but I've seen the girls. One of them, at least."

Will nodded. "Or what you believe to be one of the girls."

"What I *believe*?" I stared at him. "I'm not crazy, Will, if that's what you think."

"I know you're not." He backpedaled again, putting his palms in the air as if to hold back my anger. "Okay. Let's go with the theory that everything Iris told you today is the honest truth; nothing was embellished, nothing overblown. What now?"

"It might explain why my father took me

away." Will started to shake his head in disbelief, but I cut him off before he could speak. "Just hear me out. What if my father found out about this story somehow? Maybe he saw the girls himself, just like I have. Maybe . . ." My words trailed off. I hoped Will would pick them up.

"Okay, I'll play along. Maybe the girls were threatening you." He continued my thought. "That's reason enough for a father to resort to drastic measures to save his daughter, certainly."

"It is," I said, suddenly tearing up at the mention of my dad. I wished he were here to make sense of this, to tell me why he had taken me away from this place all those years ago.

Will took my hand. "Have you remembered anything at all from that time?"

I shook my head. "Not a thing."

"That could say something in itself," Will speculated. "I remember a lot about our childhood friendship. You don't. It suggests you might have experienced some kind of trauma that was best forgotten."

This theory had occurred to me while I was cowering in the kitchen, terrified, waiting for Will that day. The intense fear seemed familiar somehow, as though I had felt the same thing in the same place before.

"What do you remember about being here when we were kids?" I asked him.

Will smiled, thinking back. "We had a lot of fun

together. We played outside, made tree forts, went swimming."

"Did you ever see . . . you know. The girls?"

Will shook his head. "Not that I can recall. As far as I can remember, we had an altogether normal childhood."

Our conversation was at a dead end. I didn't know what else to say and neither did Will, so I decided to change the subject to a more real-world matter.

"I went to the police station today," I told him.

"Why did you do that?"

"I wanted to see the old file concerning the Sutton case."

He finished the last of his pasty and shook his head. "Let me guess. You got nowhere."

"How did you know?"

"There's not a chance the police would give you that file, Hallie. I told you that."

I sighed. "Then how can I find out more about what happened that day? I'm the only one alive who was there, and I can't remember anything about it. I thought if I could get my hands on that file, it might jog something loose in my brain."

"I said they wouldn't give it to *you*."

"But they'd give it to *you*?"

Will smiled mischievously. "I'm not sure. But this is a very small town and its old records aren't exactly housed in Fort Knox. I'll see if I can get my hands on them."

"Today you'll hear the story of your grandfather," Iris began, over the next day's morning coffee.

"He was the vet on the island, right?"

"That's right. But before he was a veterinarian, Charles was a little boy. He was born on the second anniversary of the deaths of his sisters," Iris said, her eyes closed in remembrance. "He was a happy baby, chubby and blue-eyed with a full head of blond hair. I was especially fond of Charles because we spent so much time together. I had been given the task of looking after him, you see."

I pictured a young vibrant girl with long hair blowing in the breeze, pushing a baby stroller in the garden, singing to the baby inside it. Iris?

"I was eleven or twelve years old at the time— I had grown up considerably since the girls' deaths—and my mother suggested that I be allowed to take charge of the baby as his nanny. This pleased Hannah, who was rather preoccupied. She never saw Martine after the séance on that horrible day, but not for lack of trying on her part. Martine had disappeared, her cottage on the other side of the island emptied of its contents. Nobody ever knew what happened to the witch, where she went or how she got off the island without even the ferry captain seeing her. As time passed, Hannah came to distrust her own mind and her own memories, wondering if Martine had ever existed at all."

"I know how she felt," I murmured, sipping my coffee. As I swallowed, a vision swam and wavered in the air before me: Charles as a baby, under Iris's watchful eye. I looked at Iris, questioning.

Iris explained: "You've always had the ability to see the spirits beyond the veil, Halcyon. They're showing themselves to you—the important moments in their lives."

"But how—"

Iris cut off my questioning. "You must wait. Yours is a tale for another day. Today we're talking about Charles."

Fair enough. I took another sip as she continued. "Charles was such a good-natured child, sunny and obedient and pleasant, always laughing and cooing and smiling. Perhaps that's the reason nobody thought anything of the fact that, by age two, he had not yet spoken a word."

"Two? That's pretty late to begin talking, isn't it?"

Iris nodded. "It was indeed. After his second birthday, Hannah began to voice some concern about her silent child. I accompanied her on several trips to doctors on the mainland, none of whom ever came up with any sort of diagnosis that would explain his lack of speech. So I decided to try to teach Charles to speak myself. I read to him, teaching him the alphabet and rudimentary mathematics. I'd point to the letters and make the sounds: *aaaay, beeee, seeee.* Charles did not respond in kind, but I knew he was listening and learning. When he was four years old—"

"Four?" I interrupted. "You mean to say he still wasn't speaking at *four?*"

"That's right. But he did begin wandering out of the kitchen door on his own, much to my consternation. I'd be frantic, searching everywhere—in the garden? on the cliff? But soon I learned to find him in one of two places: the barn or the back lawn."

A watery, wavy image of a young boy formed in the air above the table, a blond-haired blue-eyed child sitting in the grass by the garden with a couple of dogs. A deer stood nearby, curious, and a hawk circled above.

"Animals?" I asked Iris, doubting what I was seeing.

"The boy had an otherworldly connection to animals. That was his gift. It was almost as though he could read their thoughts and understand what they were saying. Charles spoke their language even though he never made a sound. I'd find him lying in the stall with one of the cows, or sitting on the grass with a dozen robins perched around him, or lazily petting a wayward skunk that had found its way onto the grounds.

"I never bothered him during those times," Iris continued. "I can't explain why, but I knew I shouldn't intrude. So I watched, amazed."

"It sounds magical and wonderful, Iris," I murmured, as I envisioned an enormous hawk landing on Charles's tiny outstretched arm.

"It was indeed." Iris smiled at me, a thrilled look in her eyes. "One day when Charles was five years old, I found him on the back lawn curled up with a cougar!"

I gulped. "I had no idea there were big cats on this island." With all of my wanderings, had I been in danger of meeting one?

"In those days, we had quite a few of them here, but they're long since gone. We all knew what cougars—some used to call them panthers—were capable of, especially if they were hungry. Well, of course I was terrified, so I called out for Hannah, who did nothing but collapse to the floor, screaming at the sight of her child sitting with this big cat. I ran to get Simeon, telling him to come quickly and bring his rifle. He strode out the door toward Charles and the cougar, aiming at the cat's great head.

"'Don't be afraid, now, son,' Simeon said evenly to Charles. 'Daddy's here. Stay perfectly still.'

"But for once in his life, Charles did not do as

he was told. He stood up, positioned himself between his father and the cat, and threw his arms open wide.

" 'Why would you want to shoot this cat, Father?' Charles cried out. 'Bella is here to protect me, taking her turn just as all the animals have done.'

"These were Charles's first words. At the sound of his son's voice, Simeon dropped his gun and sank to his knees.

" 'Don't cry, Father,' Charles said, running up to Simeon and throwing his little arms around his father's neck.

"Simeon picked up the boy and hugged him tight, and as he did so the great cat stood up and padded toward them. Simeon was ready to reach for his gun—I saw the look of terror on his face—when Charles said, 'It's all right, Father. I've told Bella you're not hurting me.' And with that, the cat rubbed against Simeon's legs, just as a housecat would do, before taking her place in the yard again."

"Amazing," I murmured, having seen the whole thing.

Iris nodded. "Nobody could quite believe their eyes. Later on, after dinner, when everyone had gotten over the shock that the mute Charles was sitting at the table chattering away, Simeon asked his son, 'Charles, why haven't you spoken a word before today?'

"Charles looked at him, confused. 'I don't understand, Father.'

"Simeon repeated the question. 'You haven't said one word until today, son. We were wondering if you'd ever speak.'

"Charles just shook his head. 'I've been talking for years, Father. Haven't you been able to hear me?'

"A silence fell around the table. Nobody knew what to say. The boy had been silent as the grave his entire life, of that everyone was certain. Simeon answered his son in the best way he knew how. 'No, Charles, we haven't heard you. I'm so sorry, son. I guess we just weren't listening carefully enough.'

"Charles smiled a great smile, then, and took his father's hand. 'That's all right, Father. I was listening carefully enough for all of us.' "

The compassion in my young grandfather's voice—which I was able to hear as clearly as if he were standing right next to me—was overwhelming. I dabbed at my eyes with a Kleenex. "Charles sounds like a wonderful child."

"He was a magical child, really," Iris said.

"So the animals kept coming around as he grew up?"

"They did indeed," Iris said. "Especially the wolves and the big cats. None of them ever went after our chickens or cows or even the dogs. They were here for one purpose, to protect Charles."

"Protect him from what?"

A smile spread slowly across Iris's lined face as she shook her head. "Child, were you not listening to my story the other day?"

"Of course I was listening."

"Then what do you suppose Charles needed protection from?"

The answer hit me like an icy wave as an image of three ghostly girls swept through my mind. He needed protection from his dead sisters.

· 21

I decided not to tell Will about Iris's latest tale. I had been enthralled by her storytelling, but when she left for home that day, Will's words echoed in my head and I wondered how much of her story was true. I knew how it sounded: a young mute boy able to forge an otherworldly connection with the animal world? It was the stuff of a children's book.

No, before I could tell Will any more stories, I would need to find some sort of proof. I was burning for it. On Saturday morning, I made my way up to the third floor, determined to find some old family photos that would confirm what Iris had told me.

I hadn't ventured up to the third floor yet. There were many reasons for my reluctance to explore the top of the house, all of them admittedly silly.

The third floor was accessible only by the back staircase because, I imagined, it had housed the servants, who needed to come and go from the kitchen and laundry without disturbing the main areas of the house. Even the staircase felt haunted, empty, forbidden, so I could only imagine what the floor itself might feel like. Also, at the top of those stairs there was a locked door, with no sign of a key in sight.

Well, of course I might have simply asked Iris for it. She certainly had the key or knew where it was stashed, because from time to time I heard her scurrying around up there, cleaning. But I had the overwhelming feeling that I wasn't supposed to go up there, which probably stemmed from my childhood. Whatever happened to my father and Julie Sutton had happened up there. Something about confronting that scene again made me feel queasy.

But on this day, curiosity got the better of me. It's not as if I expected to find a photo of Martine in mid-séance, but I hoped I could find a shot of Charles with some animals, at the very least. Perhaps an old photo of the girls?

I set about finding that key and finally, after nearly an hour of searching, I slipped my hand onto the sill of the high window above the kitchen sink and felt something cool and metallic, an old skeleton key on a chain. That had to be it. I closed my palm around the metal, crept up the back stairs, my heart beating furiously, and slipped the key into the lock. The door opened easily.

I found myself standing in a long hallway similar to the one on the second floor. It was dark, the shutters on the windows at both ends of the hallway drawn tightly closed against the sun. I flicked the light switch—nothing. I opened the shutters at one end of the hallway and then the other, letting bright slim shafts of light stream in through the slats. There was nothing frightening about this third floor. Being servants' quarters, it just wasn't as opulently decorated as the rest of the house. A plain red carpet sat on the hallway floor and the walls were painted a simple cream that had yellowed over time.

I grasped the knob on the first door and turned it to find a small room with a single bed (no sheets or bedding, just a bare mattress) and a little bedside table. A dresser sat against the wall, unused and empty. A small bathroom occupied one end of the hall. I imagined Iris and her mother living in these spartan rooms back when they would've been clean and comfy.

As I neared the doorway at the end of the hall, my pulse began to quicken. Had the incident with Julie Sutton, whatever it was, happened in that room? I held my breath and opened the door.

A set of twin beds, still made up with yellow and red quilts, were pushed to opposite walls; a rocking horse, its paint flaking in spots, sat between them. A rocking chair was positioned in the corner by the shuttered window. The walls were covered with a faded yellow wallpaper on which ducks, geese, and chickens paraded to a barnyard on the opposite side of the room. It was a delightful nursery, even now. I felt very much at home in this room. Had I played here as a child?

In one corner, I spied several boxes, trunks, and suitcases. Success! The boxes were clearly labeled: toys, clothes, coats. I found photos in one of the trunks, album after album, clearly marked and organized. I was about to sit down and begin going through generations of photos when I saw a box labeled NOAH and next to it, one for HALLIE. This stopped me in my tracks. My original reason for exploring the third floor forgotten, I sank to the floor and opened my father's box, finding his things neatly folded and stacked—a few clothes, books, ties, and other personal items—and, what interested me the most, two albums of photographs.

I held my breath as I opened one of them, an ache of longing and loss filling me as I saw my mother and father together for the first time. He looked younger, certainly, but it was the joy in his eyes that struck me most. I flipped through the pages, seeing the two of them on a picnic, at the lakeshore, posing arm in arm at the Grand Canyon (their honeymoon?) and she, in her youth, looking unsettlingly like the reflection I saw in the mirror each day. They had been happy then, in the early years of their relationship. These photos didn't lie.

I pushed my father's box to the side and held my breath as I opened the one with my name on it. A stuffed purple skunk gave off a vague scent of lilac and I knew that was his name, Lilac. A Raggedy Ann doll lay next to a white stuffed dog, who, like the Velveteen Rabbit, had become real as a result of all of the love I had undoubtedly given him during my childhood. His name came to me: Puppy Dog. I unfolded a tiny white sweater and a long white gown that I must have worn on my baptism day. I found a plaid jumper, which evoked the sense of autumn and sharpened number 2 pencils and a walk down the hill, lunchbox in hand, to a kindergarten class. I took a few books out of the box: *The Little Mermaid* (the Hans Christian Andersen version) along with *Hans Brinker and the Silver Skates* and an entire boxed set of *Little House on the Prairie* books, their bindings still stiff and unread. All these things had been mine.

Here, too, were photographs. I had never seen any of my early childhood—me as an infant and a toddler, happy and laughing and playing. Birthday parties and Christmases and summer celebrations. But as I flipped through these photos, I slowly realized that something seemed a little off; the images weren't entirely happy and carefree. As I aged, the pictures began to evoke a slightly ominous feeling. Guilt and secrecy and even a bit of fear were hiding behind my eyes.

Faced with the artifacts of my forgotten childhood here in this house, things my grieving mother must've put away in remembrance of the husband and daughter she believed to be dead, I was overwhelmed. No wonder she kept that third-floor door locked, I thought. Better to shut away those painful memories.

That's what I wanted to do then, too: get out of the dusty past and back down to the part of the house that lived in the present. I grabbed one box of old family photographs; I'd take them down to the sunroom and look there for the proof I was seeking. At the last second, I stashed Puppy Dog under my arm as well. I locked the hallway door behind me and made my way down the stairs, feeling a little lighter with every step.

I spent most of the the weekend going through those photographs. If it was proof I wanted, I certainly got it. I came upon a grainy shot of a young couple standing on the cliff, her long hair blowing in the breeze, his hat placed at a jaunty angle on his head: a handsome couple. But what struck me about the photo was the fact that I recognized Hannah and Simeon. *I knew their faces.* It hadn't been my imagination, then; I had actually seen them when Iris was weaving her tales. How? I had no idea.

I carefully picked up a small photo of a young boy and immediately knew it was Charles. He was lying in the barn with some animals around him, but I couldn't make out exactly what sort of animals they were. I squinted to get a closer look, and all of a sudden it was as though the photo itself enlarged and opened, pulling me into its black-and-white world. I watched as Charles gathered up his books. "Let's go!" he called to his menagerie, his sweet, cheerful voice filling my heart. I followed as he trotted out of the barn door, putting one foot in front of the other until I saw him again, this time sitting at a desk by the window in what looked to be a one-room schoolhouse. I noticed birds perched on the windowsills, dogs curled up outside the schoolhouse door, deer standing ready in the woods. *They're really guarding him. It's all true, then.*

The scene shifted and I saw children in the classroom teasing Charles—"The Pied Piper's animals are here again!"—and Charles, undaunted, running happily outside into the midst of his mismatched flock.

A flurry of animals—bats, raccoons, squirrels—swept into my vision and out again, and I saw the children, the ones who had been taunting Charles, running home, crying all the way, a squirrel chasing one, a bat diving into the hair of another.

I took it all in, mesmerized by the black-and-white images of my grandfather as a boy, a small Dr. Dolittle. I held my breath hoping the scene wouldn't fade, but soon enough it did, the barn dissolving and re-forming into a church, filled to the last pew with mourners. There was Hannah, dressed in black with a black veil over her face, sitting in the first pew, a dashing and grown-up Charles by her side, and I knew I was seeing the funeral of my great-grandfather Simeon.

In an instant, I was in this house, standing in the kitchen. There, I saw Hannah in her nightdress, her hair wild, her eyes searching, her lips mouthing words that found no sound. I stood at the window, watching her wandering outside in the rain, rubbing her hands together as though washing away blood.

Finally, I saw her stride purposefully toward the cliff: *No, Hannah!* I screamed it out, running toward her, but of course she couldn't hear me. I wasn't part of these scenes, I was only observing them. I could do nothing but watch as she stood on the edge of the cliff and simply leaned forward, falling in slow motion and hitting the ground below with a thud, a slumped and broken form, limbs splayed this way and that, lying in nearly the same spot where they had found her girls, years earlier.

I opened my eyes and found myself lying on the chaise in the sunroom. I sat up and shook my head, trying to make sense of what I had just seen. Photos were strewn about; the box I had been exploring was on its side on the floor. Had I fallen asleep? Had I dreamed everything?

Later, over dinner with Will, I opened one of the albums. "My grandfather," I told him, showing him a photo of Charles with his animals.

He studied it, a slight smile on his face. "You know, I remember him quite well. Of course he was much older than this."

"He was still alive when we were kids?" This hadn't occurred to me.

Will nodded. "Everybody on the island trusted their horses to your grandfather, in addition to their household pets and livestock."

"Iris said he had a knack for relating to animals, even at a very young age. Apparently he didn't talk until he was five years old, and then one day he just started speaking in complete sentences." I left out the part about the cougar.

Will took my hand. "You're really enjoying hearing all of these stories about your family, aren't you?"

I nodded. He didn't know the half of it. "It means the world to me." I closed the album, then. I could languish in my ancestors' pasts with Iris, but with Will, I desired nothing but the here-and-now.

Monday morning, after breakfast, Iris appeared at the back door.

"Will Archer says he knew Charles," I announced.

Iris nodded. "Of course. Everyone on the island knew him. But Charles was an old man by that time. There's much more to tell about his life up until then."

With that tease of things to come, Iris set about her cleaning. I knew the story would have to wait until her work was done, around lunchtime, so I pulled on a jacket I found hanging by the back door and made my way outside and down the back stairs to the barn. I hadn't yet been inside it. The horses were still with Madlyn's neighbors; I had felt I had enough to deal with without learning the particulars of caring for horses, too. Now I pushed open the side door, and as it closed behind me I found myself nearly overcome by the sweet smell of hay. The barn was dark, but light was streaming in through the windows above the loft, illuminating the dust floating in the air this way and that. In the corner sat a woman's bicycle with a basket on the handlebars: a few years old, but not ancient. It must have been my mother's, I thought; the tires were still inflated. What a perfect way to get around the island! Deciding to take it for a spin, I wheeled it outside into the sunshine, hopped on the seat, and pedaled out to the main road.

I didn't feel like going down into town—the climb back up the hill to the house would be daunting on a bike—so I turned the opposite way and set off. The houses grew farther and farther apart until they ended altogether, and I found myself riding through the countryside. I love all seasons, but late fall is especially beautiful to me—the leaves have already said their spectacular goodbyes for the year, trees stand ready for the chill to come, everything else is browned and yellowed and dry. It is the time before the death of winter and the rebirth brought by spring.

Soon I rode into a forest of enormous cedar and red pine trees, towering high above my head. I spied an overgrown dirt path leading from the road deeply into the woods and remembered Iris's description—was this possibly the way to Summer Glen? I steered my bike onto the path and pedaled slowly through the sweet-smelling trees, sunshine stubbornly poking its way between their great limbs.

The path opened up into a grassy field ringed by enormous ancient trees and covered with unlikely wildflowers: lupines, daisies, poppies, and tangles of wild rose bushes. What were they doing in bloom here, at this time of year? I noticed overgrown low-lying foliage I couldn't identify, smelled the heady mixture of their perfumes as I set the bike's kickstand on the ground to explore the area on foot. I saw the crumbled remnants of an ancient fireplace, on what seemed to be the flat clearing for a house, and suspected I had indeed found Summer Glen.

This is fantastic, I thought, as I held my breath and walked gingerly through the glen, not wanting to make any noise to stir up the memories that surely resided there. I closed my eyes and tried to use my "gift," as Iris called it, and almost immediately I saw before me the images of wealthy society ladies sneaking their way here, cloaks covering their faces, each hoping Martine would work her magic for them. I thought of my great-grandmother, so desperate for a child that she'd turn to witchcraft to conceive one. My eyes grew wide as the thought hit me: None of us would have been born—not Charles, not my mother, *not me*—if not for the concoction Martine had given Hannah, right here on this spot.

I heard a voice, whispering in my ear: *Children conceived out of witchcraft are witches themselves, as are their children and their children's children.* I thought of Charles's otherworldly way with animals; was that his form of witchcraft? And what about these "visions" of mine?

Suddenly, I felt as though I wasn't alone. Something—no, a lot of somethings—swirled in the air around me, brushing at me, nudging me. It was as if I were in the middle of a tornado of spirits. I ran toward the bike, but the rosebushes grew up to block my path, reaching and grabbing at me with their gnarled branches. I pushed my way through the brambles, the skin on my arms and legs tearing on the thorns until I reached the bike, hopped on, and pedaled away as fast as I could. When I was safely inside the cedar forest, I braked to look at my arms and legs, which I assumed would be ripped raw and bleeding from the thorns. But I didn't find so much as a scratch.

I pedaled toward home, wondering what, if anything, had happened in that glen.

· 23

Y ou've been to the glen," Iris stated, pulling a chicken-and-broccoli casserole out of the oven just as I burst through the back door.

I nodded, bending low to catch my breath. My leg muscles were throbbing and my throat was parched. I filled up a glass with cold water and drank it all in one gulp.

"You mustn't go back there, not yet." Iris had a stern look in her eyes.

"What is it about that place, anyway?" I asked, filling my water glass again and brushing the wet hair from my face. "I felt like . . ." My words trailed off. "I don't know what I felt like." I eyed the casserole, suddenly famished. After what I had just been through, I wanted only to immerse myself in the safety and familiarity of one of Iris's tales. I settled into my chair, took a bite of the steaming casserole, and listened as she cleared her throat and began to speak.

"After Hannah's death, life went on here in the house. We had a very companionable existence for the next few years. Charles built a thriving business while I ran the household, supervising a staff of three. I'd have breakfast, lunch, and dinner on the table for Charles every day. He had grown into such a fine man.

"Of course, he never stopped mourning his beloved mother and father. I believe that's what drew him to Amelia, the woman who would become your grandmother. I thought she bore a striking resemblance to Hannah; they had the same fiery eyes.

"Amelia's parents—a wealthy Irish couple from Chicago by the name of Fister—had built a vacation home on the island several years earlier. Charles had a bit of contact with the Fister family over the years; he had seen Amelia once or twice and never thought much about her. But the year Hannah died, Amelia came to the island with her parents. Her father, no fool, hoped to interest the handsome, rich, and single veterinarian in his daughter, so he arranged a party where they could be introduced.

"When she came to the house a few days later carrying a sick cat, I tried to send her away. I knew why she was really here. But she was too smart for me. She took it upon herself to find Charles in the barn."

Iris's eyes became black and cloudy at the thought of Amelia, which made me wonder: Had she been in love with Charles all those years? Yes, she had been his nanny, but she was barely a decade older. It was plausible. So I said, "Iris, you haven't said much about yourself in your stories of this family. Did *you* ever marry?"

"Marry?" she spat. "My life was here, in this house, taking care of the Hill family. There was neither time for nor thought of marriage for me."

"I'm sorry, I shouldn't have—"

"Never mind me. It wasn't long before Charles and Amelia were married. She was a thin, slight woman with short dark hair and deep blue eyes. She liked to wear trousers, something many women of the time didn't do, and she was quite athletic, enjoying golf and tennis and a walk with Charles and whatever animals happened to be on hand in the afternoons. When she came into this house as Charles's wife, I let her know right away that I was head of the household staff. I told her what was what and how the house was run. I was the one who had taken care of him all of these years, I was the one who was here when Simeon died and poor Hannah lost her mind. I was the one who had cooked his meals and washed his clothes."

I saw a fierce determination in Iris's eyes then, and the familiar darkening that shrouded her face when she was angry. She *had* loved him. It sent a chill through me. I did not envy Amelia, coming into this house and facing Iris.

"Of course, everything changed," Iris went on bitterly. "Our quiet, simple existence was obliterated. In the evenings, Charles used to enjoy reading in the study. I would bring him his tea and perhaps sit with him awhile, doing my needlepoint. All this ended when Amelia arrived. She was an overly talkative, grossly exuberant person. Charles became more outgoing than I had ever seen him, always laughing and smiling, especially when she was around. He was in love with her, anyone could see that."

I heard the resignation in Iris's voice.

"It was all a whirlwind of parties, dinners, travel, and people until the day she told him their lives were about to change yet again. I was busying myself making my mother's cabbage rolls for dinner. I remember it plain as day."

I could smell the simmering cabbage as she spoke, a curl of smoke rising from the heat of the stove.

" 'Oh, Iris,' she said to me, as she rushed into

the kitchen, breathless. 'Do you know where my husband is?' She was bursting with news, her eyes sparkling in anticipation. Of course, I knew immediately what it was.

"'You are with child,' I said to her matter-of-factly, stirring the rolls.

"She looked at me with wide eyes. 'Yes! I am! I've just come from the doctor. How did you know?'

"Ridiculous girl. Any fool could've seen it. 'Charles is in the barn,' I told her, and watched her run out the back door. I did not see her fall."

Iris stopped talking while a wicked smile crossed her face for just an instant, replaced quickly by a countenance of concern and caring.

"She fell?" I prodded. "Where, on the way to the barn? But it's just flat ground between here and there."

Iris shook her head as she continued her tale. "Somehow, she found her way to the cliffside."

"You mean to tell me she fell from the cliff? How did that happen?"

"I have no idea," Iris replied. "The last thing I heard, she was on her way to the barn to tell her husband she was with child."

"She died?" Why did Iris's stories, no matter how lovely and benign at the start, always seem to take a sinister turn?

"No," Iris explained. "Remember, child, Amelia was your grandmother, Madlyn's mother.

She did not die at the bottom of the cliff that day. Charles found her. She was alive, but the baby had perished.

"After that, Charles treated his wife like a china doll, as you might expect. If I thought he doted on her before, it was nothing compared to the way he became. He expected me, along with the rest of the staff, to wait on her hand and foot. Which of course we did." Iris sniffed at this; I could see her resentment bubbling just under the surface.

"Within a few months, she was on the nest again, so to speak."

"That time, she carried the baby to full term, right? That was Madlyn?" But even as I said it, I knew I was wrong.

Iris shook her head. "All of Charles's attentiveness wasn't enough to stop her from tumbling down the stairs one night."

"You're kidding me. She fell again?"

"She did," Iris confirmed, adding slyly, "It was the middle of the night, and apparently she had been sleepwalking. She fell down the front staircase. Accident-prone, that one."

But I didn't think Amelia was accident-prone. It seemed to me that someone or something had pushed her. *The girls?* As if that wasn't dark enough, a darker thought crossed my mind. I saw an image of Iris creeping about at the top of the darkened stairway.

"Iris, you didn't—" I was too afraid to finish the thought.

She silenced me with a harsh look and continued her tale.

"Amelia did a great deal of crying during those years after losing two babies. It was Charles who gave her the strength to keep going, to keep trying. If he hadn't been so gentle and kind, your mother might never have been born."

Iris set her teacup on the table with an air of finality. "I will come again tomorrow," she said, after studying my face as though she was looking for something. "You were interested in hearing the stories of your great-grandparents and your grandparents, to be sure, but I can see that you are much more anxious to hear about your mother."

She gathered up her things, a tattered old purse and an umbrella, and was gone. It was an hour or so after she left that I realized. Iris had begun her tale where my vision in the sunroom had left off.

· 24

I hopped onto the bike and rode down into town. Once the spell Iris was weaving with her storytelling was broken, I felt like some real-world companionship. I coasted to a stop in front of Jonah's coffee shop.

"Hey." He smiled at me as I walked into the otherwise empty shop. "Glad you're here. I owe you a latte."

"Sounds wonderful," I said, climbing onto a counter stool, looking forward to a quiet chat with Jonah. I didn't get my wish, however, because at that moment, a group of islanders entered the shop, ordered cappuccinos, and announced it was time for their weekly book club. I recognized many faces from the group I had encountered in Jonah's shop my first day on the island. They were friendly to him, of course, but they gave me the same icy reception they had given me that first day: cold stares and whispered comments as they sat down and took out their copies of the latest book club selection.

I truly don't know what it was about that day; perhaps after living with three ghosts, I was unafraid of this lot. I walked over and faced them.

"Hi, ladies," I said, leaning down and putting my hands on their table. "In case there's one person left on this island unaware of who I am, I'm your friend and new neighbor, Halcyon Crane. And I'm just wondering: Are you ever planning to treat me like a neighbor, or are you always going to stop talking and stare and whisper when I come into a room?" Silence from the group, as I expected. I continued. "Because it's getting tiresome. I'm not sure how long I'm staying on this island, but it'll be a while. I suggest you get used to it and start acting like human beings."

With that I walked away from them, grinning from ear to ear.

"Nicely done." Jonah laughed as he handed me a latte. Then he added, under his breath, "Call me after closing time, Hallie. There's something more I've been wanting to tell you since the night we met for drinks, but I wasn't sure . . . Like I said, it's complicated."

I nodded and walked out of the shop with my coffee. After a few steps I ran into Will.

"Hi." He smiled at me and kissed my cheek. "I've just come from dropping some paperwork off at the police station. Care to take a look at what I picked up while I was there?"

He passed me a plastic bag. I peeked into it just long enough to see a folder with SUTTON, JULIE, 1979 written on the front.

"Will—" I started, but he silenced me with a kiss.

"I've gotta run right now, but I'll come by the house later and we'll look at this together." He winked at me and then headed off down the street, toward his office. I put the bag into the basket on my bike and started the long pedal up the hill to home.

I stared at that folder on my kitchen table for the rest of the afternoon, dreading what might be inside, but when Will arrived just before dinner, I knew it was time to face whatever it contained.

Before I opened it, Will shook his finger at me. "I just need to say this: Astonishingly enough, despite the fact that it's sitting right here on this table, I never saw this file. And neither did you."

"Understood," I said, as I took the folder from him. Now was the time. I took a long sip of wine and opened it up.

The first thing I saw was an article reporting my death. On a yellowing tear sheet from the local newspaper, I read the headline under a photo of my father and me.

NOAH CRANE AND DAUGHTER HALCYON PRESUMED DEAD IN KAYAK ACCIDENT

Island mathematics teacher Noah Crane, 37, and his daughter, Halcyon, 5, disappeared during a kayak excursion early Friday and are presumed dead.

Crane left his home on Hill Cliff early Friday with his daughter for a day of kayaking around the island. When they didn't return by late that afternoon, his wife, Madlyn Crane, who is also the girl's mother, became alarmed and alerted local authorities.

Police quickly organized a search party of some three dozen islanders, all of whom used their own vessels—speedboats, kayaks, canoes—to scour the island shoreline in an attempt to find the missing boaters. The Grand Manitou Ferry Line also participated in the search.

Sheriff Chip Norton reported that islander Mira Finch spotted an overturned kayak near the Ring, a rock formation on the north side of the island that has long been a popular destination for kayakers and boaters. There was no sign of Crane or his daughter.

After searching the island's coastline with no success, rescuers enlisted the aid of the Coast Guard and other vessels to patrol the waters between the island and the mainland. However, as day wore into night, hopes dimmed of finding the boaters alive.

"We believe father and daughter may have been carried into the shipping lanes by the current, which is pretty strong on the north side of the island," Norton stated. "We hoped we'd find them alive, but, after all this time in the water, if those folks haven't drowned by now they've certainly succumbed to hypothermia. As a result, we've changed our focus from rescue to recovery."

"Well, this sort of takes your breath away," I said, after a moment of stunned silence. It's not that I didn't know this information; I knew full well that my father had faked our deaths. But reading it in the newspaper, there in black and white, made it real and tangible in a way it hadn't been before.

"Did Mira ever mention to you that she was the one who found the kayak?" Will asked.

"No, she didn't say anything at all about that day. Not a thing. I wonder why."

Will looked at me and shrugged. "That's a good question."

"It must've been pretty emotional for her, finding that kayak."

"Still, don't you think the moment she discovered who you were she might have said something?" Will went on. *I was part of the search party that looked for you. I was the one who found your kayak*—or words to that effect."

"You'd think so, wouldn't you?" But I didn't know what to think. Not really.

"The lawyer in me smells more to the story here," he said, then backpedaled a bit. "Of course, the lawyer in me thinks there's more to every story. It could be she just didn't want to dredge up the past."

I put the article aside and looked at the one beneath it. It was a longer story about my dad, Julie's murder, and our deaths, and how the three might be connected.

"I'm not sure I want to read this," I told Will.

"You said you wanted to know everything," he said gently. "This is part of it, unfortunately.

Remember, Hallie, it's all in the past. Nothing here can hurt you now."

He was right, of course. So I took a deep breath and began reading.

QUESTIONS SURROUND THE DEATH OF NOAH CRANE, DAUGHTER

The memorial service for Noah and Halcyon Crane took place last week, but questions remain about the exact nature of their deaths. Police have reason to believe the father and daughter died as a result of a murder-suicide.

At the time of his death, Noah Crane was under investigation for the island's only murder in more than 50 years. Julie Sutton, 6, the daughter of island residents Frank and June Sutton, was found dead on the Crane property in July. Police initially believed it was an accident, but soon the evidence began pointing toward foul play.

The girl had apparently fallen from a third-floor window of the Crane home. Noah Crane, upon discovering the body, called the police. When they arrived, their investigation turned up several clues. The room from which the girl fell was in a state of general disarray, lamps broken, furniture knocked over, dishes cracked, indicating a struggle had occurred. The girl's dress had been torn, presumably in the struggle, and there were marks on her neck consistent with strangulation.

"As we began piecing together the evidence of what happened that night, it started to look as though Mr. Crane was involved in this poor girl's death," said Sheriff Chip Norton, who headed up the investigation. Norton explained that Crane's footprints were found around the girl's body and his fingerprints were identified on the windowsill of the room where she fell. Strands of hair believed to be his were found in the girl's closed fist, indicating that she fought with him before she died.

Crane maintained his innocence. The police were not able to bring the investigation of Julie Sutton's murder to a conclusion before Crane's death.

Crane's wife, Madlyn, was off the island on business at the time of the incident. The only other witness to the event was Halcyon Crane, five years old. She never spoke another word after that night. Her parents had taken her to psychiatrists on the mainland, but none could determine how or why the girl stopped speaking.

According to the American Psychiatric Association, it is not uncommon for children who have witnessed a crime or have been the victims of physical or emotional abuse to be struck mute as a result of the severe trauma involved.

I looked at Will, incredulous. I had had no idea.

"I know." He took my hand. "It startled me when I read it, too."

"I stopped speaking? Do you remember that?"

"I was thinking back, Hallie, and I don't remember ever seeing you again after the death of that child. I'm not sure about it, but I'll bet my parents never let me come back to your house. I can ask them." He refilled our wineglasses.

I was beginning to think things were starting to make a kind of perverted sense. "That would explain why I don't remember anything of my life here," I mused. "Witnessing the death of a friend is certainly a severe trauma."

"It makes me wonder what you saw that night."

"I wonder, too," I said, and went back to reading the article.

The final blow to the investigation came with the deaths of Noah and Halcyon Crane. "He was our only suspect in this murder, and we were in the process of building our case against him," Norton confirmed. "His death, and the death of the only witness to the crime, puts an end to that."

Although they acknowledge it's pure speculation, police believe that Noah Crane killed himself and his daughter to escape the consequences of his actions.

Madlyn Crane declined to be interviewed for this article, but through her lawyer she issued a strong statement in defense of her husband. "The idea that Noah Crane murdered that child—and his own daughter—is a macabre, disgusting fabrication put forth by an incompetent police force in order to create a murder out of what was clearly an accident in both cases. To accuse my husband of this is a desecration of his memory, and I will not tolerate it."

I laid the article back on the pile and wiped the tears from my eyes. "You gotta love my mother for saying that. I wonder how the islanders treated her."

Will stood up and wrapped his arms around me from behind. "Like I said, I don't remember a whole lot about those days, but my parents tell me people looked at Madlyn as another victim. They didn't blame her, not really."

"What about Frank and June Sutton?" I asked him. "I wonder how she made peace with them. They lived here on this same small island for thirty years with Julie's death hanging between them."

"They had both lost daughters, remember," Will said quietly.

Of course they had.

I began sifting through the police file, which

was woefully incomplete. A sketchy incident report described the scene of the crime. My father had made the call to police. I was a witness. My mother had been out of town. Nothing I didn't know there.

The report also included notes of an interview with Frank and June Sutton. June had dropped Julie off at our house that morning to spend the day playing with me. My father was supposed to take her home after dinner. Other than the part about me not speaking again, it was all pretty benign stuff, nothing I didn't know or suspect.

Then I came to a photograph of the crime scene, and everything changed. It was the third-floor nursery, the one in which I had found the boxes of pictures the day before, and the police report was correct. The room was in disarray: lamps knocked over, comforters pulled from the beds, books lying everywhere. Obviously, there had been a fight.

I began to feel something at the moment I saw the photograph: a hand, tightening around my throat. I started coughing, first softly, then violently. Someone was choking me, constricting my airway. I stood up, knocking over my chair as I did so, and stared at Will, wide-eyed.

"Hallie." He stood up and took me by the shoulders. "What's the matter? What's going on?"

I couldn't breathe. I felt a tremendous pressure on my chest, as though I were an undersea diver whose air tank had sprung a leak. I was gasping for air but unable to fill my lungs. I was going to die, right there in my mother's kitchen.

And then, nothing. Everything stopped.

"My God, Hallie," Will said, frantic. "Should I call a doctor?"

I shook my head and sat down. "I felt like my throat was closing up," I croaked. "It was like somebody was strangling me. I couldn't breathe. I literally could not get any air."

Will crossed the kitchen and poured a glass of water for me. "Here," he said, thrusting it in my direction. "How do you feel now?"

I drank the water in one gulp. "I'm okay. I think."

"You know," Will said, slowly, "you were looking at the photo of the crime scene when your throat closed up."

I nodded.

"Whatever happened there that night, you saw it all, and it traumatized you to the point where you couldn't speak. And now you felt as though your throat was closing. Seeing this photo might have brought some of that back to you. I think we had better just close this file for now."

"No." I shook my head. "Whatever's in here, I have to see it all."

That decision may have been a mistake, because I came upon a photo of the dead girl, taken as her body lay in a heap on the ground beneath that all-important third-floor window. I recognized her.

It was a girl in a white dress. She had long braids, one still tied with a white ribbon.

As I dropped the photo and it fluttered to the floor, I put my hands over my face and turned toward the wall, my mouth open but making no sound. I don't know if I would have simply stayed in that suspended state of reality had Will not been there with me, but he wrapped his arms around me again and held me tight. Somewhere far away, I heard him saying my name.

"Hallie, what is it? What's going on?"

But I could barely say the words. I had been trying so hard to shield Will from all of Iris's fantastic stories, her tall tales, the ghosts. But at that moment I didn't care any longer. "It's her." I said it over and over.

"You recognize Julie. You were a witness to her death. Are you remembering her?"

I shook my head. "No, Will, that's not Julie. That's the girl I saw outside my window the other night. That's the girl I saw at the inn. I'm certain of it, right down to the white hair ribbons."

Will bent down, picked up the photo, and studied it. "What ribbon?"

"Tied to one braid," I said.

He shook his head, holding out the picture. "Hallie, there's no ribbon here. And no braids."

I took it out of his hand, confused. I was

272

looking at the image of a small, vaguely familiar girl—Julie Sutton—who lay on the ground, arms and legs splayed every which way. Her hair was curly and shoulder-length. She was wearing Levi's and a T-shirt. Her eyes were open. Blood was pooling near the back of her head. No white dress. No white ribbon.

I slumped to the floor, holding the photo close to my chest, and began to shake.

· 25

Will took me upstairs, ran a hot bath, and sat with me as I soaked in the water. I was a mess; there's no other way to describe it. I couldn't stop crying. Seeing that photograph—both of them, really, the shot of the crime scene and the one of the dead girl—had clicked on a switch inside me that had been in the off position for thirty years.

My shoulders shook as I tried to pull myself together. "I don't know what's the matter with me," I blubbered between sobs.

"Shhhh," Will said, rubbing my back. "Don't worry about it. You've had a series of shocks."

I sniffed. "I'm so sorry about this."

"You had an unspeakable trauma when you were a child, so bad you couldn't remember anything about it. And now you're seeing it again. Anyone would be shaken by that."

His voice was soothing and I began to breathe a little easier. He went on.

"Of course you've been seeing that poor little girl's face all over this island ever since you got here. Your memories of that night are coming back on their own."

My mind began to review everything that had happened to me since coming to the island. Could repressed memories really be the explanation for it all?

"You're back here in this house where the trauma occurred. A girl—*your friend*—was killed, on purpose or by accident, and you saw it. It was so horrible, you stopped speaking for a while and blocked it out of your mind. And now here you are, confronted with all this stuff again. I don't think there's any doubt that the girl you've been seeing and the girl who was killed are one and the same."

I must've looked confused, so he continued.

"It's your mind, Hallie. You're remembering bits of what happened, piecing it all together. You're remembering *her*."

"No, Will. The girl I've been seeing isn't Julie Sutton. The girl I initially saw in the photograph . . ." My words trailed off. How could I explain seeing another girl's face in that photo?

He shook his head. "Doesn't it make sense that something psychological is going on here? Flashes of memory coming to the surface as a result of being back, for the first time, at the scene of a crime?"

It did make sense, in a confusing, muddled sort of way. I wasn't sure about any of it. "So what do I do now?" I asked him.

He considered for a while. "You don't have to do anything, not right away. But if it were me, I'd be thinking about seeing someone for a few rounds of regression therapy."

"You mean like hypnosis?"

He nodded. "A psychiatrist can take you back to that night. Uncover what really happened. It might give you a sense of closure. Hey, you might even begin to remember your childhood here on the island and get some bona fide memories of your mother out of the deal."

That sounded good to me.

"We'll have to find a psychiatrist on the mainland who does that sort of thing," Will mused. "Jim Allen—the doctor here on the island—can probably recommend someone."

It was settled, then. Everything that had happened to me since I came to Great Manitou was the result of repressed trauma. I wasn't seeing or hearing ghosts. I didn't have a haunted house. It was just my mind that was haunted, by the spirit of a girl I had seen fall to her death. I put the incongruity of my first and second impressions of the girl in that photograph out of my mind. It didn't matter. A wave of calm came over me, and I sank low into the water, enjoying it.

The feeling did not last long.

After I climbed out of my bath, I went to bed, quickly falling asleep in Will's arms. I awoke with a start to discover myself alone. Groggily, I eyed the clock, its fuzzy symbols slowly jelling into numbers as I squinted. Nearly 2:30. Where was Will? The bathroom, surely. I waited for a few minutes, nearly drifting back into a light sleep. "Will?" I called out softly. No response. I sat up and looked around the room, but he wasn't anywhere in the suite. That's when I noticed the open door.

I crept out into the darkened hallway. "Will?" Again, no response.

Moonlight was streaming onto the wood floor from the windows at the end of the hall, creating a river of light that seemed to vibrate with a life of its own. And then there she was: a little girl, standing in the corner next to the windows. The white dress. The braid tied at the end with a ribbon. And then she dissipated, as though she were nothing more than fog burning off in the midday sun.

Just at that moment, I heard a sickening crash and knew immediately what had happened. I ran down the hallway toward the front stair, screaming Will's name, and saw him lying in a heap at the bottom. I flew down to his side.

"Oh my God, oh my God," I was muttering. "Please be all right, please don't be dead."

Will groaned and clutched his head.

"Thank God!" I said, intensely relieved that he was alive, breathing and groaning. "Are you all right?" I helped him to his feet.

"I'm not sure," he said, groggy. "That was some fall. I hit my head pretty hard."

I helped him into the kitchen, turning on every light as we went, sat him down at the table, and poured him a glass of water. Then I started opening cabinets; I knew I had seen pain reliever around somewhere.

"Take these," I told him, handing him some Motrin. "Should we call the doctor?" I wasn't sure what to do. I was afraid he had had a concussion, but I didn't know the signs or symptoms.

He shook his head. "I didn't pass out or anything. I don't think we need to wake Jim in the middle of the night for this."

"What happened? Why did you get out of bed?"

"I thought I heard something," he told me. "It was the weirdest thing. Something woke me up, I'm not sure what it was. You were fast asleep. Snoring, I might add." He grinned at me. "As I was closing my eyes again, I heard—I know this sounds crazy, but I thought I heard my name."

"Your name," I repeated.

"So I got up," Will continued. "When I got into the hallway I realized nobody was there, but I was still hearing voices. Talking. Chattering."

"What kind of voices?" I asked him, but I already knew the answer.

"Children's voices," he admitted. "I must have been dreaming somehow, still in a sleep state— you know, sleepwalking. My mind was full of that story about the dead girls you told me the other night, and maybe I was dreaming the whole thing. I don't know. But whether I was awake or asleep, I followed the voices to the edge of the stairs and stood there with my hands on the railing, listening. The voices seemed to be coming from the living room."

I did not want to hear the rest of this story. I knew where it was going, and I didn't want it to go there. But it did.

"I started down the stairs," he said. "And Hallie, I know this is going to sound absurd but I swear to you that I was pushed. I don't know if I was dreaming or sleepwalking, but I definitely felt hands on my back."

"Somebody pushed you?"

Will shook his head in amazement. "I think so."

I had fallen asleep believing that the Hill House ghosts were nothing but memories surfacing in my own head, and frankly I liked that notion. But now, Iris's stories were swirling around in my brain, her assertion that the girls had driven her cousin off a cliff, poor Amelia's sudden falls, and now Will tumbling down the stairs. These certainly weren't products of my imagination.

"I think we should get out of here right now," I said. "Let's go to your place."

Will shook his head. "My place is all the way on the other side of the island. Besides, it's almost morning. Let's just make some coffee and watch the sun come up."

There, with the lights of the kitchen illuminating the darkness, in a house built on secrets and filled with ghosts and murder, I realized that the lines between Iris's stories and my reality were blurring. Were Will and I somehow caught up in my family's grim and bloody fairy tale?

· 26

I asked Will not to go into the office the next day, but he insisted.

"I thought you didn't have anything to do in the off-season." I was terrified that he would collapse alone in the office from the aftereffects of a concussion.

"I don't have *much* to do." He smiled, pulling on jeans and a sweater.

"Then why go in? We could spend the day reading or taking a walk around the grounds."

"I've got a conference call to make—"

"Which you could do here." I wasn't letting this go.

"Yes, I could. And I would, if my files and my computer weren't down at the office. Besides, I have to go into town anyway to get feed for Belle. I won't stay long. I promise."

"Do you want me to come with you?" I yawned.

He smiled and wrapped his arms around me. "Stay here and take a nap. I'll come back after lunch. How's that?"

I relented. "Okay."

"Any thoughts on dinner?" he wondered. I shook my head. "How about if I make us a stir-fry?"

"A great lover who also cooks." I managed a tired smile. "You're too good to be true."

I walked with him down the stairs, saw him out the back door, the cold air snatching away any sleep I might have fallen back into that morning, and watched as he and Belle set off toward town. I pulled on a jacket and sat on the sunporch with a cup of strong coffee, staring out at the angry water and thinking about everything and nothing at all.

"Morning, miss." It was Iris, walking in from the kitchen.

I wanted to ask her whether she thought Will's and Amelia's falls might be connected somehow. I had intended to bring it up right away, but for some reason I can't explain, I didn't. She started in on another of her tales and I found myself fully drawn into the past, the present goings-on receding into the background like one of my wispy visions.

"Madlyn Hill was born on a spring day when the lilacs came into full bloom here on the island. She came into this world feet first and both mother and daughter nearly died during the ordeal, but Amelia finally delivered the girls with Charles—"

I interrupted. "You said *girls,* Iris. Plural."

Iris nodded. "Twins. Maddie was born first, healthy and pink and crying. Only then did the doctor realize he had more work to do, and shortly thereafter he delivered a second girl, Sadie.

"I was tending to Maddie when Sadie was born. Amelia was exhausted and near-delirious from the difficult delivery, but when the nurse rushed into the study to tell Charles that another baby was coming, he was over the moon with excitement. His joy, however, was short-lived. It lasted just long enough for him actually to see the baby."

Iris closed her eyes for a moment, as if to shut out an image too painful to recall, before she continued. "I'll never forget the sight of Sadie, so tiny and blue and delicate, like a newly hatched baby bird. She lived for only a few minutes, her mouth opening and closing like a fish out of water. I could see she did not belong in this world.

"As the doctor explained it, while the twins were in the womb, Madlyn was taking in most of the nutrients. She grew bigger and stronger as her twin withered and starved. A horrible thought, really. It was as though Madlyn ingested her sister's very life. I wish Amelia had not heard the doctor's explanation of how the twins had developed. I wish she had been told only of the death. It might have made things easier, later."

I shuddered at this, closing my eyes to the vision I knew was beginning to form.

"We buried Sadie the next day in the family plot, next to Hannah and Simeon. There was a short service, a few prayers read. Amelia was too weak to attend. And though Charles grieved for his lost daughter, in time he embraced life again. Amelia was a different matter. She was forever haunted by the thought of Sadie's death. Somewhere deep inside, in her darkest, most twisted thoughts, Amelia believed Maddie had killed her sister."

"Killed her? On purpose? That's crazy, Iris."

"You're absolutely right. After the birth, Amelia did sink into a sort of madness."

"Postpartum depression?"

"Worse. Amelia didn't get out of bed for days and days, not to wash, not to eat. She didn't want to see the baby, hold her, or even feed her. She spent most days tossing and turning in her bed and most nights wandering the hallways of the house in her white nightdress, her hair wild and uncombed. Poor Charles would find her in the nursery in the middle of the night, hovering over Maddie's crib, staring, muttering incomprehensible things. One night he caught her carrying the baby down the hall toward the stairs.

"With memories of his mother's madness fresh in his mind, Charles was terrified that he'd have to institutionalize his young wife. So he didn't call the doctor or tell anyone about Amelia's odd behavior. I believed this was a mistake. Amelia was intent on hurting the child, anyone could see that. Charles certainly did. But he decided to handle the situation himself, so what could I say?

"I did what I could, taking it upon myself to protect little Maddie from her mother, stationing myself in a hard-backed chair in the nursery as soon as the sun went down and not leaving again until it rose in the morning. Night after night, Amelia would appear in Maddie's room, wild-eyed, her face white as bone, and I'd order her back to bed. Most of the time, thank goodness, she obeyed me. But some nights I'd have to shove her out of the room."

"Did my grandmother end up in an institution?" I wanted to know.

Iris shook her head. "It took many months, but Amelia came back to herself. It happened suddenly, and nobody was ever sure how or why. One morning she simply got out of bed, bathed, and came downstairs to the kitchen as though she had awakened from a coma or a long sickness.

Whatever cloud had descended upon her had dissipated, and Amelia walked out of her room smiling, wanting to know where her husband and daughter were, as though none of the madness had ever happened.

"Charles was overjoyed. He stood there, holding his wife and crying openly, so relieved was he to see her back to herself. I credit much of her recovery to his gentle ways and loving nature. He was so patient with her during those long months.

"But Amelia was never the same as she was before the birth of her children, not quite. As Charles was holding her that day, I noticed a strange new look on her face and in her eyes. I don't want to say it was sinister, exactly, but there was something of an undercurrent to her from that day on. The way she continued to look at her daughter unsettled me quite a bit.

"In no time whatsoever, baby Maddie was crawling, then toddling, then walking and, unlike her father, talking a blue streak from a very early age. However, in a strange development that alarmed her parents and me, little Maddie directed most of her conversation toward one person: her sister.

"Her father brought a toy telephone home for her one afternoon, and Maddie would use it to call her sister. 'Sadie! Time for dinner! Come to the table!' This frightened Charles and Amelia, because of course they had not told young Maddie she had had a twin sister, much less the sister's name. Yet somehow she knew.

'Who are you talking to, dear?' Charles would ask. Maddie would simply answer, 'Sister.'

"There were many whispered and frantic conversations about this odd behavior behind closed doors, but finally Charles came to the decision that they would simply have to live with it. Maddie and Sadie had been twins together in the womb, and somehow Maddie retained the memory. He was sure stranger things had happened at other times to other families. I thought, *Yes, and in this very house,* but of course I did not say it aloud."

I shuddered as I saw my young mother holding conversations with her dead sister.

"Neither Charles nor Amelia ever knew what was really going on with their daughter." Iris smiled, her eyes shining. "But I knew. In the womb, as poor Sadie grew weaker and weaker and Maddie grew ever stronger, the two girls made a pact. Sadie would not live a day in the outside world, so Maddie would live for both of them. And right there in the calm waters of the womb, the girls joined hands and Maddie called Sadie's soul to her."

Iris paused for effect, looking at me expectantly.

I scowled. "What do you mean, she called Sadie's soul?"

"It was a gift she would possess her entire life."

"What do you *mean,* Iris?" I repeated.

"Your mother was called *soul capturer* in her work. It's how she was known professionally."

"I had heard that, yes. But I assumed it was because she had a way of capturing a person's true spirit in her photographs."

"That's exactly what it was." Iris nodded. "The photography came later, of course. But when Madlyn was just a child, she began to collect bits and pieces of people's souls, their spirits, wherever she went. They always stayed with her, hovering around her, until she learned to put them in her photographs, the way other children collect butterflies or frogs."

"I still don't quite get what you're saying."

"It was her special ability, her *gift,*" Iris stressed. "Have you not looked at one of her photographs and known exactly what the person was thinking or feeling?"

I nodded, thinking back to the first time I had found my mother's website. I could clearly see—and sometimes even hear—her subjects' thoughts.

"But I'm getting ahead of my story with all of this talk about Madlyn's photographs. I'll tell you about them, to be sure, but you have more to hear first." Iris looked at her slim watch. "But that's enough for today, miss. I'll come back and continue the story tomorrow."

• • •

She stood up and prepared to leave. As I shook the visions out of my head, I remembered I had intended to talk with Iris about Will's fall the previous night.

"Iris, I woke up last night to find Will crumpled at the bottom of the front staircase," I began. "He thought he had heard voices, children's voices, and I know this might sound silly but he felt as though someone had pushed him. With you telling me about Amelia's falls the day before . . ."

Iris stared deeply into my eyes. It made me more than a little uncomfortable. "You're wondering if something or someone in the house caused those falls."

"Well, yes."

"What do you think?"

"I think it's a very strange coincidence that certainly could have a reasonable explanation," I said weakly. It's not what I thought at all.

Iris nodded, smiling. "That's what they all say at the beginning."

I needed answers, not evasions. "Listen, Iris, if you think Will is in any kind of danger—or if I'm in danger—from someone or something in this house, I want to know it right now. Are we safe here?"

"Miss Hallie, you're asking questions for which I have no answers," she said sadly. "I am only this family's storyteller. That is my role. I cannot tell the future. I don't know what will be. None of us does."

I wouldn't let it go. "But, judging from what you've told me about things that have happened in the past—Charles needing protection, Amelia's falls, even your poor cousin—isn't the same thing happening now?"

Iris's smile sent a chill through me. "The girls have never liked strangers," she said, and she turned and went into the kitchen.

Suddenly, I felt the cold. It must've been no more than 40 degrees on that porch, and I had been sitting out there in just a jacket listening to Iris. I found myself wishing for a big pot of the stew she made so often, and oddly enough, when I went back into the house, I found just that. She must've brought it with her when she arrived that morning and left it simmering on the stove when she came to join me. As I ate a few spoonfuls of stew right out of the pot, I wished Will were already home.

An hour later, during which time I had done nothing but stare out of the back window watching for him, the ringing of the phone jarred me out of my trance.

"I know, I know," Will said. "I should be back by now, but I've been caught up in something that's going to take a while."

"How are you feeling? How's your head?"

"I'm fine. Just a headache and a dull one at that."

We hung up after he promised to come for an early dinner. I looked around the kitchen, not knowing quite what to do. I called Mira at the Manitou Inn; I wanted to find out about her being the one to discover my dad's overturned kayak the day we disappeared and thought perhaps we could get together and talk about it. No such luck. Her machine said she had gone to the mainland for a few days.

I rattled around the house for a while, wandering from kitchen to dining room to sunroom, but nothing felt quite right. I began to think about Will, and how he believed Iris's stories sounded too fantastic to be true. She had to be embellishing or outright inventing past events, he said. But now, after his fall, I needed to know the truth. Was I imagining things or was there a ghost on this property that was inclined to push people down staircases . . . ?

It hit me, then. Down staircases and *out of windows*.

· 27

I called the dogs and ran out the back door and into the wind, grabbing a thick cardigan that was hanging over a chair in the kitchen as I went past. I needed to get out of that house. My thoughts were swimming and I wanted to clear my head. I wrapped the sweater around me and made my way down the drive and onto the road, Tundra and Tika following close behind, dirt crunching under my shoes with each step.

Walking through the leafless, stark landscape, I knew only one thing for certain: I was faced with one of two highly undesirable prospects: uncovering some pretty ugly childhood memories in order to get to the bottom of these visions, or exorcising a trio of dead children from my house.

How had I found myself here, exactly? What would I be doing right now if I hadn't received the letters from Will? Maybe I'd be sitting in my living room in Washington drinking tea and listening to the seals bark in Puget Sound. Maybe I'd be wandering through my favorite bookstore.

I walked on, my feet heading in an unknown direction. I was going somewhere, even as it began to mist, the spray wetting my face.

The sight of the island cemetery surprised me. *Of course.* I wanted some proof that what Iris was telling me was real, and it doesn't get more real than gravestones with names and dates on them.

The black wrought-iron gate was rusted and weathered in spots, decaying with age. I swung it open and stepped inside, but the dogs stayed where they were, yowling in warning. I began to wander around, floating from one grave to the next, touching each headstone in reverence.

And then I found what I had been seeking. The sight of it brought me up short: a marble tombstone with the words MADLYN HILL CRANE, *1938–2009. Devoted daughter, wife, and mother.*

I sat down on my mother's grave, wondering why I hadn't visited it before. "Hi, Mom," I said out loud.

And then I leaned my head against her stone and cried, my tears mixing with the icy rain that began to fall. I don't know how long I sat there—minutes, an hour maybe. But at some point the dogs' barking pulled me back into the moment, and I knew I couldn't sit on that sodden ground anymore.

That's when I saw my own marker. HALCYON HILL CRANE, *1973–1979. Beloved child.*

It takes your breath away, seeing your own tombstone. It hadn't occurred to me before this moment, but of course I had one. Everyone thought I was dead. There had been a memorial service.

Next to my stone, my father's: NOAH THOMAS CRANE, *1940–1979. Devoted husband and father.* So that's where he came up with *Thomas.* I wondered where he got *James.*

I was standing on the Hill family plot, obviously, so I looked around at the neighboring gravestones and found them all. Hannah and Simeon. Sadie. Charles—who had died only a few years earlier—and Amelia. And then I saw the names of the three girls, Patience, Persephone, and Penelope. Their stone stark white, crumbling and ancient, almost a century old.

I sat down there, among my ancestors, feeling strangely at home. Thanks to Iris, I knew these people now. I had seen them all through her rich storytelling: Hannah, young and beautiful, when her children were born. Charles, toddling around as a baby, communing silently with animals, now lying only a few miles from where he grew up, having lived more than ninety years. My mother, whispering to her dead twin.

All the Hills had lived on the island; this was where they were born, grew up, and died. And now here I was among them. I felt, for the first time in my life, that I was part of a large family. Yes, they were all dead, but they were my people, my history, my roots. Even seeing my own gravestone there—I don't know, it felt as though ultimately I knew where I would rest. I was home.

I stood up and looked around once more, knowing I'd return to tend these graves often. I might have stayed longer, but I knew it would be an unpleasant walk home in the cold rain.

When I finally walked through my back door, I found Will in the kitchen, phone in his hand. He looked at me, stunned, and then said into the receiver: "Thanks, Jonah, but she just walked in.

Sorry to have bothered you." And then, to me: "Where in the *hell* have you been?"

My smile faltered. Except for Richard, when had a man been worried about me? I pushed my dripping hair out of my face and said, "I went for a walk."

This was met with open-mouthed silence from Will. Finally, gesturing toward the window, he said, "In *this?*"

The dogs had followed me inside the warm kitchen and were shaking their fur dry as I took off the sodden sweater I was wearing; nothing smells quite like wet wool or wet dog. "Not the smartest decision I've ever made, although it wasn't raining when I left. I got caught in it a few miles from the house."

"I called everyone I could think of." He was still standing with the phone in his hand. "Jonah, Henry, Mira, the grocery store. I even called the wine bar, wondering if you had ended up there. I couldn't imagine where you had gone." Then his arms were around me and I could feel his heart beating fast, like a bird's. "I was so worried about you," he murmured into my wet hair.

Suddenly I was freezing. Something about coming into the warm kitchen made me acutely aware of how awfully cold I had been.

"You're shivering," he said to me, pulling back from our embrace. "My God, your lips are blue. They're actually blue."

He looked at me for a moment, and I could tell he was running through various scenarios of what to do. First he poured a brandy and handed it to me. It tasted hot and spicy on the way down, warming me from the inside. "Right," he said then, leading me out of the kitchen. "Let's get you upstairs and into the tub."

As he drew a bath, I peeled off my sodden clothes. They smelled of peat and rain and centuries-old dirt. Maybe I'd just throw them away. I left them in a heap on the bathroom floor, climbed into the steaming water, and submerged. I felt safe and protected there, with the sound of the water rushing in my ears.

It wasn't until later, when Will and I were back in the kitchen eating dinner, that he asked me where I had gone. "I know you're a grown woman, but I was really worried when I got here and found you weren't home," he admitted. "After last night, I half expected to find you in a heap at the bottom of the stairs."

"Or lying under the third-floor window."

He looked at me. "Well. That's an interesting thing to say."

I twirled some noodles around my fork and considered how to continue the line of discussion I had just started. I hadn't even worked it out in my own head.

Will jumped into the silence. "Are you saying

you think that Julie Sutton's death thirty years ago is connected to what happened to me last night?"

"I'm not sure what I think—about anything."

"Anything?" He poked me with his fork.

I poked him back. "Okay, you I'm sure of." I smiled. "Everything clse is up in the air. But the thing is, whether they're fabrications or embellishments or outright lies, Iris told me her cousin was pushed or somehow driven off the cliff—she died, by the way. And my grandmother, Amelia, had several suspicious falls when she was pregnant. She lost two babies, Will!"

The ideas were jelling, becoming more real as I spoke them.

"Then, thirty years ago, we have the death of a child here in the house from being pushed or thrown out of a window. And now, you are pushed—or simply fall—down the stairs. Either we've got an epidemic of clumsiness around here or something else is going on."

"What's the something else?" he wanted to know.

Even as I said this I felt like an idiot, but it had to be said. "A ghost who likes to push people to their deaths."

We ate in silence for a few minutes, digesting, no doubt, the ridiculousness of the conversation we had been having. Then Will said, "Listen. You know how I feel about all this ghost business, but what would be the harm in calling a priest to come here?"

"No harm at all," I said. "A blessing on my new house. Let's do it tomorrow."

More silence.

"I was thinking of going at this another way," I started. "Maybe we should get a medium."

Will raised his eyebrows, as he took a bite off his fork.

"Seriously, Will, this is what these people do for a living—contacting the dead. Maybe we could find out if there's a ghost here and, if so, who it is."

He shook his head. "I don't know."

"What's the difference between a priest exorcizing the house and a medium doing it?"

Will considered this. "Aside from the authority behind the priest, not much, I guess. I'm still not sure this all doesn't have some sort of reasonable explanation. But whatever you want to do, I'll support you."

I squeezed his hand. "I want to get this ball rolling soon. Like tomorrow."

He nodded. "Whatever you want."

I stood up and began to nose around the kitchen. "Do mediums advertise in the phone book? Do I even *have* a phone book for the mainland?"

"Don't need one," he said, smiling. "I know a medium. And so do you."

"If you tell me it's you, I'll hit you very hard."

Will laughed. "No, you dope. Not me. It's Mira."

I stared at him, wondering if he was telling the truth. "You've got to be kidding."

He shook his head. "As I live and breathe. I don't know if she's on the level or not, but Mira bills herself as a—what does she call it?—a *sensitive*." As he said the word, he elongated the syllables and raised his eyebrows in mock fear. I laughed.

"It's true. She has a little cottage business in tourist season doing tarot card readings and giving walking tours of haunted spots on the island. It's quite popular, actually. People tend to get a sort of haunted-house vibe when they come to the island. Mira plays into that."

"But does she really have any ability at all—beyond the nose for a good business opportunity, I mean?"

"That's what I don't know," he said. "I've always thought she was sort of loopy. But at least she'd be a good place to start, if you want to go down that road."

We cleaned up the kitchen and headed upstairs. For now, we had other important things to attend to.

W hat does a girl wear for a séance: Jeans? A dress? Beads? In the end, I supposed the spirits wouldn't care one way or the other, so I pulled on a pair of jeans and a sweater and trotted downstairs to join Will in the living room, where he was waiting for me with wine and cheese and some other snacks.

I had called Mira that morning, and after a bit of catching up about her recent trip to the mainland I just dove right in. "Listen, Mira," I said. "I understand you are something of a—Well, I guess what I'm trying to say is, you've got the reputation for—"

"Being a medium?" She interrupted me, laughing.

I sighed. "Well, yes. I heard it from Will."

"I see," she said. "It's true, actually. I do possess a certain sensitivity." Her just saying the word made me stifle a laugh. "Why do you ask?"

I took a deep breath. I was really going to say this out loud now. I blurted it all out in one quick stream. "I'm asking because I think I might have a ghost in this house and I'd like to find out for sure and, if so, get rid of it."

Mira didn't say anything for a moment, and I was wondering if she was thinking I was as much of an idiot as I felt like, right then. But she wasn't. She said, "You know, I've always felt a certain presence in that house. I would say there's little doubt you've got a spirit or two floating around."

"Can you come over to check it out?" I asked her.

"You bet I can. What time do you want me?"

We decided that she would come for dinner that night, because I wanted Will at the house with me when whatever was going to happen happened.

After I hung up, Will trotted off to work, giving me strict orders either to stay home or, if I needed to go out, to call him and he'd come by and get me with Belle. I was cleaning up the breakfast dishes when I heard a rattling at the back door. Iris.

In all the excitement, I had forgotten she was coming back that day. Unlike the previous day, she began by taking the Murphy's Oil Soap in one hand and a rag in the other and setting off to shine the woodwork.

"You'll hear your mother's story over lunch," she told me gruffly. *Fine,* I thought. I grabbed a book and retreated to the sunroom.

Iris joined me there a couple of hours later, carrying a tray holding a bowl of leftover stew and a mug of steaming tea.

"Iris," I said, as I took a bite of the stew, "I hope you're not offended by what I'm about to say, but

I've been wondering if the stories you're telling me are the truth, or if they're embellished accounts with threads of truth running through them."

A smile crept across Iris's face. "It's the boyfriend doing the wondering, I expect."

"Well . . ." Where was I to go from there?

She nodded and closed her eyes and sat for a bit. "Do you not see them as I tell their stories?" she said, finally.

"I do. I do see them." She had a point. I hadn't told this to Will for fear of how strange it would sound.

"Then you know what I'm saying is true. You're seeing it as it happened." She looked at me deeply. Trying to discern what I believed?

"Okay—well, good, then," I said, awkwardly. "I just wanted to know." What I really wanted was for her to stop staring at me and get on with today's tale.

"I was beginning to tell you of Madlyn's gift," she began, "her ability to capture bits and pieces of the souls of others through her photography. Have you heard that many ancient cultures—and some not so ancient ones—were convinced of the power of mirrors?"

I nodded slowly. "I think so. It sounds familiar."

"Many cultures have believed that mirrors hold the power to predict the future, capture people's souls, and send bad luck to whoever is unfortunate enough to break one."

That last one I *had* heard. "Seven years of bad luck."

"Exactly. Because mirrors capture and contain bits and pieces of a person's soul. In other cultures, they believe mirrors are portals to the spirit world, allowing people and spirits to travel back and forth between the two planes."

"So?" I led her. "What does this have to do with my mother's photography?"

"Cameras, my dear, contain mirrors. And unlike the fleeting image reflected in a mirror, cameras capture images that remain."

"Of *course*," I said. "I've heard that. Many Native Americans refused to be photographed. Crazy Horse never allowed a photo of himself to be taken, even on his deathbed."

Iris smiled like a teacher whose student has finally caught on. "Yes, child. And why?"

"Because the camera would steal a bit of their soul."

"Exactly. They weren't wrong. A camera does have the ability to capture the soul of its subject, just as a mirror does. But it needs to be in the right hands to do so. Your mother had such hands. It was her gift. Oh, she didn't see it right away. Nobody did. But even from a young age, she was drawn to photography. She begged her parents for a camera for her birthday when she was, I believe, about five years old. Of course, Charles could never deny his daughter anything, so he got one for her, believing her interest to be a phase and he would be the one to end up using it.

"But Madlyn was never without that camera. She took it everywhere. When your grandfather got the first set of pictures developed, he was amazed at their quality and clarity. He had expected to see childish snaps: people's heads cut off, fuzzy landscapes. Instead, he found that his little daughter had taken beautiful, haunting portraits of himself, of Amelia, and of people who had visited the house.

"Charles especially loved Maddie's portraits of his animals, the horses in the barn and the dogs. He was astonished to find that they represented these creatures in a way that only Charles knew them.

"As you might imagine, Madlyn never wanted to do anything else. In very short order after she graduated from high school, she was working for major magazines, hired on the strength of the photographs she had taken growing up. She was on her way."

"You've told me a lot about my mother's talents and gifts, Iris, but not much about who she was as a person. I'd like to know that, too."

"Madlyn was a complicated girl," Iris said. "She was at times a delight and at times a terror, not unlike many teenage girls today. She would sink into dark moods in which she would talk to no one except—when she thought nobody was listening—her twin. At those times, it was as though her twin's spirit was attached to her, weighing her down. She continued having these dark moods her whole life, even after she met your father. Sadie never left her. But at other times, as I said, Madlyn was a complete delight. She was Charles's daughter, all smiles and laughter and goodness. Soon enough, she met your father."

I smiled at the thought of my young parents. And then another thought struck me. "Iris, you never mentioned my mother being bothered by the triplets. Charles had animals to protect him; who protected my mother?"

Iris nodded her head. "A very good question, Halcyon. Sadie, of course, was there to stand between the girls and your mother. But it was the camera, and Madlyn's unique ability to capture souls, that really kept the girls at bay. They knew not to get too close. At least, it was that way when Madlyn was young. When she met your father and brought him into this house, things changed somewhat.

"It was the summer of your mother's twentieth year. She was already a photographer of some note, living in New York City and traveling all over the world, working for *National Geographic* and other magazines. But this particular summer, she came home to the island because Amelia was in ill health. It was cancer, but nobody knew it then. She had been growing weaker and weaker, and Charles, frantic and already, I believe, grieving, contacted Madlyn and asked her to come home.

"She was a great solace to Amelia and Charles during this time, as you might expect. And they made the most of it, spending every day together, whether it was simply sitting and reading in the house or taking Amelia, who by now was confined to a wheelchair, out onto the cliff for picnics. It was as though they wanted to extract every bit of togetherness they could out of every moment Amelia had left.

"She died in August of that year." Iris sighed deeply. "Charles grieved for her every day of his life. He never got over losing her, although he did throw himself back into his practice. Tending animals gave him comfort during those first dark days.

"Madlyn, meanwhile, was due back at her New York apartment and her high-powered life the following month, and she was contemplating what she was going to do with her father—take him to New York, perhaps?—when she met Noah Crane."

I smiled, curling my feet up under me. I loved all of Iris's stories, grim though they were, but now we were getting to the best ones.

"Noah was working on the island in one of the hotels for the summer with a few of his friends from the mainland. Your mother met him one evening in a pub downtown. He was drawn to her immediately, of course, as everyone was. But the difference was, she was also drawn to him.

"She knew immediately that she would never be going back to that New York apartment. And he knew he wasn't going to take the teaching job waiting for him in the fall on the mainland. Within a few days of meeting each other, they had both decided to remain on the island and build a life together right here.

"I can see you'd like to know a little about their courtship." Iris eyed me. "They did all the usual things—dinners and dances and picnics and walks. But most of all, Noah and Madlyn talked. They were able to talk more deeply and intimately to each other than to anyone else."

It sounded familiar. It's just how I felt with Will.

Iris went on. "Your father asked about a job at the small local school here on the island. They happened to have an opening for a math teacher, which is what he was, and he didn't have a moment's hesitation in accepting the position. Madlyn, meanwhile, called all the editors at her various client magazines and informed them that her home base would now be Grand Manitou, not New York. She would still go on assignment as she always had.

"Everything fell into place so neatly and nicely, Madlyn always suspected her dead mother had had a hand in it somehow. Of course, that was true. I know for certain that Amelia was whispering in Noah's ear that night in the pub—*Turn around, turn around now*—when Madlyn was about to walk by. If she hadn't done that, my dear, you may well have never been born.

"She was also whispering *Stay, stay on the island* into their ears whenever they were together, planting that seed firmly and deeply. Yes, it was all Amelia's doing that Noah and Madlyn got together and ended up settling down here. She did it all, of course, for her beloved Charles. She was terrified to think of him alone and knew how much he needed his daughter beside him.

"Oh, Amelia was a busy one during those months after her death. But when Madlyn was married to your father and Charles was suitably provided for, she turned toward that ever-present light behind her and saw a tiny figure standing there. Sadie. Amelia ran to her, wrapping her arms around her beloved child for the first time, and the two of thcm floated away into that light together."

Iris's face was softer and kinder than I had ever seen it, perhaps in response to the fact that I was, and had been for the past several minutes, bawling like a baby.

"That was so beautiful, Iris." I sniffed, wiping my nose with a Kleenex. "But I don't understand. They were so happy. What could have gone so horribly wrong in just five years to make my father steal me away from her?"

Iris's face hardened into her familiar expression, but she grasped my hand as she shook her head. "That, my dear, is a story for another day. It is your story. The tale of Halcyon Crane."

"You can't tell me now?" I was desperate to hear it.

"You have guests coming, miss. You need to prepare for them, and I need to take my leave."

I knew better than to try to stop Iris when she was intent on leaving the house. *Let her go,* I thought. I had a séance to attend.

· 29

I made pasta with chicken, caramelized onions, sun-dried tomatoes, and a Gorgonzola sauce— a recipe pirated from my favorite restaurant back in Seattle. Will brought fresh bread and several bottles of wine (those would definitely be needed) and rattled uncomfortably around the kitchen while I cooked until Mira materialized at the front door, seven o'clock on the dot.

I found her looking—well, just like she always looked. Jeans and a striped shirt, a sweater slung across her shoulders. Funky glasses hanging on a chain around her neck, her hair pulled back in a ponytail. She seemed so—I don't know, normal?—that it startled me. This made her laugh.

"Did you expect me to show up in a velvet cloak?"

I laughed. "Get in here, Madam Mira."

Our dinner conversation covered everything from the weather to my relationship with Will to island gossip. I was skirting one of the issues I wanted to talk about with her and Will could see it, catching my eye every now and then to give me a look that seemed to say, *So? Ask already.*

After a few uncomfortable forays into the subject—"Mira, I was wondering . . . that is to say, I found out something . . . It got me thinking . . ." I finally choked out the words: "I recently learned that you found our kayak on the day my dad and I disappeared."

Will winked at me across the table. Mira twirled the pasta around her fork, considering her response.

"That was some day," she said finally. "Most everyone on the island was out looking for the two of you. I had the feeling I knew where he had gone—somehow I just *knew*—and sure enough, I was right. Still, the sight of that kayak took my breath away. I wanted to be wrong more than anything." She looked at me with a mixture of regret and anger. "Your father certainly put this island through the wringer with his little stunt."

Mira was baiting me, trying to shift the focus away from her finding the kayak toward my dad's sins. But I refused to play along. "Why didn't you tell me? We've had plenty of opportunities."

"I really don't know why," she said, flustered. "When you first came to the island, I was stunned to find out who you were. Who wouldn't be? You were dead for thirty years, Hallie. And then, as a bit more time went on—I don't know, it didn't seem to matter that I had been part of the search party that day. Everyone on the island helped, not just me."

This made a kind of strange sense. I nodded, ready to change the subject, but Mira leaned toward me and continued, in an almost conspiratorial tone. "The thing is, Hallie, all these years, and especially back then, I had the feeling there was more to the story than we were being told."

This intrigued me. "You did? How so?"

"Julie Sutton's death. Your disappearance shortly thereafter. Everyone, especially the police, believed that Noah committed suicide in the face of those allegations and took you with him because you were the one witness to his crime. I wasn't convinced. If he wanted to end his own life just as the police were bearing down on him, fine, but what would be the point of killing you? He loved you more than you can imagine. And if he *had* committed that horrible crime and somehow killed that girl, the Noah Crane I knew would've stood up and faced his punishment."

"The Thomas James I knew would've done the same thing," I said to her.

"So." Mira changed the subject as I loaded the last of the silverware into the dishwasher. "You've called me here for some ghost busting."

I laughed nervously as we took our wine and moved from the kitchen to the dining room, where I had already lit the candle chandelier. It bathed the dark room in a soft flickering light that danced along the windowpanes. The three of us took seats around the table, and Mira sat up straight and cleared her throat. She was now taking control of the proceedings, a role I sensed she was very comfortable assuming.

"Why don't we begin by you telling me exactly what's been happening in the house," she directed.

I took a deep breath and told her everything: the sightings of the girl in the white dress, the disappearing and reappearing jewelry, the television turning off and on, the shades opening and closing.

She nodded, looking from me to Will and back again. "Sounds like a haunting." I know that's why I called her here, the word still sent a chill up the back of my neck. "There's really no other explanation," Mira went on. "You know that, right?"

Will gave me a look. "Actually, Mira, there is

another explanation," he began tentatively. I could see he wasn't sure of whether to go on or not, but I nodded, giving him the signal to continue. "I had the idea that perhaps Hallie's mind is delivering bits and pieces of memories back to her," Will said. "You know, she was so traumatized by the death of her playmate that she didn't speak until after she and her father built a new life away from here."

"I do remember that." Mira nodded. "You stopped speaking altogether. Your parents were frantic."

"Considering that, I was thinking the very fact of being back in this house was triggering memories in Hallie's mind," Will continued.

"I'd go along with that theory if it wasn't for the other things happening," Mira said finally. "How can you explain the jewelry disappearing and reappearing? The shades? The television?"

"That's why you're here," he admitted. "I *can't* explain those things. If it was just Hallie seeing a girl in white around the house, I'd recommend a psychiatrist."

I continued Will's line of thinking. "The thing is, Mira, all these little happenings—a necklace gone here, a television turned on there—wouldn't bother me too much if it wasn't for some rather distressing information I've learned about my family in recent days."

Mira squinted at me. "What sort of information?"

311

"I've learned that over the years there have been a number of—well, what I would call *suspicious falls* on this property and in this house, including—not incidentally—Julie Sutton's fall out of a third-floor window thirty years ago."

"Tell me more about these falls."

I leaned in toward Mira and told her what I had learned from Iris.

Mira grimaced. "That doesn't sound good," she murmured.

"No." My account was picking up steam, heading to its conclusion. "But the last straw came the other night when Will fell down the front stairs."

Aghast, Mira looked at Will for an explanation. He told her how he thought he heard someone calling his name in the middle of the night and how he felt hands on his back, pushing him down.

"That's the reason we called you," I concluded. "It's become dangerous. If there's a malevolent spirit here, I want it out. I want to be able to live in my new house in peace."

That was the full story. Now that Mira knew, she opened her bag, spread a deep-purple velvet cloth out on the table, and placed five votive candles on it.

"Do you have any idea who this ghost might be?" Mira asked, as she lit the candles one by one.

I exchanged a sidelong glance with Will. "I

think it might be one or all of the little girls who died here in the 1913 storm: Penelope, Patience, and Persephone."

She looked at me in the flickering candlelight. "I'm not familiar with that event. What storm?"

And so I told her all about it—how nearly a century earlier a freak November snowstorm had caught Penelope, Patience, and Persephone unawares outside and how they died in one another's arms at the bottom of the cliff.

"So you don't think it's the spirit of the girl who was killed here thirty years ago?" Mira asked.

Will and I exchanged glances. I hadn't even considered this. "The reason I thought our spirit is one or all of the girls from 1913 is because of the family lore I've recently learned. My relatives have all assumed the girls were still around. Their mother especially was tormented by the thought that her daughters didn't make it to heaven. She believed it until the day she died, and even tried to contact them once. And all the falls—"

Mira nodded. "I just wanted to be sure. If you think you know who the ghosts are, it helps. Whenever possible, it's best to try to contact specific people on the other side."

She explained what was going to happen tonight. She would spend a few quiet moments meditating—going into a trance?—and then we'd join hands while she called the girls, inviting them to join our circle.

Mira took a deep breath and closed her eyes. *Here we go,* I thought. But then she opened them again. Something had occurred to her. "Do you have anything that belonged to the girls? It's really helpful to have something from the person I'm trying to contact."

I shook my head. "It was nearly a hundred years ago, Mira. Their stuff might still be around here packed in a box somewhere, but I wouldn't have the first idea where to look."

As Mira collected herself, taking one deep breath after another, grasping our hands, squeezing them tightly, all I could think of was that perhaps it was a good thing we didn't have those ribbons.

"Penelope, Patience, Persephone," Mira chanted, in a voice that was not quite her own. "Penelope, Patience, Persephone. Girls, we are calling to you. We are asking you to join our circle. Come to us, girls. Join us here at the table. "Penelope, Patience, Persephone. Penelope, Patience, Persephone."

Mira sounded just like Iris when she had said those same words, chanting, calling to the girls. Her voice was scratchy and oddly pitched, as though it wasn't she who was speaking but someone else. I was beginning to feel something, an electricity in the room prickling at the back of my neck and running down my arms.

"Penelope, Patience, Persephone."

I heard it first in a distant corner of the house, the rumbling of something awakening and coming to life. A century-old wind snaked its way into the room from where it had been lying dormant on the third floor, swirling around the three of us at the table, wrapping us like a python and constricting us. All the candles, those on the table and those in the chandelier, were extinguished in one collective *whoosh*. We were in total darkness. And then I heard it.

Say, say, oh, playmate, come out and play with me.

I tried to scream but my voice had no sound. I tried to open my eyes, but it was as though they were glued shut. I tried to let go of Mira's and Will's hands, but I could not unclench my grip. Their hands had gone cold, stonelike, completely without feeling. It was as though I were holding the hands of the dead.

Somewhere in the distance, Mira was murmuring. "You're cold as ice. You're freezing. You're frozen. You're dead."

I smelled it, then. Suddenly and immediately the room was filled with it. The scent of roses, overpowering and thick.

"Hey!" It was Will, his voice high and awkward. "Stop it!"

From Mira, in a whisper: "You're cold as ice. You're freezing. You're frozen. You're dead."

"Ouch!" Will was on his feet, trying to wrench

his hands free of ours. I opened my eyes but it was no use, I could see nothing but blackness.

The dogs burst into the room from the kitchen, snarling and barking. I could feel them circling the table and hear them panting. Finally—it must have been only a few moments but it felt like forever—Mira loosened her grip, pushed back her chair, and ran toward the wall. She flipped on the light switch, and the three of us uttered a collective gasp at what we saw.

The table was covered with white ribbons.

They were piled high between us, covering the velvet cloth, the unlit candles, and the tabletop itself. They spilled onto the floor. One lazily danced its way across the room as the dogs growled, soft and low.

Mira was standing at the light switch, her eyes wide, panting. Only then did I see Will's face. It was covered in scratches. Little rivers of blood trickled down his cheeks from what looked to be razor-thin cuts. He just stood there, open-mouthed, unable to comprehend what had just occurred.

I tried to hide my terror and slid up to Will, resting my hand gently on his arm. "Let's get you into the kitchen and clean you up." I led him into the other room and sat him down at the kitchen table, Mira following close behind us. I grabbed a clean dish towel out of a drawer and wet it down before gently and softly dabbing the blood from

Will's face. He was looking at me with the eyes of a frightened little boy.

"There's a first-aid kit under the sink in there." I pointed Mira in the direction of the bathroom off the kitchen. She returned with the kit and I opened it to find an antibacterial cream for cuts and scratches, which I rubbed on Will's face. Luckily, none of the cuts were very deep. Scratches from tiny claws. Or a child's fingernails. I wondered if they'd leave scars.

Meanwhile, Mira's hands shook as she opened another bottle of red wine. *Good thinking*. She poured three glasses of it and downed one immediately, pouring another in its place. Then, we all started to talk.

"I've experienced a lot of things in my life, but nothing like that," Mira said.

"I couldn't let go of either of your hands," I reported.

"Something was in that room with us," Will murmured, touching the scratches on his face.

"Tell me exactly what happened to you," Mira said to Will. "When did you start feeling the scratches?"

Will thought for a moment. "It was right after I started to smell the rose petals. You smelled them, too, right?"

Mira and I nodded.

"So the scratching began as soon as they came into the room," Mira murmured. "Does either of you know the significance of the ribbons?"

"Family lore has it that, a long time ago, another medium called the girls with ribbons. They used to wear them in their hair every day."

Will's eyes were wide, but Mira did not seem at all surprised by this news. "Sometimes that's how the spirits of the dead come to us," she murmured. "They'll place something significant to them around us, so we'll notice they've been there. It's quite common, actually. Sometimes it's a butterfly hovering close by for an unusually long period of time. One woman I know sees an eagle perched on a tree outside her window and knows it's her dead son sending a message of protection. Another family finds pennies in strange places—in their shoes, in the bottom of a bowl of pasta, frozen into a compartment in an ice tray. It's how the dead tell the living they're still around, still watching."

Neither Will nor I said anything. We both just sat there, holding hands, shaking our heads in disbelief at what had just occurred. If only all we had to be concerned about was pennies or hovering butterflies.

Finally, Mira said, "Well, at least we accomplished one thing tonight."

"What's that?" I wanted to know.

"It's absolutely clear that you've got a ghost. Three of them, actually. Penelope, Patience, and Persephone."

"So now what?" I asked her. I was truly at a

loss. I had no idea what came next. And I was suddenly very, very tired. All I wanted to do was to fall asleep in Will's arms without any worry about mischievous, murderous ghosts.

"We go on to Phase Two tomorrow." Mira smiled.

"Which is?"

"Getting them out of here," she said. "I'm assuming you still want to stay in this house, right?"

"Right."

"And I'm assuming you want the girls gone?"

"Definitely."

"Well, there are ways to take care of that," she promised, pushing her chair back from the table. "But I think we've all had about enough for one night."

I didn't want her to go, I'll admit it. I was afraid to stay in the house. Suddenly, I had an idea. "May Will and I come with you and stay in a room at the inn tonight? I'm really not excited about spending the night here."

"You can have your old room." Mira smiled, patting my hand.

"We could go to my house, you know," Will offered, as he dabbed at his face.

I shook my head. "You live clear on the other side of the island and Mira's just down the road. Plus, Tundra and Tika won't fit in your buggy and I'm not leaving them here alone." I turned to Mira. "We *can* take them to your place, right?"

She nodded quickly. "I don't usually allow pets, but I can make an exception tonight for these girls."

And that's how the three of us came to leave my house together that night. In retrospect, I see it was a mistake. Hindsight can be particularly cruel when one goes down a wrong road. Perhaps if Will and I had braved the night in that place— faced the girls head on—we would have been spared what happened the next day. On the other hand, I don't have any way of knowing what might have befallen us if we had decided to spend the night in the house after those spirits had been called, awakened, and stirred up. Who knows what manner of horror we might have experienced?

PART THREE

Y ou're not going back there alone," Will said
to me, over breakfast at Mira's the next
day.

When we arrived at the inn after a damp, rainy
ride in Mira's carriage, we simply fell into bed
and into a deep sleep, dogs curled up at our feet,
not awakening until midday. I didn't even have a
change of clothes with me, so I thought I'd head
back to Hill House in the light of day and pack a
few things.

"It's daytime," I said stupidly. "Nothing's going
to happen to me. And anyway, I've been living
there for two weeks now. If they wanted to do
anything beyond tease me, they've had plenty of
opportunities. I'm not afraid now. I was last night
but I'm not afraid now. I'm really not."

How afraid did that sound?

Mira had run into town for some groceries, so
she couldn't dissuade me, and Will wasn't convinced by my bravado. He was shaking his head,
and only then did it occur to me: The scratches on
his face were all but gone. I could barely make
out their faint trails on his cheeks. It was as
though they, too, were phantoms or figments con-
jured up by Mira's call to the dead, dissolving
with the light of day.

"I just wish you'd come into town with me," he

muttered, knowing he wasn't going to win this battle.

"It's a beautiful day," I told him, as though that meant anything whatsoever in the context of what we were discussing.

But it was true. It was one of those rare late-fall days, just as you're preparing for the onslaught of snow and chill and cold, that surprises you with a burst of summer, a day of respite and reprieve from the harsh weather that will certainly be descending in very short order.

"Here's what I'll do," I began, by way of compromise. "I'll pack some things for us, just in case we decide to stay here at Mira's again tonight. I'll clean up all the debris from the séance, and then I'll take a picnic lunch outside and wait for you. And I'll keep the dogs by my side the whole time. How's that?"

The sky was a deep cloudless blue and the temperature must've been climbing into the sixties—not a heat wave but, in late November on this island, quite an unusual occurrence. I leaned against Will as we walked toward my house, the dogs running in long circles around us.

"You know what didn't occur to me until just now?" I said. "Iris. She'll be there. I won't be alone."

Will smiled. "Small comfort. Like she can do anything if the ghosts try to push you down the stairs. But it's something, anyway." He kissed me as he veered into the barn to hitch up Belle, who had spent the night in a stall vacated by one of my mother's horses.

I ran up the steps, took a deep breath, and opened the back door. Iris was already here: the glasses were washed and put away, chairs pushed neatly under the table. I opened the door to the dining room and found her, broom and dustpan in hand, sweeping up the ribbons. The scent of roses was still overpowering.

She gave me a sharp look. "What happened here?"

Suddenly, I felt like a small child caught in the act of doing something wrong, something forbidden. Had we? I was almost afraid of saying the words, but I managed to squeak out, "We tried to contact the girls."

"Tried? I'd say you succeeded." She sniffed as she picked up the dustpan full of ribbons and made her way to the kitchen door to dump them. "That was a mistake, Halcyon. The last time someone contacted those girls, somebody died."

I remembered the story of Hannah's séance and shivered at the thought of poor Jane going over the cliff.

"I think it's time you heard the tale of Halcyon Crane," Iris said, and walked out the back door, leaving me alone with my fears and my questions.

It took a moment before I followed. Iris had gone down the drive and into the garden, where she was sitting on one of the stone benches. As the dogs curled up on their beds in the kitchen, I trotted down the drive and joined her.

"You need to fully realize your gift," she said to me there in the garden. "You need to own it and use it, now that you've called the girls to you in this very real way. You are more powerful than they, and much more powerful than any supposed medium you had here. Now is the time, Halcyon, to realize who you are."

I sighed. "I have no idea how to do what you're suggesting. I've tried, but I—"

"That's why I'm here, child: to teach you, to unlock your sight with my stories. And now I'm convinced that this last one, *your* tale, you need to see on your own. It's the only way." She fished a few black-and-white photographs out of her apron pocket and handed them to me. "Look deeply, Halcyon, and then empty your mind of all thought. Let your spirit drift in the ether. When you're hovering there between worlds, call the spirits to you, your mother and father, and they will show you what you need to see." She fell silent, leaving me to ponder the photographs in my open palms without benefit of her explanation.

I saw me, as a baby, my mother and father smiling broadly. A birthday party with just one candle. My father lying in the grass with me sleeping on his chest. I let myself become absorbed in the photographs until I could almost sense the moment in time they contained—the smell of the grass that day, the taste of sugary frosting . . . I closed my eyes and tried to clear my mind of other thoughts, listening to the sound within my own ears, feeling the soft breeze on my face, until another scent swirled about me: a familiar cologne. *My father's cologne.*

I opened my eyes but was unable to see what had been in front of me. There was no stone bench, no garden, no cliff beyond, no Iris. Only my dad, younger than I, sitting in a room in Hill House that I took to be his study. He was staring out the window absently, running a hand through his hair. How full it looked, back then. My mother, obviously pregnant, swept into the study wearing a long purple dress and dangly earrings and kissed him on the forehead.

"Money's not the issue, Madlyn, you know that." My father sighed. "I'm just worried about what kind of father I'm going to make. Am I ready for this? Are we?"

Madlyn laughed, a musical trill that sounded familiar and sweet. "Nobody's ever ready to have a child, silly. They come into our lives when *they're* ready."

Noah looked into his wife's eyes and collapsed in the face of her optimism. "I guess you're right. This baby's coming, whether we feel ready or not."

• • •

That scene dissolved into thin wisps of smoke taken aloft on the breeze, to be instantly replaced with the image of me, wriggling in my bassinette, my father leaning over me, beaming. "Let her sleep, Noah." My mother smiled at him and led him out of the room.

I saw another image then. My mother, her long auburn hair pulled back in a scarf, was sitting at the desk in her bedroom suite, squinting and scowling at a group of photographs she had laid out in long rows. I watched her gather them up in a hurry and shove them into a file when my father came into the room.

"I'm worried about Halcyon," he said to her.

"What else is new?" My mother rose from her desk and took him in her arms. "You've got to be the most doting father on this planet. What is it this time, my love?"

"Madlyn, I know we've talked about this before, but you really have to listen to me this time. I've been trying to tell you, honey, our little girl is blind." *Blind?* My father went on. "She never makes eye contact with anyone, not even you. She doesn't react to toys or faces or animals. You've got to face it, honey. We need to take her to a doctor."

His earnest, pleading words sent a familiar chill up my spine. I watched a curly-haired toddler, unsteady on her feet, turn and walk directly into a wall. But that image didn't jibe with the next one that floated in front of my eyes: me as a toddler, looking directly at a woman whom I recognized as Hannah and laughing as she covered her face with her hands and then dropped them, crying, "Peek-a-boo!" before she dissolved into the air as my mother swept into the room. Image after image flickered into view then, like a slide show, me talking and laughing and playing with Hannah and Simeon and Amelia. I wasn't seeing what was in front of me—but I *was* seeing beyond the veil into the world of the dead.

Noah tried again one afternoon. "Madlyn, I think we might have another problem with Hallie. I know it sounds crazy, but I heard her talking to your mother today. And it's not the first time."

Madlyn laughed. "That's ridiculous. She has an imaginary friend, that's all there is to it." But I could hear what my mother was thinking. She herself had spent her childhood talking to a dead twin, so to her this was normal behavior.

"How can she talk about pretty white ribbons and that brown furry teddy bear and the red leaves in the garden when she's blind?" Noah wanted to know.

"Honey, don't question it," Madlyn told him, turning him around and rubbing his shoulders. "This house has a way of doing strange things to people. Don't worry about it. My dad didn't *talk* until he was five years old, and look at him now."

Another image materialized: Will, as a boy! With me in the garden, right where I was now sitting. He was chasing me around one of the benches and suddenly I stopped, turned, looked directly at him, and leaped on him. I knew I was seeing the first moment of my own sight. Will's was the first face—other than a ghost's—I had ever seen. A warmth overtook me and I laughed, watching my young self lying on top of Will, tickling him mercilessly. I grinned, thinking of the night before. Not much had changed.

"I can't believe it," Noah murmured tearfully to Madlyn as he held me tightly in his arms.

"It's just like my father and his speech," Madlyn whispered over my shoulder. "I don't care why it happened or how, only that she can see now. That's all that matters."

As I learned from the next vision, I had not lost my ability to see beyond the veil, and I saw how frazzled my dad was becoming with my mother's constant denials that nothing out of the ordinary was happening. "Hallie! Halcyon Crane!" he would call as he pounded through the trees in front of the house, looking for me yet again. I would disappear during the afternoons, exploring the house and the grounds and especially the woods. More often than not, he'd find me lazing in the grass watching the sailboats come and go in the harbor, or brushing the horses with my grandfather, or playing in the shade of one of the great oak trees that stood near the cliff. But on this day I wasn't in any of those places, and it was getting dark.

Noah's breath started to catch in his throat as he ran through the grounds, calling my name, the exposed roots and gnarled branches clawing at his shirt and his hair. He was lumbering through the stand of trees in front of the house, nearly blind himself with the fear of never seeing me again. "Hallie!" His voice was shrill, frantic.

"Here, Papa," came my voice from within the trees. Noah stopped and looked around wildly, but he couldn't see me. "Not there! I'm over here!" Suddenly, a rustling in the bushes. "Boo!" I cried, leaping onto my father's legs and holding on tight. Beads of sweat had begun to dot my father's forehead. He bent down and scooped me up, holding me close to his heart. I saw that I had been perilously close, three or four steps, from the edge of the cliff.

He held me tight; I could smell the baby shampoo in my hair, mixed with wildflowers and lavender and water and night.

"What's the matter, Daddy?"

Noah put me down and knelt beside me, face-to-face. "You know the rule about the cliff."

I squirmed and shrugged. "I was just playing."

"I don't care, young lady. You've been told never to play by the cliff alone."

I looked at him with innocence in my eyes. "But I wasn't alone."

Noah shook his head and sighed, confusion and dread apparent on his face. "Who was with you?"

"My friends," I explained. "We were playing hide-and-seek."

A dark shadow crept over my father's face. A childhood game had become dangerous. It had led me to the cliff edge.

What I saw next made me suddenly cold: me on the bluff with three ghostly playmates—the girls. We were sitting across from one another, playing patty-cake and singing:

Say, say, oh, playmate!
Come out and play with me.
And bring your dollies three.
Climb up my apple tree!

The sound wrapped around my throat like an ice-cold hand. I saw my father scooping me up away from them into his arms. I saw them waving at me. I saw his terrified face before I put my hands over my own.

"But I play with them all the time, Daddy! And other people, too! Grandma and great-grandmother, especially. Grandma fell and lost a baby."

My stomach began to tighten and I was having trouble breathing. *This is it,* I thought to myself. *I'm about to learn everything now.* I had an overwhelming urge to get up and run from that bench, to shake the vision from my eyes, because I knew what I was going to see next—my repressed memories of the day Julie Sutton died.

The memories had stayed hidden in some dark recess of my brain for a reason, I thought, in a wild attempt to justify not hearing the rest of the story. Maybe I shouldn't know what happened. Up to now I had been just fine not knowing, after all. Why dredge up the past? But then again, what was the point of hearing all these family tales from Iris if I wasn't going to hear—or see—my own?

Somewhere, very far away, I heard Iris's voice. "Keep looking, Halcyon. It's right there before you."

But I didn't see Julie, not just yet. What I saw was my mother, entranced with her photography, her own gift, oblivious to everything going on around her. The capturing of souls was a heady thing; it intoxicated her, I could see it in her eyes. Every time she developed one of her photographs, she was like an addict, insatiably drawn to what she would find there. I saw it clearly: This gift, this obsession, left very little time for other things, like husbands and children. That's why she didn't see I was in danger. And I knew then this part of the tale was cautionary. I made a mental note to remember that I, too, risked addiction. I needed to keep my eyes on what was really important.

"So what if she's having visits from previous occupants of this house?" my mother said to Noah, waving off his fears. "They're my *relatives,* for heaven's sake."

"Maddie, I think we should leave the island," he pleaded. "Let's get away from here."

"Are you kidding?" she spat back at him. "Leave my father here alone? No, Noah. Absolutely not."

I saw more arguments, then. Doors slamming, tears from both of them. "This is a wonderful place to grow up," Madlyn told her husband. "Hallie has friends and a great school and a whole island to explore—without cars to run her over. You've got a fine job, and I can do my work from here. These are my roots and they're Hallie's roots. You can't seriously want to take her away from all of that because you think she sees ghosts."

She said that last bit with a kind of sarcastic venom that Noah had never before heard from his wife, and I saw the defeated look on his face. Nobody was leaving the island. Desperate, grieving, and frightened, he whispered into my ear that he'd protect me as best he could, promising to watch me with a hawk's keen eye.

Then the scene shifted, and I saw somebody new on the island shopping for groceries. She followed my father and me out of the store and touched him on the sleeve. He turned and saw a young woman. She looked into his eyes and said, conspiratorially, "I can see that your daughter has quite a gift."

I could almost hear Noah's heart beating. He took a deep breath and whispered, "What do you mean, a gift?"

"The sight. I have it, too."

He grabbed the young woman's arm and hustled her over to a quiet corner of the street. "Listen, I don't know who you are or how you know what you know, but I really need to talk to you," he said to her.

Now I saw the woman's face more clearly than I had before. Mira? *It couldn't be.* And yet there she was, her face younger and brighter than I knew it to be, but plain as day.

I watched my father meet Mira for a clandestine dinner on the mainland that evening. Of course they couldn't be seen together on the island— word would get back to my mother in a flash—so they picked an out-of-the-way restaurant not far from the ferry dock. He told Mira everything: how I didn't see until I was three years old but was constantly talking about visual things and people and animals, how I regained my sight in an instant one day, how I was immersed in stories of my ancestors' pasts, how I had always played with imaginary friends but now those games were turning dangerous.

"What does your wife say?" Mira asked him shyly.

"She discounts it, all of it. She is totally in denial and says I'm insane to be worried. I've tried everything to make her understand, but she won't listen, she won't . . . ." His words trailed off into a sigh.

I watched as a coy grin appeared on Mira's face and knew she was very glad to hear this. I saw images of the two of them meeting again and again, intimate dinners and rendezvous at out-of-the-way hotels. They had had an affair? I felt sick. All those times she had been so friendly toward me, so helpful, she had never once said anything about this.

Then I saw Julie Sutton's parents drop her off at the house for the afternoon. My father found us playing in a third-floor room, sitting on the floor with a tea party spread out before us. I was pouring imaginary tea from a pot and chattering away to Julie and to the stuffed bears I had positioned as the other guests.

"You girls are playing so happily up here, honey." He smiled at me, relieved to find me immersed in a normal child's activity—a tea party with a real live friend—and went on his way down the stairs.

But then came the screaming: high-pitched, horrible screams. My father flew back into the room and found me, scratches bleeding all over my face, locked in a struggle with, to him, what was an unseen foe. But I could see exactly who it was.

I saw myself screaming, holding my arms in front of me to fend off a girl in a white dress: Patience—but her face was not the face I had come to know. It had morphed into a grotesque worm-eaten skull, its flesh paper-thin and flaking. Her eyes were gone—only empty black holes remained—and she was yelling, "We weren't invited to this party! You didn't invite us to this party!"

Julie was crying and cowering in the corner, and then Persephone was upon her, scratching and pushing her, tearing at her dress, and finally putting her tiny hands around Julie's throat.

Seeing all this, I was stunned into a stupor. I couldn't shake the images from my view and I couldn't move; the images held me captive even though I wanted to get up from that bench and run more than I had ever wanted anything in my life. This scene now before me was what my mind had locked away.

• • •

I kept screaming and fighting against this unseen enemy—unseen by my father, that is. I knocked over lamps and tore bedding off beds, I fell and tumbled and screamed. My father was just standing there—paralyzed with shock, I assumed—until one of them—Penelope—knocked into his legs and he felt, with certainty, her presence there.

He dove into the fray and tried to grab whatever it was that was torturing me. In doing so, he turned Penelope's wrath against him. She flew at him, scratching his face and biting and tearing his shirt—he could not see her, but I was seeing it all—until he was backed into the wall near the open window.

I couldn't catch my breath. There I was again, on top of a roller coaster, about to plunge toward the ground whether I wanted to or not.

In the confusion, with me fighting off Patience and my dad fighting off Penelope, Persephone saw her opportunity and took it, pushing Julie out of the open window. I ran to the window and watched her fall. She locked eyes with me as she tumbled all the way to the ground, mouthing my name. The last thing I saw was her terrified face before her skull hit a rock, making a sickening cracking sound.

My father didn't see exactly what happened, but he saw me leaning out of the window. When he looked out the window, he saw, to his horror, the body of Julie Sutton lying on the ground.

"Oh, my God," I murmured to myself. "He thought I did it!"

Noah flew through the house, down the stairs, and outside, stopping only when he reached Julie. I watched from the window as he attempted CPR, but it was useless; she was dead. He called the police and the Suttons.

"It was the girls," I whispered. "They killed Julie. But my father thought it was me. That's why we left the island."

The vision swirled into view again. My mother was away when it happened, so my dad asked Mira to come to the house that evening. She did, and he told her everything that had occurred during the day—by that time, of course, the whole island knew there had been a death at Hill House. And Mira hatched the plan for escape—leaving the island. Within Noah's panic, she saw a clear road leading to what she wanted, so she took it.

"I'm going to take the blame, Mira," I heard my father say. "Just so long as none of this touches Hallie."

Mira shook her head. "Your daughter is in grave danger," she told him slyly. "I can feel it. This is not the end of the matter. You need to get her out of here. With you in prison, who is going to watch over Hallie? Your wife?"

Noah sat down hard on one of the kitchen chairs, defeated.

"Listen," she said, in low conspiratorial tones. "I know a man on the mainland. He can come up with a whole new identity for you. For us. We can run away together and start a new life somewhere, pretending that this never happened."

I put my head in my hands, feeling the beginning throb of a migraine. Or was it my father's head I felt hurting? Somehow, I could see it in his eyes. He never intended to take Mira with us; she was merely his means of escape.

"I've given Madlyn several chances to see that something is very wrong here," he murmured, nodding. "Hallie's in danger, that's never been more clear. But Madlyn won't see it. All she keeps saying is that she herself was perfectly safe growing up in that house. But Hallie's life could very well be at stake."

Noah arranged everything with the man on the mainland: a new driver's license, birth certificate, college degree, everything. And he waited for the right time. Meanwhile, the police investigation was turning nasty, as was island opinion. Everyone was horrified by Julie Sutton's death and there was only one person who could be responsible: Noah Crane. He allowed the police to believe that he was the one who killed that poor girl. Never once did the harsh eye of blame come to rest on me.

I saw my father and Mira cooking up an escape plan. She would tow a fishing boat to the designated site; she would find our overturned kayak, thus making everyone think we had died. Noah would send for her later, when he reached our destination.

Still, he waited and wondered. Was leaving really the right thing to do? The last straw came the day Madlyn showed him the latest photo she had taken of me, swinging in the backyard. Noah saw it loud and clear, his mute daughter calling out: *Help me.* That was it for my father. He tried, one last time. "Can you not see she is in danger here? Can you not see that, Madlyn?" But she was as blind as I had been during my first years of life.

It was time to go. In the middle of the night, Mira towed a fishing boat to the enormous arched rock formation known as the Ring, where she left it moored securely, along with a change of clothes and some supplies. The next day, after kissing my mother goodbye, Noah Crane paddled the double kayak toward the north side of the island with me sitting still, as I knew to do, in the front seat. Young as I was, I knew that keeping one's center was the most important part of kayaking. If you lost it, you'd tip. My dad had taught me that.

Noah knew we were just minutes away from death, a death he had carefully planned. He was paddling toward a remote part of the island that could not be seen from shore, a spot that few people frequented. It was a tricky thing, dying. The calm weather that was perfect for kayaking on this great lake called many people to the water. It was difficult to find the solitude he needed. He scanned the horizon. If he saw any other people nearby—a kayak, a sailboat, even a swimmer—he would have to abort the plan and try another day.

My dad's face was stern and determined. He was so close. The plan seemed to be falling into place perfectly. Nobody was around, as far as the eye could see. Just a few more strokes. He poured on the steam, as though he were paddling for his life; in a way, he was. His arms began to ache, his muscles tiring. Still, he couldn't stop now. It was really happening. He was really doing it.

If Madlyn didn't believe we were dead, she would surely hunt us down and bring me back to the island; my father would go to jail. But Noah wasn't worried about failure on this day. He was a methodical man, and he had calculated every eventuality. His plan would work.

The image shifted slightly, and I saw my dad withdrawing money from his bank account again and again and again, sums not large enough to attract notice, but enough. It was easy for him to squirrel this money away for himself, and he had traveled to the mainland to open a bank account under his new name, Thomas James. He had managed to stockpile almost six figures. He had a few thousand more stuffed into his jacket pocket. Not a fortune, but enough to start us in a new life.

I could see it on his face; the enormity of this thing was overwhelming to him. What he was doing was illegal, never mind the crucl immorality of taking a child away from her mother. He still loved Madlyn and knew he always would. But love comes a distant second to the safety of your child. He told himself that, over and over, until it took root in his soul.

I saw my dad think of all these things that day, as he paddled his kayak under the Ring. Local legend had it that the Ring was the gateway to the spirit world. It would be our gateway, too.

"See that, Daddy?" I called to him, silently, from my mute world. (I was not to speak a word for two years because of the trauma.) I was staring back toward shore. Then I turned my head and looked back at him, the fear apparent in my eyes. Noah had no idea I was also seeing the girls, standing on the shoreline, angry. He tried to say something to me, but the words caught in his throat. If he had had any moments of doubt about what he was doing, they were put to rest. Thank God he was getting his daughter away from this accursed place.

He passed through the Ring and found what he knew would be there, a fishing boat tethered to a rock on the sandbar, all gassed up, ready to go. Mira had stuck to their agreement. *Now,* Noah prayed. *Please let us get away.* He slowed his paddling and floated onto the bar.

"Hallie, we're going to do something fun today," he said, in a voice that was not quite his own. "Are you ready?"

I nodded and smiled, always up for a fun adventure with my dad.

"Okay," he began. "I want you to climb out of this kayak very carefully and stand on the sandbar. Can you do that?"

Of course. I was delighted that my father trusted me enough to do this important thing. He had never let me get out of the kayak before until we were on shore. But I wasn't afraid. I knew I could do it. I slithered out of my seat and stood on the sandbar, wiggling my toes inside my sandals.

Then my dad did the most curious thing. He got out of the kayak, too, and turned it belly up, shoving it out into the water. Then he threw his wallet and hat into the water. I watched it all float away.

"This is our boat now," he said, motioning toward the fishing boat. "Look. I've got some things in there for you."

What could those be? I waded to the boat and looked in. Two backpacks, a hat, an old jacket, and a blanket sat on the bottom of the hull.

"Climb in," Noah said. "This is the surprise I

was telling you about. We're going on an adventure, just you and me. Now, I want you to crawl into the boat and get under the blanket, and stay there until I tell you to come out. You're hiding. It's a game. Can you do that for me?"

Sure! It was simple. I hid under blankets all the time. I did as I was told, shivering with anticipation, wondering what would come next.

Noah untied the boat and started the engine. As we puttered slowly away, he put on a fishing hat with a wide brim and an old jacket he had stuffed in the boat. He took out a fishing rod and laid it over the side. Anyone watching from shore would see a lone man out fishing, not a father and daughter in a kayak.

It was done. We were dead, or would be, hours from now, when Madlyn began wondering why we hadn't come home. Noah imagined the frantic search, the cries of anguish when the kayak was found, the funeral of father and daughter. He pushed those thoughts out of his head and focused instead on the next tasks he would have to accomplish: finding an isolated spot to ditch the boat, hailing a taxi, getting to the airport. I saw all this swirling around my father's head like an ethereal to-do list.

Thomas James was glad his daughter was obediently huddling under the blanket so she couldn't see the tears in his eyes as he steered the boat toward the opposite shore.

This vision blurred, and I heard crying, a baby's cry, and knew the tale wasn't over. I saw Mira holding an infant. Was this my father's child? I sat there in stunned silence for a moment or two as the vision floated out of view. Was there anything else about Mira I didn't know? She had never told me she was a mother. I wondered if the baby had survived. Did I have a brother or a sister somewhere? Had my dad known?

I shook my head, sweeping the last wisps of the vision away, and suddenly became aware of my surroundings again. Iris was still sitting next to me on the bench. She now seemed impossibly tired, as though this tale had sucked the life out of her. I also saw that the bright November day had turned dark and foreboding, as it had on so many other days here. Clouds were swirling and turning above us; the wind was changing direction; the horizon looked dark and threatening. A storm was brewing. It was time to go inside.

"Iris," I said, taking her cold hand in mine, "let me help you into the house." But Iris shook her head.

"My work here is done for the day, miss." She started to stand up from the bench on what looked to be painful and creaky legs, but then I remembered what I wanted to ask her.

"May I ask one more thing before you go?" I spoke gently, holding her steady.

"What is it, child?" She was dead tired; I could see that clearly.

I began hurriedly. "Iris, my father took me away from here because of the girls. They're still here, and they have harmed Will—pushed him down the stairs and scratched him. I want to live in this house for the rest of my life. It's my legacy, my family history. I don't know how to thank you for telling it all to me. But right now, I need to know one more thing: How do I get rid of the girls?"

Iris's smile was weary. "They're just children, Halcyon, and spirit children at that. You are a living adult. As such you are much more powerful than they are. You now know how to use your gift. You must simply tell them what to do."

"And what is that, exactly?"

"To go, of course," she said. "They have been earthbound for too long now, doomed to stay in a house where they have committed murder and mayhem for generations. They are confused and lost without their mother and father. They view new people coming to the house as intruders, strangers to be feared—especially other children—Jane, Charles, Amelia, all the poor babies, Julie Sutton. And now your Will intrudes. You must tell them their family is waiting, Halcyon, or he will continue to be in danger. They're not aware that they are dead, you see. It's time for them to go where they belong."

"That seems too easy," I said, unconvinced.

Iris wrapped her arms around my shoulders and brushed her paper-thin cheek against mine, pressing her lips to my face. "I have done what I was to do, Halcyon. I have kept your family's lore safe and tucked away in my heart until you arrived. And I have shown you their faces and told you their stories and, in the doing, helped you unlock your gift. You're correct, child, in knowing that you belong in this house. Three little girls, even murderous ones, cannot take that away from you."

I got the strangest feeling, then, that Iris had somehow taken us outside of real time and space, as though *we* were shadowy figures floating somewhere in the ether as she told her stories.

When I finally pulled away from her, I was up to my calves in snow. How long had I been standing there in Iris's embrace? I whirled around, and all I could see was a wall of white. No house, no trees, no garden, no Iris. Only the blizzard that had suddenly descended upon me.

· 31

Why hadn't I noticed that it had started to snow? Had I simply lost all awareness of everything around me? I couldn't see the house, and I had no idea which way to turn. *It's just like the storm that killed the girls.* This idea gave me a very sick feeling in the pit of my stomach, but I knew I had to be strong in order to get Iris and me back to the house.

"Iris!" I called, reaching blindly into the snow for her. "Iris!" But there was no answer. I bent down to the bench—perhaps she had simply sat down?—but she wasn't there. She had wandered off into the storm.

The last thing I wanted to do was look for Iris in a raging blizzard. I wanted to get back to my warm house. But I knew I had to find her. And so I put one foot in front of the other, slowly and slower still, calling out her name. I rubbed my bare arms for warmth. That's all I'd need, to freeze to death out here. Then I'd be another of Iris's strange family tales. But whom would she tell? The last Hill—me—would be gone.

Then I heard it, soft and faint in the distance. "Hallie! Hallie! Where are you?"

Will! All of a sudden I remembered I had told him that morning I'd meet him on the cliff for a picnic. Surely he didn't think, in this weather . . . But there it was again. "Hallie! Hallie!"

"I'm over here!" I screamed. "By the garden!"

"Hallie?" But his voice was getting fainter and fainter. He was going the wrong way.

I started running toward the sound of his voice, stopping only when I remembered that there was an actual cliff somewhere nearby.

"Will!" I called out, and then, remembering, "Iris!" I had two people to find in this storm.

But I heard no response from either of them. I could see nothing but whiteness swirling in the air before me. I had no idea where I was, and no idea how to get back to the house. I was lost.

"Will!" I tried again. "Will!"

The silent snow wrapped around me. Panic was setting in as the whiteness descended around me, piling up at a very rapid rate. Now it was nearly to my knees, and I was having great difficulty moving around. I thought how restful it would be simply to sink to the ground and let that blanket of snow cover me. I slumped to my knees, almost giving up.

But then I heard it: laughter. "You're ice cold!" I heard a voice say. "Hallie! You're ice cold!"

I heard the voices clearly. It was the girls, I was sure of it. "Come on! You can't stop now! You're ice cold. Come and find us!"

Were they trying to lure me off the cliff? No. I remembered how Hannah always believed they had saved her life in that storm. Their voices were getting louder and louder, as though the words were being shouted into my own ear. I put one foot in front of the other and began to move. "You're getting warmer! Warmer now, Hallie!" A few more steps and then: "Colder! Colder! Turn around before you freeze!" I turned and walked another couple of steps. "Warmer! You're getting hot!" A few more steps. "You're burning up! You're burning!"

My foot hit something hard and tall. I recognized it immediately as the stone wall adjacent to the stairs leading from the drive to the house. I was home. I was saved. I climbed the stairs blindly, feeling each one with my foot as I went.

"Hallie!" I heard, louder now. It was Will.

"Will! I'm at the stairs! Follow the sound of my voice!" I just kept shouting until he collided with me. *Thank God.* We stood there for a moment, holding each other.

"Iris is out there," I said to him. "We've got to look for her."

"Hallie, I'm getting you back up to the house. Right now. You're freezing."

He led me up the rest of the stairs, one by one. I nearly died of joy when we reached the back door. I opened it and fell into the kitchen, shivering. Will ran to the living room and got me an afghan, which he immediately wrapped around me.

"My God, how long have you been out there?"

"I have no idea," I said, through chattering teeth. It was then I noticed a pot of stew on the stove and smelled the bread in the oven. "Did you make that?" I asked him, knowing he hadn't. He shook his head. It must have been Iris. Who else would've done it?

Much later, after we had showered and eaten and thoroughly warmed up, I told Will the tale of Halcyon Crane. He kept shaking his head, muttering things like *Unbelievable* and *Wow*. I don't know whether he took what I said at face value—especially the part about the girls saving me—or if he believed Iris was embellishing my story the same way she embellished the others.

I wasn't sure either, but at that moment I didn't much care. I was back in my house with the man I loved, and we were both safe from the storm. Iris had made it, too, as evidenced by the fine dinner she had prepared. I took Will up to bed that night with the distinct feeling that everything was going to be all right.

· 32

I had it out with Mira after the storm passed. She had been planning to come to the house the night of the storm to help me exorcise the triplets—"Phase Two," she called it—but there was no way she could get through the snow. So she came by a couple of days later when the island had begun to dig out.

"Thanks for the offer, but I think I can get the girls to leave on my own," I told her.

"On your own? Are you sure?"

"No, I'm not," I admitted. "I still might need your help. But the way I'm seeing it now, the girls aren't the only demons of the past that my coming here has stirred up. Other things need to be exorcised, too."

Mira seemed worried. "I'm not sure what you mean."

So I confronted her with what I knew. She tried to deny it, sputtering and posturing and pretending that she was the wronged one—how could I possibly *think* such a thing?—but I stood firm and she basically collapsed under the weight of the truth.

"I'm sorry, Hallie," she said finally, after pulling out a chair from the kitchen table and sitting down hard. "I looked for you and your father for years. The man who I put him in touch with for new identity papers disappeared around the same time, so I couldn't get your location or new name from him. It was impossible to find you, and then I realized Noah didn't want me to. It's true that I was furious when your father left me. I've been holding that grudge ever since. But I really felt as though I was helping him back then. He needed to get you out of here."

"Why didn't you tell me?"

She made a face. "I'm not exactly excited about anyone else finding out. I don't know the statute of limitations, but I might be charged as an accessory to murder. Or whatever they charge people with for helping murderers."

Oddly enough, I felt for her. I don't know if it was pity or empathy or something else, but seeing the way she was so resigned, I just couldn't hate Mira. She was right. She had helped my dad, her selfish motives notwithstanding, and in doing so she had probably saved my life. Right then and there, I forgave her.

"But what about the child, Mira? Did you have my father's child?"

At this, Mira's face went white. "Who told you that?"

"The source is not important," I said to her. "I just want to know if it's true. No more lies, Mira. I've lived half a lifetime based on lies. I want the truth now, once and for all."

She shook her head. "I've kept this secret for thirty years, Hallie. Nobody on this island knows who his father is."

"His? So you do have a child. A son, then?"

Mira looked at me and smiled. "I thought you knew I had a son. Everyone here on the island knows him. He runs the coffee shop."

I sat there, open-mouthed. Finally, I managed to say, "Jonah? Are you kidding me? Jonah is your son? My dad's son?"

She nodded in confirmation. I could hardly believe what she was saying. My thoughts were racing. Jonah was my half brother? That would explain why he felt so familiar, so like my dad in so many ways.

"He has known who his father was for some time," Mira told me. "In fact, what he's been going through the past couple of weeks isn't so different from what you went through. He thought his father was dead all these years—that's what I had told him—and now he finds out that he was alive and living just north of Seattle until just before you arrived. When you think about it, it's exactly what you went through after learning about your mother."

"Not exactly," I said to her. "He had you to come to for answers."

"And when he did, I told him the truth. I looked for your—and his—father for years. I tried everything I knew to find him. But he had disappeared into thin air. Jonah was angry with me at first, sure. But I think he realizes I was just as much a victim as he was."

A painful thought occurred to me. "Mira," I said carefully, "did my dad know about the pregnancy before he left here with me? Did he leave you, knowing you were carrying his child?"

She shook her head. "Even I didn't know it then. If I had, you can be sure I would've told him. I loved your dad, Hallie. I wanted to spend the rest of my life with him."

My mind continued to swim. So this is what Jonah had wanted to tell me. I thought back to our evening at the wine bar, and now it made perfect sense that he had asked so many questions about my growing-up years. He was trying to learn about the life that might have been his and about the man who was his father.

I sighed and looked at Mira, feeling a mixture of confusion, defeat, and regret. "What a tangled web this is," I said to her.

She smiled a weak smile. "Do you have anything to drink? Stronger than tea, I mean?"

And so we opened up a bottle of wine and sat together drinking it, talking about what was and what might have been. We both saw that nobody, not my mother, not my father, not Mira, not me—and certainly not Jonah—was to blame for any of it. The affair notwithstanding, everyone had acted with the best of intentions, and this was simply how it had turned out. All our lives had been thrown into turmoil as a result of the epic tale of my family, and now, after thirty years, several deaths, and more than a few otherworldly occurrences, the circle was closed and we were back where it all began.

Much to Mira's relief, Jonah wasn't ready to tell the whole island who his father was. Neither was I. It would be between us for a while. But the fact that we were siblings was not lost on either of us. We saw more and more of each other, becoming good friends. We even decided that one day when I stopped reeling from the tales I had heard from Iris about my mother's family, we'd look together for our father's family on the mainland. Other stories about other ancestors were swirling out there in the wind, waiting to be learned.

One day not long after this, I ran into the Suttons downtown. I took a deep breath, walked over to them, and told them I had gone to the police to request the file on the case. "I wanted to find out for myself what the evidence against my father was, and I can see how it looked suspicious," I said to Julie's parents. "But all I can tell you is that I don't believe my father would have ever intentionally hurt your daughter. I'm sorry that I can't give you a better explanation of the accident that day. I know you want it as much as I do."

They accepted my apology—what else could they do?—and we went our separate ways. I assumed word got around that I tried to dig into the case and uncover the truth, because not long after my meeting with the Suttons, I noticed a great thawing in island opinion about me. People stopped staring and whispering, and I became a prodigal daughter of sorts, one of their own who had left and returned. Some of that goodwill, I believe, came from what I decided to do with my days during tourist season.

One snowy afternoon while Will was at work, I found myself at the front door of my mother's art gallery downtown. It hadn't been opened since her death. According to Will and Jonah, it was one of the more bustling and popular shops on the island during the summer months, selling not only my mother's photographs but other pieces crafted by local artisans: jewelry, pottery, watercolors, the occasional sculpture. The thought of it sitting there, unused, had begun to nag at me. The moment I turned the key and stepped inside the dusty building, I knew I had found what I would be doing with my summers.

"I'm going to open the Manitou Gallery in the spring," I announced to Will that night over dinner.

"That's fantastic!" He smiled and lifted his glass. "I know people have been wondering about the fate of the shop. To a new chapter!"

A few days later I was at the shop, taking care of the many details that needed to be completed before spring came—dusting and cleaning and calling the artists whose work was displayed there, many of whom lived elsewhere during the winter, to let them know the shop would be open before the first tourist ferry arrived.

In the back room where my mother had her studio, I noticed several boxes labeled MOSAIC MATERIALS. I found them filled with old cracked pottery, tiles, and pieces of what seemed to be foggy antique mirrors. I picked up one of the larger mirror bits, and it seemed to me I could see the hint of a face within it, as though it had captured the reflected image of the mirror's previous owner when he or she gazed into it long ago. Could that be true? Could they be reflecting an image of the past? I remembered what I had seen that first day in my mother's house—her image reflected in the mirror in her bedroom. A jolt of possibility traveled up my spine.

I began to work with the shards, arranging them on a small table, and before I knew it, day had passed into night and I was staring at a colorful mosaic I had created. In the coming weeks, I created many more, becoming immersed in crafting them, positioning the mirrors just so. Will commented how beautiful and haunting he thought the pieces were, although he didn't understand what I meant by reflected images of the past. Perhaps I was the only one who could see them. Was it my particular family gift? I wasn't sure. But I was beginning to think a new Crane woman would have artwork to sell in the shop when it opened in the spring.

I was turning off the lights before bed one evening in Hill House when I found the girls standing before me in their white dresses, white ribbons in their hair. They looked so pretty and sweet, not at all like the ghouls I had been seeing. They were just little children.

"Come play with us, Halcyon," Persephone said, extending her small hand to me. I noticed slight smiles creeping as one across their faces, their eyes hesitantly anxious.

I folded a stray afghan and set it on the chaise. "Playtime is over now, girls," I told them.

"You never play with us anymore." Penelope pouted; the others narrowed their eyes.

The force of their gaze gave me a chill. My voice wavering just a bit, I said, "That's because it's time for you to go."

"Who says so?" Patience wanted to know, her chin jutting defiantly forward.

I put my hands on my hips and faced them. "I say so. It's time for you to go home."

The girls smiled then, eerie ice-cold smiles. "But we *are* home." Patience grinned, as the three of them dissipated into the air like wisps of smoke swirling around me.

And then I felt it, the poking and prodding and pinching of unseen fingers, on my face, my arms, my legs, my hair. Three pairs of hands on the small of my back, pushing me forward. I stumbled to my knees.

"Stop it!" I screamed into the empty room, covering my face with my hands. And just like that, their assault ended. The air in the room began to seem lighter and fresher, as it is after a spring rain. I stood up. Could they be gone, as easily as that? I took a deep breath and closed my eyes, thinking it was over.

It wasn't. They were there again, in the doorway leading to the living room. But instead of the innocent little girls in white dresses who had been with me moments before, I saw a macabre vision of the moment of their deaths, three children frozen together, silent screams of terror coming out of their gaping mouths. I quickly turned away, only to hear their giggles echoing throughout the room.

Now they were walking slowly toward me, the flesh hanging on their worm-eaten, eyeless faces, the skin on their arms rotting and falling away with every step, their white dresses now black and tattered with dirt and decay. It was as though they had risen from their graves.

"You don't frighten me!" I shouted at them with conviction, but my trembling legs told me otherwise. What would they do when they reached me? What would I do? I tried to run from the room but found I could not move. Was it fear or something else holding me firmly in place?

My mind was swimming. Iris had said I could get the girls to leave, but how? I thought of the stories she had told me. I thought about Hannah and Simeon, about the old witch Martine, and about Iris's doomed cousin Jane, driven over the cliff by these demons. I thought of Charles, whose animals protected him, and of Amelia and the unborn children she lost when she was pushed and fell. I thought of my mother and my father, driven apart because she couldn't accept his fear of the girls, and finally I thought of poor Julie, who spent her last moments on earth in terror, battling these unseen enemies. I'm not sure where it came from, but I had an idea. I recited the names of my relatives out loud, over and over—"Hannah, Simeon, Charles, Amelia, Madlyn, Noah!"—as though the names them-selves were incantations. Or prayers.

Then I whirled around to face the girls, their ghoulish faces dancing ever closer to my own. "This is going to end now," I growled at them, with every ounce of strength inside of me.

And then I saw them, my ancestors, hovering and shimmering near me as though I were seeing their reflections on a glassy lake or in one of the antique mirrors at the shop: Hannah and Simeon, Charles and Amelia, and—my breath caught in my throat—my own mother and father. The girls must've seen them, too, because they dropped their horrible façades and in an instant were the sweet-looking little girls they had once been.

"You're leaving now," I told them. "You have been very naughty for a very long time and caused this family untold grief."

"But Halcyon—" Penelope started.

"But nothing," I told her, pointing toward our ancestors. "Look. Your parents are waiting for you."

As I spoke, Hannah and Simeon had their arms outstretched. "Come, girls!" Hannah called to her daughters. "It's time to come inside! It's getting cold out there!"

"Mama!" Penelope cried, as the three girls ran to their parents. "Where have you been? We've been looking for you for so long!"

And then all of them were gone, dissipated into the air like fog when the sun shines. It was truly over.

· 33

When spring came, I found myself wandering with the dogs on the other side of the island, ending up at the old cemetery. I decided to tidy the graves of my relatives, pulling weeds, dusting off headstones, talking to all of them. Visiting. Telling them my news: Will and I were happily in love. Maybe there would soon be a new generation of the family whose stories would intertwine with theirs.

Later that night, I had the strangest dream. I was back in the cemetery, among the graves of my Hill ancestors. I noticed the gravestone of Iris's cousin, Jane Malone. As I bent down to pull some weeds near her grave, I felt a chill wind rush through me.

"Grave tending, miss?"

I wheeled around and my eyes couldn't quite take in what I saw.

"Iris? My God! Where have—"

I was going to ask her where she'd been; I hadn't seen her since the storm. But my words trailed off, because just then Iris's face began to change. Before I knew it, I was looking at a woman I didn't recognize.

"I thought you deserved to know the truth," she said, her speech now heavy with a French-Canadian accent.

I couldn't make sense of what I was seeing. "Iris, I—" I started, but she cut me off.

"Not Iris, *chérie*. It's time we dispensed with that ruse. My name is Martine." She smiled, and as she did the age seemed to evaporate from her face, her deep wrinkles replaced by rosy, smooth skin. She reached up and ran a delicate hand through her hair, shaking out the gray. It was now long and flowing and auburn. She moved at the waist, and her dress, now a vibrant green, swayed this way and that. "It feels wonderful to finally shed that skin."

Martine? I leaned against a tombstone, afraid my quaking legs wouldn't support me. I tried to speak but couldn't formulate any words. I wanted nothing more than to run away from this woman, as fast as my legs could carry me. But where would I go? I couldn't get away, not really.

"When Iris went over the cliff that day along with her poor cousin, I saw my opportunity." Martine smiled.

"Opportunity?" I croaked.

Martine smoothed the folds of her dress and sniffed. "Hannah had done a pitiful job raising

364

my three children. That was my mistake, giving the spell to someone so weak."

My skin went cold. "*Your* children?"

"Oh, *chérie*, you are so naïve. Of course they were part of me. I gave them to her. They were as much my children as they were hers. But when I saw what she did to the girls—my three babies— I had to step in before she could hurt the others who would come later."

I shook my head. "What do you mean, step in?"

"I mean just that. I stepped in. I had been planning to leave the island. I had had enough of these wealthy people who would scorn me outwardly, only to come creeping to my back door when they needed something. But then I saw how incapable Hannah was of raising children—the girls died because of her!—and I knew the herbs I gave her would allow her to conceive again and again. Something had to be done. Someone had to protect future children. So when poor Iris went over the cliff—"

"Iris died?"

"No, Hallie." Martine shook her head. "She went over the cliff, just as her cousin did. But I saved her. I knew I could use her to live within the house and watch over my children and grandchildren, so I put her body around mine like a cloak. Just as I said: *I stepped in.*"

"How—" I started, my eyes growing wide.

Martine laughed and shook her head back and

forth, her long hair blowing in the breeze. "I'm the Witch of Summer Glen. A little thing like that isn't so difficult."

I sat down, hard, on the cold ground next to the grave, not quite knowing how to formulate coherent thoughts out of the muddle that was my mind. Finally, I said, "So you were Iris, all those years?"

She nodded. "I had to look after them: Charles, Maddie, even the girls, such as they were. I had brought them all into the world, so to speak. I had a responsibility."

An undefined anger was bubbling up in my throat. "You certainly didn't do much to protect *me*."

"You?" Martine laughed again. "You didn't need my protection. You were stronger than all of them combined. So like me. That's why you were able to rid the house of those naughty triplets. Soon after you left with your father, I left as well. Look at the gravestone, my dear."

I shuddered, thinking I was going to see my own name there. Instead, I noticed a small stone. *IRIS MALONE. Faithful daughter, servant, and friend. 1905–1976.*

"Wait. Iris died? But—"

Martine shrugged. "My work was done. And I was so tired of that horrible black dress."

"So—" I couldn't quite grasp what she was saying to me.

"When I learned you were coming back to the island, I decided to put on that dress once again. You didn't know anything about your family— my family. I had to tell you, *ma chère*, to make sure you kept their memories and mine alive. You needed to know the truth, about them and about yourself. And there was only one person who could tell you. Me."

With that, my eyes popped open and I was sitting up in bed, Will breathing low and shallow next to me. The room was dark except for a shaft of moonlight shining in through the window.

"What's the matter?" Will murmured groggily.

"It was just a dream," I whispered. "A crazy dream."

"Curl back in." He held out his hand to me. And so I did, slipping down under the covers, snuggling next to the man I loved.

Acknowledgments

I grew up in a family of storytellers. Some of my earliest memories involve sitting at the kitchen table, listening to my parents, grandparents, cousins, aunts, and uncles tell tales about the people and places in their pasts, so it's no wonder I should grow up to tell stories for a living. My first acknowledgment, then, goes to my family. To my mom and dad, Joan and Toby Webb; my brothers, Jack and Randy Webb; and Gram, Elma Maki. I know how proud you are to see me fulfill my lifelong dream. Your confidence in me is what got me here. And to everyone else who has ever sat around my parents' kitchen table and *raconteured*, thank you for a lifetime of inspiration.

To my wonderful, funny, fabulous agent, Jennifer Weltz. The gratitude I feel for your belief in me, your hard work on my behalf, and your friendship is boundless. I wouldn't be here without you. Writers—you may have written the next best seller, but without a great agent all you've got is a ream of paper. Thanks to everyone at the Jean Naggar Agency for your unwavering support.

To my talented editor, Helen Atsma. Thank you for believing in a first-time novelist, for loving this story as much as I do, and for your wise, insightful, and careful editing. Your skill has made this book infinitely better, and working with you to hone this tale was an absolute joy.

To my long-suffering friends who have endured the process of me doing something so audacious as writing a novel and trying to get it published, Sarah Fister Gale, Kathi Wright, Mary Gallegos, Bobbi Voss, and Barb Smith Lobin. I fully expect you each to buy a case of these books and give them out as gifts. (Just kidding, though it's not a bad idea.) Really, what I want to say is, thank you for your encouragement and for making me laugh every day. And to my sounding board, plot untangler, and kindred literary spirit, Randy Johnson. Thank you for being so happy to see my dream come true. Next it will be your turn.

Finally, to my spouse, Steve Burmeister, and my son, Ben. I know living with a writer, especially this writer, isn't always easy. Your love means everything to me. I'm so happy to be walking through the world with you two, creating the tales we will tell others around our kitchen table.

One last word about the story itself. Although it was modeled after Mackinac Island, Grand Manitou Island is a figment of my imagination and, now, yours. This novel is a work of fiction, save one thing: the 1913 storm that killed the Hill triplets. That was very real and remains the worst storm in the history of the Great Lakes.

etc.

extras . . .

essays . . .

etcetera

more author
About Wendy Webb

more book
About *The Tale of Halcyon Crane*

. . . and more

Meet Wendy Webb

Wendy Webb grew up in Minneapolis and has been a journalist there for nearly two decades, writing for most of the major publications in the region. Currently, she lives in the gorgeous Lake Superior port city of Duluth with her spouse, photographer Steve Burmeister; her son, Ben; and their enormous Alaskan malamute, Tundra. She is at work on her next novel. Please visit her website at www.wendykwebb.com.

A Conversation with Wendy Webb

Although you are making your fiction-writing debut with *The Tale of Halcyon Crane*, you've worked as a journalist for more than twenty years. Was it difficult to make the switch from nonfiction to fiction? What were some of the challenges?

It was difficult at first. I didn't realize how different the two styles of writing actually are. One of the cardinal rules of fiction writing is "Show, don't tell." But as a journalist, you "tell" a story, and as I'd been writing that way for so long, it was second nature to me. It took a while before I even understood the difference between showing and telling well enough to break that habit. Also, plotting and pacing a novel was a completely new experience for me because it's something you never have to do when writing a magazine article. The timing of when to let a bit more of the story unfold is an art unto itself. And consistency—you never even think about it as a journalist, but I found myself constantly going back to make sure Halcyon was wearing the same outfit she left the house in fifty pages earlier.

Loving, lively animals play a role in *The Tale of Halcyon Crane*—from the animals that Hallie's veterinarian grandfather cared for to the boisterous dogs Hallie inherits from her mother. Do you have pets?

We have a 130-pound giant Alaskan malamute named Tundra. Readers will notice Madlyn's dogs are also mals, Tundra and Tika. Tika was our husky-samoyed cross; she passed away about five years ago. I believe there's a special connection between people and their pets that fits very well with the magical realism I like to convey in my writing. Pets sense our fears and our sadness, and want only to help. There's something enormously comforting about that. I also love the unqualified joy my dog experiences in the moment—going for a walk, chewing on a bone, giving me a hero's welcome when I walk in the door after a long day.

The Great Lakes clearly occupy a special place in your heart. Have you spent a lot of time on or around the lakes?

I grew up in Minnesota and have a great love for Lake Superior, where I now live. It's a spiritual, mystical place filled with ancient lore and legend. Many local residents actually do have a vague sense that the lake itself is a living thing, which is how the native peoples in this area viewed it. Here's an example: A few years back, a man set out to swim across all the Great Lakes. But he couldn't make it across Superior despite many attempts. In the press, he had been "trash talking" the lake, saying its reputation for being dangerous was a myth. People here thought the lake simply wasn't letting him pass because of it. I think all of the Great Lakes hold that kind of fascination for residents and visitors.

Any special hobbies?

I like to row and kayak on Lake Superior, and we've got a cabin in the Boundary Waters Canoe Area Wilderness that separates Minnesota from Canada, where we spend a lot of time. It's a gorgeous area that offers the best of both worlds—unspoiled wilderness and beautiful lodges with great restaurants.

My friends joke that my two major vices are expensive wine and lots of new books, and I love nothing better than a morning of kayaking or rowing followed by an afternoon sitting with a glass of wine on the deck of my cabin overlooking our lake, reading a great book with my dog at my side. And it doesn't hurt if my son and husband are there, either.

Have you read any good spooky fiction lately?

I'm always reading. My favorite book in the genre that I read last year was *The Spiritualist*, by Megan Chance. I read it in one day, sitting on the aforementioned deck of my cabin. It's absolutely fabulous. This year, one of my favorite books is *The Little Stranger*, by Sarah Waters. It's deliciously creepy and I could not put it down. I highly recommend those two novels for people who want a little tingle up their spines.

The Tale of Halcyon Crane begins on the West Coast, north of Seattle. Do you have any personal connection with that area?

I lived in Bellingham, Washington, for a couple of years, and I absolutely love that area. It reminds me of Minnesota in a way. But of course, here on Lake Superior we don't have seals or whales. One of the things I loved best about living out there was that I could actually hear the barking of the seals from my house. It's a very relaxing sound. The San Juan Islands are hauntingly beautiful—maybe I'll set a novel there one day.

Your tale is filled with ghosts. Do you believe in them?

I must admit I do. I think this world is filled with things we can't see and don't quite understand. I dedicated the book to my brother, who died of a sudden heart attack a few years ago. Since he passed away, several of us in the family have had odd experiences we can't really explain. Here's just one: I was sweeping the wood floor in my bedroom shortly after my brother's funeral. After doing the entire room, I turned around and saw several pennies strewn on the floor . . . the floor I had just cleaned an instant earlier. It really happened, folks. I can't tell you how or why.

On Writing
The Tale of Halcyon Crane

I come from a family of storytellers. Some of my earliest memories involve sitting at our kitchen table, listening to my parents and relatives tell stories—some of them hilarious, others tragic—about my family's past. These tales were filled with unforgettable characters and fantastic situations, and I know them all as well as I know my own name.

But as much as I loved hearing these stories, I've always wanted to spin tales of my own. In Halcyon, I found a woman whose background is the opposite of mine: I grew up hearing everything about my family; Halcyon knows nothing about her past. It isn't until she is in her thirties that Halcyon learns of her childhood abduction and sets out to find some answers. What happened all those years ago? Who was her mother? Who were her ancestors? And most important, who was *she?*

I wanted to include an element of magical realism in the story because I love the notion that something otherworldly can be right around the corner, waiting for you on any given Monday; that the world is filled with things we don't understand and many of us can't see, and that fairy tales, Grimm's especially, could really have happened. I love the goosebumps and tingles up my spine I get from shows like *Medium* and *The Ghost Whisperer* and books like *The Ghost Orchid*, by Carol Goodman, and I wanted to write a story that would give people that same type of deliciously haunting, eerie feeling.

I decided to set the story on Mackinac Island because the Great Lakes hold a magic and mystery unlike anyplace else. Many people think the lakes are actually living things, with moods ranging from benevolent to murderous.

I fictionalized Mackinac's name—calling it Grand Manitou Island instead—so I could be free when writing about the specific places, happenings, and people there, but readers who have been to Mackinac will recognize it right away. When you go there, you really feel like you've traveled back in time—I think it has to do with the fact that there is no motorized traffic and everyone gets around by horse-drawn carriage. It's a place filled with beautiful Victorian homes, grand hotels, great restaurants, fudge shops, wine bars . . . and a very creepy old cemetery. It seems to me that the whole island is teeming with spirits—if anyplace in the world is haunted, it's Mackinac Island.

There does happen to be a Grand Manitou Island in Lake Nipissing in Ontario, but it's not inhabited. I've since learned that this Grand Manitou Island also has a reputation for being haunted, interestingly enough.

What better place for a woman to go looking for the ghosts of her past?

Another reason I set the story on the Great Lakes was because I wanted to work in a real-life tragedy that occurred there: the worst storm in the history of the region, which happened in November of 1913. I came upon newspaper accounts of the storm when researching another story. They called it the Frozen Hurricane, and it destroyed harbors, piers, and shorelines, demolishing buildings, tearing up concrete streets, dumping feet of snow on land, and, most horrifyingly, sending nearly every ship on the Great Lakes that day to the bottom, all hands aboard. One of the newspaper accounts told of drowned sailors, frozen together, floating out of the fog and in to shore. When I read that, I knew I had to include it somehow in my story.

Halcyon does eventually find the answers she seeks, and in doing so gains a greater awareness about who she really is. We're all on journeys of one sort or another—some of us to the past, looking for answers; some of us tentatively moving forward, unsure of what the future holds, and I very much hope *The Tale of Halcyon Crane* speaks to that journey.

Questions for Discussion

1. Hallie's father talks about seeing Madlyn at the nursing home the day before he died. Do you think he really saw her spirit, coming for him? Why or why not? Do you believe the veil between the living and the dead is lifted as a person passes from one life to the next?

2. Hallie has twice been sidelined by men she loved: her husband and her father both were different men than she believed them to be. How did their deception—non-malicious though it was—affect her? Did she do the right thing by ultimately trusting Will?

3. Each child born of the spell from the Witch of Summer Glen has a special otherworldly ability or gift. With Hallie, her gift develops as she stays on the island. Do you think Hallie simply grew more aware of her innate talent, or did being on the island somehow change and enhance her abilities?

4. What is the significance of mirrors with respect to Hallie's ability to "see"?

5. Why couldn't Madlyn understand the danger the island posed to her young daughter, Hallie? Was Madlyn a good mother?

6. Was Hallie's father justified in taking his child away from his wife and their home? Did you think he could have handled that situation differently—perhaps more openly and truthfully?

7. Mira befriends Hallie, but she also harbors a great secret that isn't revealed until the end of the book. Did you understand Mira's decision to keep the truth to herself for so long, given that she barely knew Hallie, or should she have revealed it sooner? What secrets would you keep from a friend?

8. Did you enjoy the way Hallie's "tale" is slowly revealed to her? Are there storytellers in your family who have kept family lore alive?

9. Forgiveness is one of the themes in this novel. Who most needed to be able to forgive? Who most needed to be forgiven?

10. Have you ever seen a ghost? Do you know anyone who has? What are some of the best ghost stories you know?

Center Point Publishing
600 Brooks Road ● PO Box 1
Thorndike ME 04986-0001 USA

(207) 568-3717

US & Canada:
1 800 929-9108
www.centerpointlargeprint.com